The Methuen Book of
MOVIE STORIES

The Methuen Book of
MOVIE
STORIES

Selected with an introduction by
SHERIDAN MORLEY

Methuen

First published in Great Britain in 1994
by Methuen London
an imprint of Reed Consumer Books Ltd
Michelin House, 81 Fulham Road, London SW3 6RB
and Auckland, Melbourne, Singapore and Toronto

A CIP catalogue record for this book
is available at the British Library
ISBN 0 413 67960 8

Phototypeset by CentraCet Limited, Cambridge
Printed in Great Britain
by Clays Ltd, St Ives plc

*For Barry Burnett in London
and Don Smith in New York*

Contents

Introduction

Although I have only been writing about the movies as the critic of the *Sunday Express* for the last three years, they have been a part of my life ever since I can remember. I am the son and grandson and nephew and godson of actors who have between them made several hundred films, going right back to 1917 when my grandmother Gladys Cooper made her first appearance in the silent melodrama entitled *The Sorrows of Satan*: half a century later, she was to be found playing Rex Harrison's mother in the movie of *My Fair Lady* 'because dear,' she disarmingly explained, 'nobody else was nearly old enough.'

When therefore Methuen suggested that I might like to follow my anthology of *Theatre Stories* with a similar collection devoted to the cinema, I did not need asking twice. Again, I laid out for myself certain guidelines: I wanted to limit the collection to genuine short stories, which at once ruled out novel extracts or non-fiction. Secondly, although the stories would of course focus to a large extent on Hollywood, I wanted also to consider the ways in which European writers viewed the movies world-wide, to go beyond the usual selections of Scott Fitzgerald and Budd Schulberg and Gavin Lambert and Nathanael West. I wanted to come right up to date with Martin Amis and Ethan Canin and J. G. Ballard and Robert Coover, but I also wanted to go right back to P. G. Wodehouse and a story by Rudyard Kipling which is I believe the first ever to refer (in 1904) to what was then 'The Biograph'. Above all, I wanted to include some stories about the cinema by women writers; they are not easy to find, though Katherine Mansfield and, bending the rules, Alison Lurie are here.

Again, I wanted to try to achieve a balance between what

might be considered the 'battlefield' reports of writers like P. G.
Wodehouse and Scott Fitzgerald, who actually worked for
Hollywood studios, and those who kept their distance (somehow one doesn't see Katherine Mansfield on a back lot in
Culver City), and those like Graham Greene and John O'Hara
who made considerable contributions to the movies, but usually
managed to stay as far away from California as possible.

   When I was a child, I lived there for almost a year and
although, going back now to cover the Oscars or write about
movie people, I can never quite recapture the past of forty years
ago, it has never ceased to haunt me. In 1949, Hollywood was
the last outpost of the British Empire: just as surely as we had
colonised Africa and India and Australia, British actors and
writers and directors arrived in Los Angeles to colonise the
Beverly Hills as an invasion of expert settlers. They, after all,
could speak the English language at a time when many silent
stars were still having trouble mastering basic American, let
alone the art of moving and chewing gum at the same time.

   Expatriate European writers had been arriving off the train at
Los Angeles station as early as 1882: 'Here from the uttermost
end of the great world,' wrote Oscar Wilde to Norman Forbes-
Robertson in March of that year, 'I send you greetings.' By
1916, Beerbohm Tree had already pitched camp there for a
silent-screen *Macbeth* ('It's really not bad, for so young a
country'), and within another five years the romantic novelist
Elinor Glyn had been brought out to advise on period details
('Baronial Scottish castles do not have lines of spittoons on their
dining tables, even gold ones').

   By then, the advance guard had become a platoon: actors,
many of them on road tours of America after none-too-dis-
tinguished stage careers back home, suddenly found themselves
a place in the sun where the ability to wear uniform, ride
military (as opposed to cowboy) style and soon to speak would
be enough to guarantee them a living and a salary the like of
which they could never have expected from the provincial
British touring theatre of the period. Writers, too, were being
dazzled with the prospect of Hollywood gold: as early as 18 July
1920, the *New York Times* was able to report that 'practically all
the best-known authors and playwrights of England are about

to turn their talents into the field of the movies, and many are coming to America within the next six months to learn screen-drama writing ... for instance, Mr G. Bernard Shaw is co-operating with the new form of picture narrative, while arrangements have also been made with Sir James M. Barrie.'

Shaw in fact never succumbed to the temptations of Hollywood: 'There is only one difference between Samuel Goldwyn and me,' he declared, 'whereas Goldwyn is after art, I am after money.' Barrie however took the shilling, drafting an, alas, unmade screen version of *Peter Pan* for Charlie Chaplin and his original Captain Hook, Gerald du Maurier. Before long, Elinor Glyn was coaching Gloria Swanson not only in acting her scripts but in how to behave at cocktail parties, and the whole uneasy marriage between Hollywood and its expatriate writers was already well made, if only to head for periodic and acrimonious individual divorces.

Most writers of this period have left us some sort of written or recorded memoir (many can be found in my *Tales From the Hollywood Raj*, 1983) but sadly few have left us fully-fledged short stories. The form has never been especially popular or fashionable, least of all in Hollywood itself, where a novel could always lead to a screen treatment but a short story seldom made the length required on film. Exceptions usually came from this side of the Atlantic: the 'omnibus' pictures made in the late forties and early fifties, consisting of three or four Maugham stories, for instance, linked by the author himself in pioneering TV-host style. If Hollywood ever linked disparate short stories, it was usually under a true-crime or science-fiction umbrella, audiences presumably being reckoned generally incapable otherwise of handling more than one story at a time once they got inside a cinema.

Then again, those who did want to write about, as well as for, Hollywood often chose the novella or the novel rather than the short story, and many from Budd Schulberg through Nathanael West and Evelyn (*The Loved One*) Waugh to Scott Fitzgerald himself did some of their very best work in this genre. Since then we've had Gavin Lambert focusing on *The Slide Area*, where Hollywood itself gently tumbles down the cliffs of Malibu, Jonathan Schwartz's *The Man Who Knew Cary Grant*, and David

Freeman's *A Hollywood Education*, as well as Ronald Harwood's *One. Interior. Day.*, among others which are in fact made up of interlinked stories. Those who believe, since the movie, that the same is true of Raymond Carver's *Short Cuts* should be reminded that it was the director Robert Altman who moved these to California from their original setting further east.

But the movie short story does not of course need to be Hollywood based: Noël Coward wrote 'A Richer Dust' about a British-born film star returning in 1945 to his family having refused to come home and fight the war: 'If,' his old mother tells him, 'anyone mentions your tubercular lung, do remember that we had to tell them something.'

If I write here about some of the writers you will not find in the following pages, it is because those who are included need precious little introduction or explanation or addition from me, and would be unlikely to welcome it. Any editor of anthologies very rapidly discovers that the dictates of space, copyright and authorial approval (one writer of immense distinction solemnly told me that he never allows his work to appear in collections where other authors are involved, presumably for fear of contamination) make for a delicate balancing and juggling act worthy of Barnum or Bailey themselves.

But what fascinates me about the writers who are here is the sheer diversity of their approach to the silver screen: some hate it, some tolerate it, some love it, some regard it as a force for nothing but evil, others celebrate its manic power to entertain or regret its loony wastefulness of creative resources.

Space permitting, I would have liked to explore whole sub-sections of the species: stories about movies on location around the world, for instance, at which Bryan Forbes excels in novel form, or the relationship of crime writers like Raymond Chandler and Erle Stanley Gardner to the shadier twilight of Hollywood's meaner streets. But there again, we are in danger of crossing over the borderline into novels or screenplays or memoirs, none of which fit the brief here. The short story is something else entirely, with its own energy and dynamism, and there is no law to say that you ever have to have worked in or even near a studio in order to write one about some aspect of the movies.

Here as in my collection of *Theatre Stories*, I've also tried to go for those that have not been over-anthologised elsewhere: though this is the first such anthology (I think) to have been published over here in the last twenty years, I have for instance excluded Scott Fitzgerald's 'Crazy Sunday' on the grounds that it is the one movie short story even those who have never read movie short stories will know, and gone instead for his much lesser-known 'Magnetism'. Equally, Graham Greene's 'The Blue Film' may be unfamiliar to those who need no reminder of the movie classics *Brighton Rock* and *The Third Man* (itself an original screenplay rather than a story), while Moravia and Narayan are welcome reminders that not all movie stories have come from Britain or America, despite the fact that the vast majority still do.

So we are, given the limitations of the short-story form, inevitably dealing here with the hour rather than the day of the locust: but I still believe that somewhere in these pages you will find, as I already have in assembling them, almost every aspect of the ever-uneasy relationship between the writer and the movies. When I was writing *Tales From the Hollywood Raj* a decade ago, I took as one of my principal themes two sayings by expatriate British character actors of the 1930s, both famous for playing officers and gentlemen of that other Raj: 'Hollywood is a chain gang,' said Clive Brook in 1933, 'where we lose the will to escape: the links of our chain are forged not of cruelties but of luxuries: we are pelted with orchids and roses, we are overpaid and underworked'; while Cedric Hardwicke simply added 'God felt sorry for actors and writers, so he gave them a place in the sun and a swimming pool: all they really had to sacrifice was their talent.'

Many would argue that they didn't even have to do that: where would *The Last Tycoon* have worked, literally or figuratively, if not in Hollywood itself? In *Sunset Boulevard*, which forty years before Lloyd Webber was already Hollywood's most acidly brilliant valentine to its own deadly values, Gloria Swanson tells William Holden, as the opportunist young screenwriter, 'You people made a rope of words and strangled this business'; but in truth the business only lives on because of the words.

Those that follow are about the making of movies or the way those movies have been perceived, but not in specific title detail for they are not memoirs: the stories here are of the experience of films and filming, for those involved in their making and those who simply agree to their viewing. I know of no more perennially enthralling subject, and I only wish we had two volumes here – there are at least another eighteen stories I'd have liked to bring to your attention. Some other time, maybe.

Sheridan Morley
London, April 1994

JAY MCINERNEY

The Business

Like everybody else, I'd heard all about Hollywood before I moved out here. Still, you think things will be different for you. You say to yourself, sure this is a jungle, but I'm Doctor Livingstone.

I graduated from Columbia with a degree in English Lit. and went to work for a newspaper in Bergen County, just across the river from Manhattan, keeping my cheap apartment on West 111th Street where I lived with my girlfriend. My thesis was a post-structuralist tome on film adaptations of major American novels, and within a year I'd wangled the job of movie reviewer and entertainment reporter. I loved the movies – always have. The idea of being a screen-writer came to me during a pool interview with a writer-director who was in Manhattan flacking for his new picture. It wasn't the fact that he didn't seem particularly bright or that he made his ascent sound so haphazard and effortless. It was the way he looked, sitting there, smoking a cigarette as the light coming through the window of the forty-floor corporate tower hit his face: I could see the pores in his skin and the stubble of his beard and there was something green stuck between two of his teeth and I suddenly thought – I could be there, sitting where he's sitting with two days' growth and a green thing on my teeth.

I didn't quit my job that day, but I started writing screenplays, renting the films I loved and studying the structure, thinking about what they had in common. I was encouraged in this by my Aunt Alexis, who had once been a contract player at Paramount. She'd been in a couple of westerns with John Wayne and was briefly married to a director. After her divorce she moved to New York – the director made her quit the movies and it was too late to go back, she said, but she still talked as if she were a member of a warm, extended family called 'the business'. She claimed some tolerably famous names as friends, and avidly studied *Variety* and the *Hollywood Reporter*. I knew from the family that she'd been somewhat badly used by 'the business', but she wasn't bitter. She gave acting lessons in New York, occasionally did community theatre. When I'd moved to New York, she more or less adopted me. My parents were divorced, fading into the orange sunsets of Arizona and Florida respectively.

Alexis lived in thrifty elegance in a splendid pre-war building over near Sutton Place, a duplex she'd occupied for years, the first couple of them with her third husband, and which she wouldn't have been able to afford if not for rent control. Even with a severely depressed rent she'd had to subdivide the apartment and sublet the more luxurious lower floor, which was separated by two doors from her own quarters upstairs. The centerpiece of the downstairs apartment was a spectacular canopy bed replete with rose-colored chintz drapery. Alexis herself slept in the upstairs parlour on a pull-out sofa and cooked on a hotplate, since the kitchen was downstairs. At this time the lower floor was occupied by the manager of a rock group who was burning holes in all the upholstery. Alexis knew because she snuck down whenever he wasn't home and snooped around. She was trying to decide what to do: she needed the rent, plus she had introduced this guy to the landlord as her nephew, since he refused to let her take a subtenant.

Alexis encouraged me in my screen-writing ambitions and read my earliest attempts. She also gave me the only good advice I've ever gotten on the subject. 'Dalton Trumbo once told me the secret of a screenplay,' she said, mixing herself a negroni in the closet which served her as kitchen, pantry and bar. It was six in the evening and the fading light was slicing through the mullioned windows at a forty-five-degree angle – that second-to-last light which is thick and yellow with doomed bravado – making the dust swimming through the big old apartment seem like movie mist.

'He was a lovely man, much misunderstood,' she said. 'That McCarthy stuff – terrible. But as I was starting to say, Dalton said to me one night – I think we were at the Selznicks' and I said, "Dalton, what's your secret?" and he whispered something in my ear which I won't repeat. I gave him a little slap on the wrist, not that I was really mad. I was flattered and told him so, but at the time I was still married to the fag. This was before I found out he was that way. So I said to Dalton, "No, no, I meant – what's the secret of a great screenplay?" And he said, "It's very simple, Lex. Three acts – first act, get man up tree, second act, shake a stick at him, third act, get him down from the tree."'

When Alexis was really in her cups she told me she'd call up Sam Cohn or some other great friend of hers and fix me up, the exquisitely carved syllables of her trained speech softening, liquefying like the cubes in her glass. But the fact is she didn't have any juice in the industry. I didn't mind. I eventually landed an agent on my own, at which point I figured it was time to make the leap of faith. Plus my girlfriend announced that she was in love with my best friend and that they'd been sleeping together for six months.

I sublet my apartment in New York and got a place in Venice three blocks from the beach. It was February and I loved it, leaving the frozen, rotten city for a place where I could wake up smelling flowers and the ocean. At the same time, Venice of all places in Southern California reminded me of New York – everything had a certain shabbiness, and there were bums all over the place. The crime rate was pretty impressive, just so I wouldn't get too homesick – just so I'd know I was on the same planet. But basically I felt the same way about California that Keats did about Chapman's Homer. I quit smoking, got on the Pritkin diet, started sleeping regular hours.

One thing I didn't do was rush out to join AA, which was just becoming the really hip thing to do then. If I had I probably would have met some girls. But I was still under the thrall of the idea of the writer as holy lush. Who could imagine Raymond Chandler sober? One of my favorite Hollywood stories involved Herman Mankiewicz, the other genius behind *Citizen Kane*. Mankiewicz found himself one night in the home of one of

Beverly Hills's newest *nouveau riche* hostesses, a woman who had recently learned the correct sequence of forks and knives for a seven-course dinner and who took this knowledge very seriously. The legendarily unmanageable writer arrived for dinner drunk and got drunker, till finally he evacuated the contents of his stomach all over the dinner-table. As the guests looked on horrified, Mankiewicz turned to his hostess and said, 'Don't worry – the white wine came up with the fish.'

In Venice I had a little terrace off the back of my second-storey studio. I'd wake up early most mornings and take my computer out there to work. It overlooked a tiny courtyard choked with cactus and palms and flowering bushes. I grew up in the intemperate zones and I still get a little thrill when I see a palm tree. My landlady believed that nature should be allowed to take its course and she just let it all grow. The couple across the courtyard believed in nature too; they fucked at all hours with the shades up and I couldn't help seeing them, usually her bobbing up and down on top of him, facing me. I guess she was performing. Maybe she thought I was a casting director – all the world's a couch. Anyway, I appreciated it. That was as close as I was getting to carnal knowledge.

My second screenplay opens with this very scene: close on couple making love, girl on top, camera pulling back out the window, pulling back, reverse angle on the guy watching this scene from the terrace across the way. Eventually the girl and the guy on the terrace meet and have this incredible affair. She decides to leave her boyfriend for him, the writer, but of course the boyfriend turns out to be a coke dealer involved with some very heavy Colombians, and it turns out the girl knows a lot about the inner workings of the gang and has information that could implicate the boys in a murder. Except she doesn't know it . . .

Believe it or not, this screenplay attracted the interest of a fairly important producer. That was when I first met Danny Brode. The producer had a first-look deal with the studio where Brode was the new vice-president of production. Brode scheduled a meeting for me – my first with a studio executive. I spent about three hours in the morning trying to figure out what to wear and whether or not to shave. Finally I shaved and put on a white shirt, tie, blazer and jeans. Brode made me wait an hour and finally, when I was ushered into his dazzling white office, he shook my hand and said, 'What, you got a funeral or a wedding to go to today?' and when I looked baffled, he said, 'The tie, dude.' So I knew I'd worn the wrong thing and I knew he knew I'd worn the tie for him.

Brode was wearing jeans and a work-shirt which barely held him in. Standing about five foot six, the man weighed 350 if he weighed an ounce. He could have been a sumo wrestler. If his cheeks had been breasts they'd have filled D-cups, and his chin would have made another man's pot belly. Not exactly the guy to be handing out advice on appearances. Anyway, he told me he'd been running late all day and could we take the meeting in his car: he had to drive out to the valley to check on the mixing for a film in post-production.

So we go out to the parking-lot and get in his car, which is this four-door Maserati sedan. I didn't even know Maserati made sedans but I figured Brode was too big to drive around in their sports model – maybe they made it especially for him. We drive out to the valley and he spends most of the time on his carphone, but in between he listens to me pitching like crazy. Finally he says, 'Instead of a writer, how about if this guy is an artist? We move the thing from Venice to San Francisco, and the guy's got this big like studio full of canvases and he sees the couple screwing from his studio. The art thing is very hot right now, and we'll get a lot more visuals this way.'

I don't know, I probably would have made my hero into a female impersonator; I was dying to get into the game. I'd exhausted my savings and my Subaru needed new brakes and I hadn't met a girl yet who wanted to go out to dinner with an unemployed screen-writer. My ex-best friend had just written to say he and my ex-girlfriend were getting married and he hoped I didn't have any hard feelings. I pretended to think about Brode's suggestion deeply for a minute and then I said, 'I like it. I think I could work it.'

He dropped me at the gate of the sound studio and gave me a card with the number of a car service. 'We'll work it out with your agent.' I stood around for an hour baking in the sun waiting for the car which finally came and took me back to the studio. I bought a bottle of Spanish bubbly and knocked it back on the terrace that night while my neighbors traded orgasms.

I called Alexis in New York. She told me that I was now part of the big, happy family which was the business, and we talked for an hour to the accompaniment of her ice cubes tinkling in the crystal highball glass.

I thought about calling my old girlfriend: in my drunken state I could imagine her chagrin when she realised what she'd given up. But I passed out instead.

'Martin, darling, I'm going to make you a rich man,' my agent told me a week later. She'd grown up on Long Island and had only been out here a couple of years but she talked just like something out of *What Makes Sammy Run* – they must give you a copy at LAX Arrivals or something; I don't know why I didn't get mine.

The deal was three drafts at scale, which wasn't a great deal but it was more money than I made in a year at the newspaper and I was thrilled. Plus, it was a foot in the door. 'Danny Brode is really big,' my agent said without a trace of irony. 'That man is going places and he can take you with him.'

'I don't want to go to the fat farm,' I said.

'You better start watching your mouth around this town,' my agent said. 'It's a small community and if you want to be part of it you've got to play by the rules. Bo Goldman and Bob Towne can maybe afford to be smartasses but you can't.'

'Could you send me a list of the rules?' I said. I was so happy I couldn't help being full of myself. The next week my agent took me to lunch at Spago's. She introduced me to several people she described as important players, calling me 'Martin Brooks, the writer'.

Then I started writing. I wrote a draft making my hero into a painter. I flew up to San Francisco to get atmosphere, talked to gallery-owners and artists. Just dropping the name of the studio was enough to open doors. I implied that a major star was interested in the lead. Back home I was able to get an interview with a narcotics squad investigator for the LAPD who filled me in on the inner workings of the drug cartels.

Ten weeks after the papers were signed I handed in a draft. The next day I got a package Federal Express – a bottle of Cristal attached to Danny Brode's business card. That was how it was printed on the card: Danny Brode. Just an ordinary guy, right? No need to wear a tie here. Anyway, drinking that bottle of Cristal was the high point of the whole experience. The hangover set in a couple of weeks later.

My agent called. 'Basically they are thrilled with the script. Absolutely ecstatic. But they want to talk to you about a couple of tiny little changes.'

I said, 'No problem, we're contracted for three drafts, right? I mean, I make another ten grand or something for a rewrite, don't I?'

'Don't worry your genius brain about it. Just take the meeting and we'll see what they want.'

What they wanted was a completely different story. Brode had fallen in love with his idea of the art world backdrop and now he wanted to make it a movie about the way commerce corrupted artists. Columbia had a project about the art world in development and he wanted to beat them. We could keep the drug element – the big shot gallery-owner would be involved in the coke trade. I sat in his huge white office, trying to figure out where the white walls and the white leather furniture began and ended, trying to see the virtues of his new idea, trying to recognise some shred of my own script.

I nodded like an idiot and said it sounded really interesting. I practically told him he was a genius and that I didn't know why I hadn't seen his idea in the first place. Back home, though, I got mad. I called my agent and screamed at her about the stupidity of studio executives and about the way art was corrupted by commerce. She listened patiently. Finally I said, 'Well, at least I get paid to be a whore.'

She said, 'Try and pick out the virtues in his concept. I'll work on the money.'

'What do you mean, "work on the money"? It's in the contract.'

'Of course,' she said.

I sat down again trying just to be professional about the whole thing, which is to say, trying not to give a shit. Three weeks later I delivered the new draft. I'd just bought a new car, a little Beamer, with my first check. One morning when my agent called me to talk about another project, I said, 'When am I getting paid for my second draft?'

'We're calling that a polish instead of a draft.'

'What do you mean, a "polish"? It was a whole new story. I knocked myself out. Are you trying to tell me I'm not getting paid? What about the contract?'

'Look, Martin. You're new at this. Brode says it's a polish and he wants you to do one more polish before he shows it to the big man.'

I was beginning to understand. I'd already been in LA a year. 'You mean I get paid for a second draft, but it's not a draft unless fat Brode says it's a draft.'

'Let's just say it behoves us to please Danny Brode at this point and give him some slack. Believe me, darling, you don't want to get known as a difficult writer. Give him one more polish and I promise you it will be worth your while in the long run.'

I threatened to go to the Writer's Guild and she said she would hate to end our professional relationship, but I had to trust her on this one.

Maybe you've heard the one about the agent who's approached by the Devil. The Devil says, 'I'll give you any client you want – Redford, Newman, Pacino, you name it – in exchange for your immortal soul for all eternity.' And the agent says, 'What's the catch?'

I stopped trusting my agent from that moment on, but I followed her advice. I wrote a total of three drafts and got paid for one. The project was in turnaround within six months. I didn't see Brode for a couple of years but my agent was right, in a sense. That deal led to others – even though my first baby died, I was bankable; I'd had a deal and that led to other deals and within a couple of years I had my first movie in production and I'd moved into a place in Laurel Canyon, although I continued to sublet the place in Manhattan, maintaining a tie to my pain and to a world which still seemed more real than the one in which I lived. And whenever I needed a villain for a story, someone rich and powerful to harass the leads, I was always able to draw on my impressions of Danny Brode.

Brode became even more rich and powerful over the next couple of years. He married the daughter of a major Hollywood dynasty and shortly thereafter was running the studio which the family controlled. Consolidation of power through marriage was established procedure in this particular family and on one side they were related to one of America's major crime syndicates. Brode's father-in-law was alleged to be responsible for some untimely deaths, and in the film community it was whispered that a premarital conference had been held in which Brode had been made to understand that if he ran around on his wife, he would fall precipitously from grace. This was considered bizarre, since everybody fucked around in proportion to their power and wealth, people who ran studios and owned casinos most of all. I mean, that was practically the whole point of being successful. But the old boy was apparently over-fond of his first daughter.

'Some nice Faustian elements in this situation,' I said to the lunch partner who first filled me in on this story. I once heard someone say there are only seven basic stories, but in this business there's only one. In Hollywood the story is always Faust.

'Some nice who?' my lunch partner said.

I said I was just thinking of a German film.

Brode got even fatter. In a town where everybody had a personal trainer and where a green salad was considered a main course, there was something almost heroic about his obesity. I saw him sometimes at Morton's or wherever, and after a while – I'd say from the time CAA took over my representation and I started dating actresses – he even began to recognise me. I heard stories. My first agent was right – the bitch. It's a small town.

One of the stories I heard was about a novelist I knew from Columbia. After his first novel made him famous, he star-tripped out here to soak up some of the gravy. Success came on him pretty quickly and he ran so fast to keep up with it that he got out in front of it. He bought a million-dollar co-op on

Central Park West and a beach house in Maine, plus he had a little problem with the 'C' word. He'd sold his book to Brode's studio outright, which is to say he got paid the same no matter whether it went into production or not. By the time the second payment was due, this writer was pretty desperate for money – he was overdue on both his mortgages, his girlfriend had an insatiable wardrobe and his wife was socking him for a big settlement. Brode knew about this. So when it came time to pay off, he called the writer up to his house in Malibu and he said, 'Look, I owe you a quarter mil, but at this point I don't know if we're going to go into production. Things are tight and your stock's down in the wine-cellar with the cabernets. Let's just say I either could give you seventy-five and we could call it even. Or I could tie you up in court for the next ten years.' The writer started screaming about the contract, his agency, the Writer's Guild. And Brode said, 'Talk to your agent, babe. I think he'll see it my way.'

Even in Hollywood this was not standard procedure, but the writer's stock had dropped: after being hot for a season, he'd cooled off fast, and the agency, after a lot of thought, decided to go with Brode and advised the writer to take the seventy-five and shut up.

By the time I heard this story, I wasn't even surprised. I'd learned a lot in three years.

I did well by local standards, and it wasn't surprising that I found myself doing business with Brode again. Several production companies were interested in an idea of mine when Brode called my agency to say he wanted to work with me. CAA packaged a deal with me, a director and two stars. The story was set in New York. This was the one I'd been wanting to do from the beginning. Let's just say it was a story of betrayal and revenge. The one-liner on the project, devised by my agent, was: 'A Yuppie *Postman Always Rings Twice*.' For a variety of reasons, some of them aesthetic, it was important to me that the movie be shot in New York. Brode wanted to do it in Toronto and send a second unit to New York for a day. It was a money issue; Toronto was cheaper.

I knew I didn't have the juice to change anybody's mind

when two or three million dollars were at stake, so I worked on the director. He was a man with several commercially successful films behind him who was dying to be an *auteur*. He wanted the kind of respect that Scorsese and Coppola got and he didn't understand how it had eluded him so far. An autodidactic actor had recently introduced him to the work of Dostoevsky – an author I should check out, he assured me, Russian, as a matter of fact – and within weeks it had worked a change on his demeanor: he had grown a beard and started scowling. It wasn't difficult to convince him that the New York critical and intellectual fraternity would take his film much more seriously if it were *authentic* – that is to say, if it were shot in New York. I said you couldn't fake these things, not even in the movies. Look at Woody Allen, I said. You think he'd shoot a movie in Toronto? You think they'd publish him in the *New Yorker* if he did?

That did it. Brode kicked and screamed, but the director was adamant and very eloquent on the subject of authenticity. And in Hollywood directors count. In the end, after I'd given them my third draft, they headed off to New York with long lines of credit and suitcases full of money for the friendly local teamsters.

I flew out for pre-production; the director had decided he liked having me around and Brode had no objections; so long as I didn't ask for a consulting fee, they were happy to pay my expenses in New York. Brode's assistant, a woman named Karen Levine, would be on location, while Brode would fly out once in a while to check in. Levine was petite, blonde and terribly swift and efficient so that at first I hardly noticed her. In Los Angeles one can become accustomed to thinking of beauty as something languid, sexiness as a quality that inhered in the slow-moving, self-conscious forms of actresses and professional companions. Karen was no odalisque. But I started noticing her more and more. Despite the legendary informality of Southern California – the indiscriminate use of first names, the gross over-extension of the concept of friendship – it was unusual to encounter a human being who sailed straight between the whirlpool of craven servility and the shoals of condescension. Karen did and I liked her for it. It occurred to me that she was doing more than working for Brode, but I enquired discreetly

and the buzz was that they were strictly business and that Brode
was living up to the terms of his contract with his father-in-law.

When I heard Karen say she was looking for a place in New
York for the three months of filming, I thought of Alexis, who
had finally thrown the rock manager out of her first floor and
lost several thousand in the process. I figured the studio could
afford a rent high enough to make up some of what Hollywood
had taken out of her in the old days, and I knew Alexis would
be thrilled by her new proximity to 'the business'. Plus I liked
the idea of doing Karen a favor.

I brought Karen over one afternoon. We were both staying at
the Sherry Netherland, and I walked her over to Sutton Place. I
wanted her to see New York at its best – she'd grown up in
Pasadena and was a little nervous about the idea of three
months in dirty, dangerous Manhattan. It was a cool day at the
end of April. The air was crisp, swept clean by a light breeze.
Across the street the Plaza glowed white in the sun. We went
up to 60th and across to Park Avenue, where the daffodils were
blooming in the center median and the doormen stood guard at
the entrances of the grand old buildings, then over past Bloom-
ingdales and down to 57th. Karen looked casually tremendous
in an Irish sweater and jeans. I felt like a boy returning to his
own country having made good in the colonies, although I
eventually learned that the two people I most wanted to impress
had moved to Cambridge.

Alexis greeted us in a flowing caftan, kissed Karen on both
cheeks and ushered us into the upstairs parlor where she'd laid
out a tea service that would have done Claridge's proud. Karen
was impressed. Alexis took us on a tour, pointing out the
treasures – pictures of herself and the Duke, herself and Bogie,
a signed first edition from Faulkner, a set of candlesticks given
to her by Red Skelton, the love seat on which she'd traded
confidences – here she winked – with Errol Flynn. Some of this
stuff I hadn't even heard before. She was laying it on a bit thick,
but Karen managed to seem both attentive and relaxed. Then
we went downstairs and I knew Karen was hooked as soon as
she saw the big canopy bed, floating in the middle of the

panelled bedroom, wreathed in rose-colored chintz, like a feminised pirate galleon.

Before Alexis had mixed her second negroni — 'I don't usually drink in the afternoon but this is an occasion, are you sure you won't have one?' — it was decided. Karen would move in for three months. Alexis would introduce her to the landlord as her niece. When we finally left at six, I asked Karen out to dinner. She said she had a lot of work to do but she'd love to some other night.

Shooting started. I hung around, visiting the set every couple of days. Brode flew in almost every weekend, which surprised me. He seemed to be taking an excessive interest in the project. Each visit he managed to make someone miserable. Three weeks into shooting it was me. He had decided he didn't like the ending as it stood in the script and he wanted me to rewrite it. He wanted something more upbeat. I kicked and screamed and told him about the integrity of the story. I tried to go through the director, but Brode had worked on him first, and he was impervious to my warnings about what the *New Yorker* would think of the new ending. Apparently he was thinking about his two points of the gross.

'It comes down to this, Martin,' Brode told me as he sawed into a veal chop at Elaine's one night. 'You write the new ending or we hire somebody else. I'll give you another twenty-five; call it a consulting fee.' I watched him insert half a pound of calf's flesh into his maw and waited for him to choke on it and die. It occurred to me that he was too fat for anybody to perform the Heimlich manœuvre on him successfully. I could say to the police officers — hey, sorry, I tried to get my arms around him but no go.

I rewrote the ending. For me it ruined the movie but the public bought almost a hundred million dollars' worth of tickets and I was nominated for an Oscar the next spring.

I visited Alexis frequently and used these occasions to knock on Karen's door. One night she let me take her to dinner. I told her about my ex-girlfriend in New York, how she'd run off and married my best friend. I'd never told anyone before. Karen was appalled and sympathetic. She'd adopted the uniform of feminine night-time New York, looking very sexy in a small, tight black dress. At her door we exchanged a long, encouraging kiss, but when the kiss began to develop a life of its own, she pulled back and said she had to be up at five.

One evening I went over to visit Alexis. As she was mixing two negronis, she said, 'Who's Karen's boyfriend, anyway? I take it he's some big shot.'

'I don't think she has a boyfriend,' I said, somewhat alarmed.

'I can't understand how someone as pretty as Karen could let that fat man touch her.'

Feeling relieved, I said, 'That wasn't Karen's boyfriend, that was her boss.'

Alexis snorted. 'Call it what you want. I know about girls and their bosses.'

'It's not like that with Karen,' I said.

'Don't tell me what it's not. I have to listen to them. And now I have to buy a new bed.'

'What are you talking about?'

She put a finger to her lips, walked over to the stairway door, opened it and listened. Then she motioned for me to follow her down.

The canopy bed was wrecked. The satin-skirted box-spring, which had previously seemed to float above the floor, was now earthbound; the bedposts and the chintz draperies were tangled and splayed.

'Her boss,' Alexis said, sounding for once as tough and as cynical as someone who has been hard-used by men and their institutions, as someone who has had to sing and dance for her supper and then some, revealing in those two syllables the bitterness and anger that I always thought she would have been entitled to feel. 'I've had bosses like that,' she said, her eyes distant, looking back in time. After ten or fifteen seconds in which I contemplated the grotesque implications of the wreckage she shook her head and smiled. 'But thank God I never had one that gross. Poor girl's risking her life every time she climbs into bed with that whale.'

Brode had flown back to the West Coast that morning, so I had a whole week to think out my strategy. When he got back to town, I called a meeting. The only time he could meet me was breakfast. He told me to meet him over at the Regency at seven-thirty, the Regency being at this time where all the big players from LA stayed when they were in town, and where the local robber barons and power-brokers breakfasted. When I arrived at eight, he was just finishing off a plate of ham and eggs.

'I'm just leaving,' he said. 'What's up?'

'I want to do another movie. I think you might like this one.'

'What's the pitch?' he said. 'I've got exactly three minutes.'

'It's a mob story,' I said.

'Pretty well-worked turf,' he mumbled.

'You'll like this,' I said, fishing in the bread basket to retrieve a piece of toast which Brode had somehow overlooked. I leaned back in my chair and surveyed the room, rotten with titans of industry and finance and entertainment. It was easy to pick out the movie people – the others wore Hermes ties under bespoke suits of discreet cut and color. Brode was partially covered by a blue Oxford cloth shirt, open three buttons down to expose a wedge of black hair and white flesh. I caught the eye of a local mogul whose expression betrayed aesthetic outrage at Brode's physical appearance and for a moment I found myself on the fat man's side. At least, I thought, Danny Brode looks like what he is. His fellow diners were almost to a man bloated in every way but the obvious one. They'd all made their deals with the Prince. And I saw that I had been too hard on my adopted home town, and realised that I would not be coming back to New York except to visit. For the first time I could remember, I identified myself with the business from which I derived my livelihood, confederate with Brode and all of the unabashed and unbuttoned men of the West, the land-grabbers and gold-diggers and claim-jumpers and deal-makers, all the restless self-seekers tramping their brethren underfoot in their rush to the beach-front property of the Pacific. These men knew that there was only one story, even if they didn't know who Faust was.

But I had a story of my own to tell.

The story I pitched to Brode concerned a young mobster whose career takes a fast turn for the better when he marries the daughter of a major don. But there's a catch. The don tells him if he ever screws around on his daughter, he'll be a very sorry scuba diver, fifty feet under without oxygen. After the marriage, the new family member does very well. But it seems there's this young wise guy within the organisation who happens to live in the same building as this very attractive girl . . .

The story had a sort of farcical scene involving a broken bed. The broken bed led to very dire consequences for some of the parties concerned.

Brode scratched the congealing egg yolk on his plate with the tines of his fork as he listened to the pitch, his pink face taking on color with each sentence. At the end he looked into my eyes to see if he might be mistaken about what he was really hearing.

Then he said, 'What do you want?'

'I want to do another movie with you. OK, maybe not this one, but something else. And I want to produce.'

'I could have you . . .' He didn't finish.

That was how I became a producer. In the end we came to terms that were very satisfactory from my point of view. I don't think Brode felt it was the best deal he'd ever made in his life. I knew that I'd have to watch out for him. But the project I eventually wrote and produced made money for both of us, which made me feel a little safer when I went to sleep at night.

A year later I flew back to New York for Alexis's funeral. One of ten mourners, I cried when they lowered the coffin into the ground out in the cemetery in Queens. The last time I could remember crying was on a day that should have been happy for me. I'd just gotten a call from an agent in California who read my script and decided to represent me. I waited two hours for Terry, my girlfriend, to come home from work. I bought flowers and champagne and called everyone I knew. Finally Terry got home and I almost knocked her over. We'd talked about moving to California together if things worked well for me. I poured champagne on our heads and talked about our future in the promised land.

'We can live near the beach,' I said, following her into the bathroom where she rubbed a pink towel back and forth across her dark hair. 'We'll have a car and we'll drive up to Big Sur on the weekends.' That was when she told me she'd been sleeping with my best friend. One minute I've got champagne streaming down my face and the next minute tears, looking at pink lint from the towel in the dark strands of my girlfriend's wet hair. I thought about that as I listened to the words of the minister at the cemetery. I remembered that day years ago in a one-bedroom apartment on West 111th Street as being the last time I cried. I don't think it will happen again.

ALISON LURIE

extract from
The Nowhere City

The empty sound stage was like the inside of an immense dark
cardboard box; a vast cube of obscure space. Against the distant
walls hung painted drop cloths representing in meticulous detail
the landscape and architecture of the imaginary planet Nemo,
setting of Glory's current picture, a science-fiction musical
comedy. Assemblages of platforms and steps rose here and there
in the darkness like hillocks on a plain, among herds of folding
chairs. On the dusty ground, black electrical cables and wires of
all sizes were coiled and crossed, in some places resembling a
nest of enormous snakes. Steel and aluminium skeletons supported the spotlights and floods, and the immense cameras on
their travelling booms. More hanging lights, microphones,
ropes, flats, and cables disappeared into the shadows far above.

All these lights were dark now; the only illumination came
from the long strip of hot sunshine slanting in from the open
doorway, fading as it fanned across the cement; and from the
electric bulbs around the make-up mirror in Glory's trailer
dressing-room.

It was hot everywhere today; densely hot and smoggy out-
doors; only a little less so where Glory and her agent Maxie
Weiss were sitting in front of her trailer on two wooden chairs.
Glory's make-up was caked with sweat, for she had been
working for three hours, rehearsing dance numbers; or standing
about waiting in the excruciating boredom of film-making while
other members of the cast rehearsed, or while the choreogra-
pher conferred endlessly with the director, the assistant director,
the musical director, the dance coach, the man in charge of the
extras, and his and their assistants. The tower of pink-blonde
hair, though skewered to her head with innumerable pins, had

begun to fray at the edges; her rehearsal clothes (black tights and loose sleeveless white top) were wrinkled and damp.

She sat in the naturally graceful pose of a dancer, one leg tucked under her, the other pointed out along the floor, drinking from a Thermos bottle a health-food drink called Frozen Tiger's Milk. Maxie was eating two pastrami sandwiches which had been wrapped in waxed paper; he looked hot, fat, and worried. He would have been lunching at Scandia, an air-conditioned restaurant near his air-conditioned office on Sunset Strip, and Glory would have been at the studio lunchroom, if they had not had to confer about a crisis.

The trouble had all started yesterday. It had been a bad day for Glory, an unlucky day. While she was eating breakfast, her girlfriend, a starlet named Ramona Moon, had called up to warn her that Pluto was square with Neptune in her fourth house and she ought not to engage in any new or important professional ventures. Also she should avoid all occasions that might lead to serious emotional conflict; in fact about the best thing she could do would be to get right back into bed and stay there. Glory was not, like Mona, a follower of astrology; all the same, it would have been better if she had listened to her.

The first thing that happened was that she broke off one of her finger-nails starting the T-Bird. The traffic on the way to the studio was hell, and when she got there Roger, the best make-up man, was out sick. Then, while they were waiting around between takes, Petey Thorsley, a little dancer who was playing one of the other natives of Nemo, came over. He leaned on the back of a chair, in his green rubber costume with pink polka-dots and webbed hands like a duck, and remarked to Glory that Dr Einsam had been seen eating cheesecake in Zucky's out in Santa Monica with a brunette, and what was the story? 'You tell me, don't ask me,' Glory said, thinking that Mona had been right. 'Gee, that's all I know,' Petey said, his wire antennae quivering. 'Listen, don't let it get you down. My friend said she was nothing anyhow, kind of an intellectual type . . . Aw hell, Glory, I'm sorry.'

'That's OK, Petey, it doesn't bother me,' she had replied, manufacturing her smile.

Her real mistake had been to think that the stars were through

with her after that one. She grew careless when nothing more
went wrong on set the rest of the day; when she even got off
early and beat some of the traffic driving home. She forgot
about astrology; she had a big evening ahead.

There was a première that night of a picture called *Dancing
Cowboy*, starring Rory Gunn. Rory was also the star of the
musical that Glory was making now, and in which she had for
the first time what might be called a second female lead, even if
she did have to play it with antennae and green hands. As it
was, naturally, top priority that Rory Gunn should be well
disposed towards Glory, ever since the picture started Maxie
had been putting out stories about how much she thought of
him as an actor, and what a tremendous thrill it was for her to
have the chance to play with him. For that evening he had
arranged that after the showing, when Rory was on his way out
of the theatre, Glory would rush up to him and kiss him in a
spontaneous demonstration of her admiration; kind of kooky,
but loveable, and really *sincere*. He had cleared this with the
studio and with Rory's agent, and alerted the local papers and
also two wire services. Glory had a new dress for the occasion,
short white bouffant satin printed with pink roses, and she had
borrowed a white mink stole from the studio. So it was all set.

Rory Gunn came out of the theatre first, right on schedule,
taking it slow and giving the crowd behind the ropes a good
look at his profile. Glory was close behind him, but at the door
of the lobby she held back a couple of seconds, waiting for a
good clear space to open up between her and the photographers.
Then she stepped out, saw Rory, did a big take – excitement,
adoration – and began to run.

She had waited a moment too long. As she approached Rory,
a girl in the crowd, one of his fans, broke through the police
line and also started racing towards him. They got to the star
about the same time, and Glory stepped in front of the kid, but
before she could open her mouth to speak this juvenile delin-
quent put her hand in Glory's face and gave her a violent push.
Glory staggered back on her three-inch pink satin heels; tripped,
screamed, and fell on her ass on the sidewalk, with a noise of
ripping cloth. From this position she saw the girl fling her arms
around Rory Gunn and kiss him passionately, while he just

stood there looking dumb. Without stopping to think, boiling with fury, Glory scrambled up in the ruins of her dress, one shoe off, limped forward, and slammed the kid in the jaw. Even as the blow went home she knew she had made a terrible mistake; she heard a louder howl rise from the crowd and the flash bulbs popping, like all Mona's unlucky stars machine-gunning her down together.

Maxie had done what he could to mop up the mess. First he got the girl back into the lobby and started talking to her; come on, after all, he told her, Glory is a fan of Rory Gunn's same as you are; you ought to appreciate what she felt like when you shoved yourself in like that; besides you ruined her new two-hundred-dollar dress for her. It went over pretty well: at least the kid stopped crying, and Maxie got a taxi around to the stage door and sent her home before newspaper guys could get to her again. In the morning he ordered two lots of flowers delivered to the kid's house: some daffodils and a whole lot of other spring stuff from Glory, and three dozen red roses from Rory Gunn. Of course Maxie couldn't kill the story – but he spoke to the guys, giving them pretty much the same line: that Glory was so stuck on Rory Gunn and his marvellous performance in *Dancing Cowboy* that she just saw red when anybody got in her way. This story had appeared in the morning papers which lay about on the floor at Maxie's and Glory's feet. As he said now, it could have been a lot worse, even the photos.

'Uh-uh,' Glory uttered. 'Listen, thanks for everything, Maxie,' she added in a dull, throaty voice, and drank some Tiger's Milk. 'You're a doll.'

'That's OK. At least you appreciate.' Maxie wiped his face and began stripping the crusts off half a sandwich. 'I wonder should I check up on that kid again this afternoon, how she's feeling, is she OK?'

'No,' Glory said. 'Let's drop it.'

'Maybe you're right. I sent flowers already; we don't want to start a correspondence.'

'Yeah. Besides, she hit me first,' Glory pointed out, not for the first time.

'She's a fan,' Maxie said. 'It doesn't make any difference what she did. You can't sock a fan. Also she's only fourteen years old. A kid.'

'Yeah, well, shit: how was I supposed to know that? You tell her next time she wants to push somebody in the face bring her birth certificate.'

Maxie winced. It always bothered him when Glory's language became too vulgar; he was trying to put her across as basically a sweet kid. He shifted around and sat sideways in his chair, facing her. 'Something else I got in my mind,' he said. 'I want to suggest a new image. We got to black out this picture you don't like fans. I thought of a gimmick this morning we could use, maybe. I want to put out a release – how does this sound? – Glory Green, now working in Superb's big new musical, etcetera, has a very *personal* relationship to her growing number of fans all over the world. Glory reads every day all the letters she receives, and she says she picks up lots of acting tips and good advice about her career from the girls and boys who follow her pictures: how does that sound?'

'OK,' Glory said listlessly.

'Swell. Also I thought I'd call up Camilla at *Screen Scoops*, offer we could give her an exclusive. Maybe she can send somebody over this weekend and get some pictures. Like an example, I see you sitting at your antique writing-desk, nice outfit, serious expression, big piles of mail, dictating to your secretary. I like that.'

'OK,' Glory repeated. 'My secretary? You think I should have a secretary? Don't you think that looks kind of too snooty?'

'Oh, nah. Everybody has a secretary. Liz Taylor has a secretary. Look at it this way: it shows how you're real serious about your responsibilities; it's like your business, these fan letters. I want to build up a nice picture. Anyhow, you got to get a secretary to answer the mail.'

Glory put the Thermos down and, turning her head slowly, looked at her agent through her fog of depression. 'Aw, Maxie,' she said. 'Do we really have to play this scene? I don't think I can make it.'

'Don't aggravate yourself. It'll be no trouble.' Maxie registered Glory's expression, and sought its probable cause. 'Hey, you had a conversation with Iz this morning?' he asked. 'Maybe he called you.'

Glory shook her head. 'Why should he call me? He's got nothing to talk to me about,' she said in a strained voice. 'He doesn't give a shit what happens to me.'

'Aw, Glory, baby. He's calling you all the time already. This last month he's phoned you eight, ten times.'

'Theven times,' she corrected him. 'Exactly theven times.'

'That's what I mean. He's obviously carrying the torch. And look at you: six months, and you're still very involved emotionally. I don't understand. Next time he phones, why don't you be a little nice to him?'

'That's how you thee it,' Glory said. She opened her mouth to relate Iz's latest betrayal, but could not bring herself to do so, and remained silent, staring into the dark spaces of the sound stage.

'Incidentally,' Maxie said, following his own train of thought. 'I spoke to Bo Habenicht this a.m.' Bo was Rory Gunn's agent. Maxie waited for Glory to ask 'Yeah?' As she did not, he continued. 'Rory's happy as a kid about the statement you gave. You know it's all gravy for him, that scene. Also he really appreciates your compliments. He wants to take you out some time this week, maybe tonight if you can make it.'

'You mean you and Bo want Gunn to take me out,' Glory said as flatly as was possible for her. This 'commercial socialising', as he called it, was one of the things Iz picked on most about her profession. 'What's the matter with him, doesn't he know I'm married yet?'

'Aw, come on now.' Maxie laid his sandwich down on its waxed paper. What with the trouble last night and his nervous stomach (he had something inside there that was probably planning to be an ulcer) he had got practically no sleep. But this was his job; he gathered his forces. 'What's the difference to you? All I'm asking is you should sit a table with Rory an hour or so in a couple of night spots. I'm not suggesting to spend a weekend with him.'

'With that fag? You better not. That guy's so minty he gives me the creeps.'

'Baby, you got to think of the publicity angle. If you show

around town with Rory a couple times, all this trouble could blow over; it even could be to your advantage. Also, the studio would like it. How do you think it's going to look to them, you turn down a date with Rory Gunn? You should be flattered.'

Glory paid no attention to this hard sell, but continued with her own thoughts. 'I'll bet that's the first time in the fruit's life he ever had two women really fighting over him. No wonder he was stunned.' She gave a short laugh.

With a grating noise, the sliding door to the building slid open behind them. The strip of smog and sunlight widened across the floor, and a party of five or six new starlets entered the sound stage, accompanied by a minor studio executive named Baby Peterson, who was showing them over the lot.

'Glory, baby!' he called out. 'Hey, c'mon over here, girls! I want you to meet a kid who's really making it.'

Squeaking and tripping over the electric cables, the starlets crossed the floor towards Glory. They were all very young, more or less beautiful, and immensely got up, with laquered hair, nylon eyelashes, and layers of petticoats – exquisite dolls, dressed for a party by some little girl too old to play with dolls. One by one they held out their pink, sharp, manicured hands to Glory while Baby told her their brand-new studio names.

Glory responded politely. Four years ago she had been a kid like these; she had been through all it had taken to get them here and all they were about to be put through. They were the usual assortment – a couple of brunettes, one sultry and the other the ladylike type; a redhead who moved like a dancer; and some blondes of varying shades, at whom Glory looked hardest because there was a remote chance that one of them might be competition some day.

'And this is Maxie Weiss, one of the best agents in the business, or should I say the best, baby?' Peterson gave Glory a quite meaningless wink. It was unknown whether he was called 'Baby' because of his predilection for this epithet, or whether it was a nickname retained from his childhood, an era now some distance away. Detractors claimed that Baby was really over sixty; he admitted variously to fifty and forty-five, but dressed and deported himself like an extremely young man or boy. He had a deep tan and very white teeth, and wore a seersucker suit, perforated shoes, and some well-made artificial hair.

'And how're you, Glory; how're you doing today?' he asked noisily, meanwhile putting his arm round one of the blondes and pinching her haunch in a friendly way. 'Is the sun smiling on you?' It had sometimes been suggested that Baby had his dialogue written for him cheap by hack writers that had been dropped by the studio.

'Just fine, Baby.' Of course it was impossible that Baby had not seen the papers this morning. He would not speak about the brawl in front of these kids, but the look he gave her was greedily searching under the smile and the tan. Glory certainly pulled a boo-boo last night, it said. Is she cracking up, maybe? Is she already on the way out? 'How're you feeling yourself?' she counter-attacked, turning a sexy smile on and then fading it off, like an electronic door opening and closing in a supermarket.

'Ah, I'm in great condition. I was working out in the gym two hours this morning.' To demonstrate his vigour, Baby grabbed another one of the starlets, this time the redhead, with his spare arm, and squeezed her with some difficulty to his chest. 'I'm ready for anything!' This time he winked at Maxie.

'Isn't he a great guy, huh!' the blonde said, rubbing against Baby. He pinched her again, in gratitude.

'Well, got to get back to work,' he added in a heavily kidding voice. 'It was really fine to see you, baby. All right, girls.'

Squeaking, they trooped out.

'That guy makes me sick,' Glory said as they disappeared. 'He's a creep, that's what he is.'

'Aw, he's not so bad.' Maxie had returned to his sandwich. 'He's got good intentions.'

'He has my ass. Do you know he was blowing off to Petey Thorsley last week how he's screwed with two hundred and thirteen girls, or some number like that.'

'Yeah? Whew.' Maxie sighed, as when one hears of an exhausting athletic feat.

'The little blonde in pink wasn't bad-looking,' Glory went on, testing for reassurance.

'I liked the redhead better. She had a good walk.'

It was not exactly the right answer; what Maxie should have said was that none of the bunch would ever rate a look if she was around, or to that effect.

'Yeah, but did you get a look at her expression when Baby grabbed her like that. She really didn't like it.'

'Oh, she'll learn to play along.'

'Maybe,' Glory said, drinking from the Thermos.

'If she can't, there's plenty others where she came from.' Maxie's tone was quite neutral; still, it implied that the clients of a successful press agent, too, were not irreplaceable. He had the tact not to point his moral, but allowed a minute of silence for it.

'How about half a pastrami sandwich?' he asked then. 'I eat any more on a day like this, I'll get acid indigestion.'

'Uh-uh . . . You want some Tiger's Milk? It's good for your stomach.'

'Uh, no thanks.' Maxie could not control a tone of distaste for this drink, which he knew to be made of orange juice, powdered skim milk, brewer's yeast, vitamins, minerals, and raw egg. He shifted around and sat sideways on his chair again, facing Glory directly, but not looking at her.

'What I don't like to picture,' he said, beginning to fold the waxed paper around what was left of his sandwich. 'It's how Rory is going to feel when he hears you turned him down. Naturally, he's going to be hurt.' He finished wrapping the sandwich and put it into the paper bag. 'Aw yeah, he's going to think, all these nice statements she put out, she won't even have supper with me. She can't stand to talk to me for a couple hours with food. Actually she must hate me, probably.'

'Ah, Maxie, you know it's not like that,' Glory protested throatily. 'I mean, considering he's a complete lunk-head and a screaming queer, Gunn's a pretty straight guy. And he's a real dancer. He's got a style that won't quit.'

With the shrewdness born of hard experience, Maxie did not speak; he only looked at his client with a sad expression, waiting.

'You really figure he'll be all broken up if I don't go out with him?' Glory asked, in a tone half ironic, half serious.

Maxie shrugged. 'A guy like that, naturally he's sensitive.

Already he's got the idea he can't make it with girls, not even as a friend . . . An incident like this comes along and proves it, there's still less chance he's ever going to be able to relate normally.'

'Gee, you sound like my husband,' Glory said. She frowned, gazing up into the darkness above them. Maxie said nothing.

WILLIAM SAROYAN

OK, Baby, This is the World

One Saturday at noon I took a cab at Paramount and rode to the Brown Derby on Vine Street and all the way down I listened to the radio. There were two programmes: a football game in the Middle-West, or maybe in the East, and music, a song: 'The World Is Mine Tonight'.

I wanted the music, and the driver wanted the game. He asked if I would mind if we listened to the game, and I told him I wouldn't mind at all.

I think Notre Dame lost. Navy won. It was an upset. Notre Dame was supposed to win. Easy. I didn't care one way or another who won or lost. I didn't even listen to the winning and losing part of the game. I listened only to a couple of mediocre plays. Nobody got anywhere, although a half-back was injured.

I learned later that Navy won. Three to nothing, I think. It was rather nice to know how the game turned out, but it wasn't amazing.

I wouldn't have been amazed if Navy had won by a score of six hundred and twelve to five hundred and ninety-seven, and I don't believe I would have been amazed if Notre Dame had won by a score of twenty-one to nothing.

I believe I wouldn't have been amazed if Navy, fearing defeat, had sent in a new team armed with machine-guns, and destroyed the Notre Dame team, including substitutes, the coach, the assistant coach, and several innocent bystanders, making a score of sixty-one to nothing.

I wouldn't have been the least startled if the mob of one side of the stadium had met the mob of the other side of the stadium in the centre of the field and fought it out hand to hand.

The song, 'The World Is Mine Tonight', is better than mediocre. In the song love wins, two to nothing. It's pleasant, but
not amazing. I knew love would win before the song ended,
before it began, before it was written. Love won in another song
once, three million to nothing: 'I Can't Give You Anything But
Love, Baby'.

It was the same with Roosevelt, too. I knew Roosevelt would
win, too. Navy, love, and Roosevelt are always good bets. I
thought I would send Hearst a cablegram or a telegram, but I
didn't know where to reach him. There would have been two
words in the message: HA HA. The telegram would have cost
me anywhere from sixty cents to two dollars, but I didn't send
it. A lot of rich people in San Francisco were angry with me
because I had told them Mr Landon had no more chance than I
had. They said if that was so, then goodbye Democracy. I said,
All right, goodbye. Twenty years ago, when I was eight, I
suppose I would have been horrified if there had been a
threatening of goodbye Democracy.

I got out of the cab, bought a paper, and walked into the
Brown Derby for lunch. The headline said the rebels were near
Madrid, but don't think for a moment that I was amazed. I just
took the paper to the table and when the director came in and
sat down I said, The Fascists are near Madrid.

We ordered lunch. I had cold meats and the director had cold
meats. It was a good lunch and I dare say the Navy–Notre Dame
game was a good game. The election was an excellent election.
Mr Landon telegraphed Mr Roosevelt: *The nation has spoken.*

I never did find out what Mr Hearst said. Bugs Baer said
something about Maine.

If the NRA Eagle comes back, he said, Maine will get a squab.
Ha ha.

What's wrong with Maine? In Frisco they put up a sign before
the election. It said: *Remember Spain and vote with Maine.*

They forgot.

It looks like we're going to have a solid Fascist Europe, I said
to the director.

He didn't care. Maybe I didn't care, either. I hadn't bet a
nickel on whether or not we were going to have a solid Fascist
Europe.

A little girl came up to the director with a scratch pad and asked the director if he would sign his name on the blank page.

The little girl was thrilled and unconsciously I reached for my pencil. I would have been glad to sign my name seventeen times. She didn't ask me to, however. Most people under twelve don't know who I am and people over twelve seldom, if ever, care to have my signature on a blank piece of paper.

The director laughed and said, Who *am* I?

I don't know, the little girl said. I know you're *somebody*.

Christ, I'm somebody myself. And even though she little suspects it, so is the little girl. Her name is probably Alice.

The director signed his name modestly, the little girl thanked him, very much without pausing to read the name, returned to her table where her mother and her aunt welcomed her home after triumphs abroad, and the director said, What are you doing?

When? I said.

If he meant all the time, he had me.

When you work, he said.

I'm working on a movie about a young doctor, I said.

Is it any good? he said.

I don't know, I said.

What happens? he said.

Well, I said, he's a young doctor. A society girl is in love with him. He's in love with a nurse, only he doesn't know it.

Is that all? the director said.

Not exactly, I said. There are certain minor themes and complications.

For instance? the director said.

Well, there is a child prodigy, I said. He is a genius. He is expert on the violin, although only eight years old. Well, this boy, Michael Bartok, has a bad right arm. No, a bad left arm. We spent two days deciding which arm should be bad. We chose the left arm. The bad doctor who is the greatest surgeon in America abandons this boy on the operating table to go to a rich patient in Long Island. The boy's arm gets worse and worse, and it looks like he'll never be able to play again. His mother goes crazy and shoots the good young doctor, our hero.

Why? the director said.

I don't know, I said. I've given the matter a lot of thought, day and night, but I've never been able to find out. She just shoots him, that's all. It's very exciting, and she is an excellent shot. He doesn't die, though, because he likes the nurse. He starts to get well and the nurse comes in and takes the thermometer out of his mouth and kisses him.

Oh, boy, the director said. Did you make up the story?

No, I said, but I wouldn't be surprised if I could make up one just like it.

Well, where do *you* come in on this thing? the director said. What are *you* doing?

I'm sort of bringing the dialogue to life, I said.

Oh, said the director. How?

I don't know *how*, I said.

We ate in silence for a while. Two famous actresses with two famous actors went down the aisle. They went down the aisle just like two famous actresses and two famous actors.

This town stinks, I said. In a way, though, it's the most magic place in the world.

It's impossible for a writer to write about this town or the people of this town, the director said.

I don't know, I said. I don't think it's impossible. It's not easy, but it's not easy to write about any town or any people. Especially, I said, if you can't write.

No, he said. A writer can write about San Francisco and the people of San Francisco, but nobody in the world can write about Hollywood and the people of Hollywood. All the actors and actresses are phony.

I believe that everybody in the world is partly phony and that nobody in the world is altogether phony and that a writer's job is to determine how much of anybody is phony and how much real and to make something of it, one way or another. I believe also that the phoniest people in the world are often the most real people in the world, and the most genuinely tragic people in the world.

I used to get sore, but I don't any more because I don't know who to get sore at. It's too easy to get sore at people you never meet like Hearst and Hitler and Mussolini. I don't believe I've ever been really sore at Hearst and Hitler and Mussolini. And I can't get sore at the people I know because I know them. God almighty, they're all right, even if they're rats. Even if they're rats, they're not *always* rats. Sometimes they're not even house mice.

Anyway, the director said, Everything is phony down here and no writer has ever come to this place and written anything about this place that was worth anything. Take the people from Ohio in this town, he said. Girls who've won beauty contests. Even they're phony, even when everything they do is tragic. They're phony because when they suffer, as they do, they suffer because they want to be actresses. Everything everybody wants down here is not worth suffering for.

I didn't agree, but I didn't say anything because I knew it would take me an hour to show why it is not possible for anything to be phony if one suffers for it. That isn't a very subtle thing to know, but it is a difficult thing to explain.

Do you like the work you're doing? the director said.

It's very interesting, I said. It's not exactly writing, but it's different, and interesting.

This doctor, the director said, is he a good character?

He isn't a character at all, I said. He's somebody in a white coat to be photographed. Everybody will believe he's a doctor because they want to believe.

Well, does he say anything worth hearing? the director said.

He says a couple of things here and there, I said.

All right, the director said. What does the young doctor say?

Well, I said, he greets a lot of people and says goodbye to a lot of people in the picture.

Does he say anything special? the director said. Does he say anything *you've* written?

Yes, I said. The picture begins with this young doctor holding up a new-born baby by its legs and slapping life into it. The young doctor says, OK, baby, this is the world, so inhale and exhale and be with us a while. They're not going to be kind to you out there because nobody was kind to them, but don't hate anybody. There's nobody to hate. You're going to be pushed around, and so forth and so on. That's the idea. He tells the baby how it is and what to expect and the story begins.

The director was very kind.

That's very nice, he said.

It's nothing, I said.

It's a nice speech, the director said.

It's like this, I said. The young doctor's been around a little, so he tells the baby it's lousy, but it's the only thing there is, so the baby might as well take it easy and like it. The young doctor says, It's the world. It's not good. It's not bad. But most of us are crazy about it.

That's very good, the director said.

He means it, I said. He knows it's both things at the same time, lousy and good, and he's still young enough and naïve enough to wonder what's going to happen to the baby in the world, and of course he can't wait, so he tells the baby what happened to *him* in the world. Your heart is going to break a thousand times before you're twenty, he says, or something like that, but instead of crying about it you're going to learn to laugh, and so on and so forth. It's lousy, I said.

No, the director said, it's very good.

It's not really good, I said. The young doctor is a good guy, an easy-going guy, and he's got to talk when he brings a baby into the world. He feels half-way glad about it and half-way miserable about it. He listens to the baby bawling and it makes him laugh. I don't know who you are, he says to the baby, or who you are going to be, but whoever you are, whatever you do, for Christ's sake don't hurt anybody. But don't let anybody hurt you either.

You see, I said, it doesn't make sense. If you're not going to let anybody hurt you, you're going to have to hurt somebody. There's no two ways about it.

It's a good speech, the director said.

I didn't want to work on this story, I said. They assigned me to it. I need the job badly. I'm paying a lot of old debts. It's a good job. I'm making more money a week than most people in this country make in three or four months. I'm paying a lot of debts.

OK, baby, this is the world, the director said.

That's right, I said.

It's a swell opening for a picture, he said.

The rebels are near Madrid, I said.

This is the world, the director said. That's fine.

Shall we go? I said.

All right, the director said.

We left the Brown Derby and drove out to the director's home in Beverly Hills, changed our clothes, and went out to the tennis court and played three sets of tennis.

Every once in a while the director would make an excellent drive and say, OK, baby, this is the world.

As I said before, though, I wouldn't be surprised if they got up and ran to the centre of the field and proceeded to kill one another. What the hell, they're alive, and bored, and not overbright; what else is there for them to do, anywhere?

There are too many people, and Fascists are only people, too, so to hell with it. They think they're right and they're willing to die for whatever they believe, so what's the use being amazed about anything?

P. G. WODEHOUSE

The Rise of Minna Nordstrom

They had been showing the latest Minna Nordstrom picture at the Bijou Dream in the High Street, and Miss Postlethwaite, our sensitive barmaid, who had attended the première, was still deeply affected. She snuffled audibly as she polished the glasses.

'It's really good, is it?' we asked, for in the bar-parlour of the Anglers' Rest we lean heavily on Miss Postlethwaite's opinion where the silver screen is concerned. Her verdict can make or mar.

''Swonderful,' she assured us. 'It lays bare for all to view the soul of a woman who dared everything for love. A poignant and uplifting drama of life as it is lived today, purifying the emotions with pity and terror.'

A Rum and Milk said that if it was as good as all that he didn't know but what he might not risk ninepence on it. A Sherry and Bitters wondered what they paid a woman like Minna Nordstrom. A Port from the Wood, raising the conversation from the rather sordid plane to which it threatened to sink, speculated on how motion-picture stars became stars.

'What I mean,' said the Port from the Wood, 'does a studio deliberately set out to create a star? Or does it suddenly say to itself "Hullo, here's a star. What ho!"?'

One of those cynical Dry Martinis who always know everything said that it was all a question of influence.

'If you looked into it, you would find this Nordstrom girl was married to one of the bosses.'

Mr Mulliner, who had been sipping his hot Scotch and lemon in a rather distrait way, glanced up.

'Did I hear you mention the name Minna Nordstrom?'

'We were arguing about how she became a star. I was saying that she must have had a pull of some kind.'

'In a sense,' said Mr Mulliner, 'you are right. She did have a pull. But it was one due solely to her own initiative and resource. I have relatives and connections in Hollywood, as you know, and I learn much of the inner history of the studio world through these channels. I happen to know that Minna Nordstrom raised herself to her present eminence by sheer enterprise and determination. If Miss Postlethwaite will mix me another hot Scotch and lemon, this time stressing the Scotch a little more vigorously, I shall be delighted to tell you the whole story.'

When people talk with bated breath in Hollywood – and it is a place where there is always a certain amount of breath-bating going on – you will generally find, said Mr Mulliner, that the subject of their conversation is Jacob Z. Schnellenhamer, the popular president of the Perfecto-Zizzbaum Corporation. For few names are more widely revered there than that of this Napoleonic man.

Ask for an instance of his financial acumen, and his admirers will point to the great merger for which he was responsible – that merger by means of which he combined his own company, the Colossal-Exquisite, with those two other vast concerns, the Perfecto-Fishbein and the Zizzbaum-Celluloid. Demand proof of his artistic genius, his flair for recognising talent in the raw, and it is given immediately. He was the man who discovered Minna Nordstrom.

Today when interviewers bring up the name of the world-famous star in Mr Schnellenhamer's presence, he smiles quietly.

'I had long had my eye on the little lady,' he says, 'but for one reason and another I did not consider the time ripe for her début. Then I brought about what you are good enough to call the epoch-making merger, and I was enabled to take the decisive step. My colleagues questioned the wisdom of elevating a totally unknown girl to stardom, but I was firm. I saw that it was the only thing to be done.'

'You had vision?'

'I had vision.'

All that Mr Schnellenhamer had, however, on the evening

when this story begins was a headache. As he returned from the day's work at the studio and sank wearily into an armchair in the sitting-room of his luxurious home in Beverly Hills, he was feeling that the life of the president of a motion-picture corporation was one that he would hesitate to force on any dog of which he was fond.

A morbid meditation, of course, but not wholly unjustified. The great drawback to being the man in control of a large studio is that everybody you meet starts acting at you. Hollywood is entirely populated by those who want to get into the pictures, and they naturally feel that the best way of accomplishing their object is to catch the boss's eye and do their stuff.

Since leaving home that morning Mr Schnellenhamer had been acted at practically incessantly. First, it was the studio watchman who, having opened the gate to admit his car, proceeded to play a little scene designed to show what he would do in a heavy role. Then came his secretary, two book agents, the waitress who brought him his lunch, a life insurance man, a representative of a film weekly, and a barber. And, on leaving at the end of the day, he got the watchman again, this time in whimsical comedy.

Little wonder, then, that by the time he reached home the magnate was conscious of a throbbing sensation about the temples and an urgent desire for a restorative.

As a preliminary to obtaining the latter, he rang the bell and Vera Prebble, his parlourmaid, entered. For a moment he was surprised not to see his butler. Then he recalled that he had dismissed him just after breakfast for reciting 'Gunga Din' in a meaning way while bringing the eggs and bacon.

'You rang, sir?'

'I want a drink.'

'Very good, sir.'

The girl withdrew, to return a few moments later with a decanter and siphon. The sight caused Mr Schnellenhamer's gloom to lighten a little. He was proud of his cellar, and he knew that the decanter contained liquid balm. In a sudden gush of tenderness he eyed its bearer appreciatively, thinking what a nice girl she looked.

Until now he had never studied Vera Prebble's appearance to

any great extent or thought about her much in any way. When she had entered his employment a few days before, he had noticed, of course, that she had a sort of ethereal beauty; but then every girl you see in Hollywood has either ethereal beauty or roguish gaminerie or a dark, slumbrous face that hints at hidden passion.

'Put it down there on the small table,' said Mr Schnellenhamer, passing his tongue over his lips.

The girl did so. Then, straightening herself, she suddenly threw her head back and clutched the sides of it in an ecstasy of hopeless anguish.

'Oh! Oh! Oh!' she cried.

'Eh?' said Mr Schnellenhamer.

'Ah! Ah! Ah!'

'I don't get you at all,' said Mr Schnellenhamer.

She gazed at him with wide, despairing eyes.

'If you knew how sick and tired I am of it all! Tired . . . Tired . . . Tired. The lights . . . the glitter . . . the gaiety . . . It is so hollow, so fruitless. I want to get away from it all, ha-ha-ha-ha-ha!'

Mr Schnellenhamer retreated behind the chesterfield. That laugh had had an unbalanced ring. He had not liked it. He was about to continue his backward progress in the direction of the door, when the girl, who had closed her eyes and was rocking to and fro as if suffering from some internal pain, became calmer.

'Just a little thing I knocked together with a view to showing myself in a dramatic role,' she said. 'Watch! I'm going to register.'

She smiled. 'Joy.'

She closed her mouth. 'Grief.'

She wiggled her ears. 'Horror.'

She raised her eyebrows. 'Hate.'

Then, taking a parcel from the tray:

'Here,' she said, 'if you would care to glance at them, are a few stills of myself. This shows my face in repose. I call it "Reverie". This is me in a bathing suit . . . riding . . . walking . . . happy among my books . . . being kind to the dog. Here is one of which my friends have been good enough to speak in terms of praise – as Cleopatra, the warrior-queen of Egypt, at the Pasadena Gas-Fitters' Ball. It brings out what is generally considered my most effective feature – the nose, seen sideways.'

During the course of these remarks, Mr Schnellenhamer had been standing breathing heavily. For a while the discovery that this parlourmaid, of whom he had just been thinking so benevolently, was simply another snake in the grass had rendered him incapable of speech. Now his aphasia left him.

'Get out!' he said.

'Pardon?' said the girl.

'Get out this minute. You're fired.'

There was a silence. Vera Prebble closed her mouth, wiggled her ears, and raised her eyebrows. It was plain that she was grieved, horror-stricken, and in the grip of a growing hate.

'What,' she demanded passionately at length, 'is the matter with all you movie magnates? Have you no hearts? Have you no compassion? No sympathy? No understanding? Do the ambitions of the struggling mean nothing to you?'

'No,' replied Mr Schnellenhamer in answer to all five questions.

Vera Prebble laughed bitterly.

'No is right!' she said. 'For months I besieged the doors of the casting directors. They refused to cast me. Then I thought that if I could find a way into your homes I might succeed where I had failed before. I secured the post of parlourmaid to Mr Fishbein of the Perfecto-Fishbein. Half-way through Rudyard Kipling's "Boots" he brutally bade me begone. I obtained a similar position with Mr Zizzbaum of the Zizzbaum-Celluloid. The opening lines of "The wreck of the *Hesperus*" had hardly passed my lips when he was upstairs helping me pack my trunk. And now you crush my hopes. It is cruel . . . cruel . . . Oh, ha-ha-ha-ha-ha!'

She rocked to and fro in an agony of grief. Then an idea seemed to strike her.

'I wonder if you would care to see me in light comedy? . . . No? . . . Oh, very well.'

With a quick droop of the eyelids and a twitch of the muscles of the cheeks she registered resignation.

'Just as you please,' she said. Then her nostrils quivered and she bared the left canine tooth to indicate Menace. 'But one last word. Wait!'

'How do you mean, wait?'

'Just wait. That's all.'

For an instant Mr Schnellenhamer was conscious of a twinge of uneasiness. Like all motion-picture magnates, he had about forty-seven guilty secrets, many of them recorded on paper. Was it possible that . . .

Then he breathed again. All his private documents were in a safe-deposit box. It was absurd to imagine that this girl could have anything on him.

Relieved, he lay down on the chesterfield and gave himself up to daydreams. And soon, as he remembered that that morning he had put through a deal which would enable him to trim the stuffing out of two hundred and seventy-three exhibitors, his lips curved in a contented smile and Vera Prebble was forgotten.

One of the advantages of life in Hollywood is that the Servant Problem is not a difficult one. Supply more than equals demand. Ten minutes after you have thrown a butler out of the back door his successor is bowling up in his sports-model car. And the same applies to parlourmaids. By the following afternoon all was well once more with the Schnellenhamer domestic machine. A new butler was cleaning the silver: a new parlourmaid was doing whatever parlourmaids do, which is very little. Peace reigned in the home.

But on the second evening, as Mr Schnellenhamer, the day's tasks over, entered his sitting-room with nothing in his mind but bright thoughts of dinner, he was met by what had all the appearance of a human whirlwind. This was Mrs Schnellenhamer. A graduate of the silent films, Mrs Schnellenhamer had been known in her day as the Queen of Stormy Emotion, and she occasionally saw to it that her husband was reminded of this.

'Now see what!' cried Mrs Schnellenhamer.

Mr Schnellenhamer was perturbed.

'Is something wrong?' he asked nervously.

'Why did you fire that girl, Vera Prebble?'

'She went ha-ha-ha-ha-ha at me.'

'Well, do you know what she has done? She has laid information with the police that we are harbouring alcoholic liquor on our premises, contrary to law, and this afternoon they came in a truck and took it all away.'

Mr Schnellenhamer reeled. The shock was severe. The good man loved his cellar.

'Not all?' he cried, almost pleadingly.

'All.'

'The Scotch?'

'Every bottle.'

'The gin?'

'Every drop.'

Mr Schnellenhamer supported himself against the chester-field.

'Not the champagne?' he whispered.

'Every case. And here we are, with a hundred and fifty people coming tonight, including the Duke.'

Her allusion was to the Duke of Wigan, who, as so many British dukes do, was at this time passing slowly through Hollywood.

'And you know how touchy dukes are,' proceeded Mrs Schnellenhamer. 'I'm told that the Lulubelle Mahaffys invited the Duke of Kircudbrightshire for the weekend last year, and after he had been there two months he suddenly left in a huff because there was no brown sherry.'

A motion-picture magnate has to be a quick thinker. Where a lesser man would have wasted time referring to the recent Miss Prebble as a serpent whom he had to all intents and purposes nurtured in his bosom, Mr Schnellenhamer directed the whole force of his great brain on the vital problem of how to undo the evil she had wrought.

'Listen,' he said. 'It's all right. I'll get the bootlegger on the phone, and he'll have us stocked up again in no time.'

But he had overlooked the something in the air of Hollywood which urges its every inhabitant irresistibly into the pictures. When he got his bootlegger's number, it was only to discover that that life-saving tradesman was away from home. They were shooting a scene in *Sundered Hearts* on the Outstanding Screen-Favourites lot, and the bootlegger was hard at work there, playing the role of an Anglican bishop. His secretary said he could not be disturbed, as it got him all upset to be interrupted when he was working.

Mr Schnellenhamer tried another bootlegger, then another. They were out on location.

And it was just as he had begun to despair that he bethought him of his old friend, Isadore Fishbein; and into his darkness there shot a gleam of hope. By the greatest good fortune it so happened that he and the president of the Perfecto-Fishbein were at the moment on excellent terms, neither having slipped anything over on the other for several weeks. Mr Fishbein, moreover, possessed as well-stocked a cellar as any man in California. It would be a simple matter to go round and borrow from him all he needed.

Patting Mrs Schnellenhamer's hand and telling her that there were still bluebirds singing in the sunshine, he ran to his car and leaped into it.

The residence of Isadore Fishbein was only a few hundred yards away, and Mr Schnellenhamer was soon whizzing in through the door. He found his friend beating his head against the wall of the sitting-room and moaning to himself in a quiet undertone.

'Is something the matter?' he asked, surprised.

'There is,' said Mr Fishbein, selecting a fresh spot on the tapestried wall and starting to beat his head against that. 'The police came round this afternoon and took away everything I had.'

'Everything?'

'Well, not Mrs Fishbein,' said the other, with a touch of regret in his voice. 'She's up in the bedroom with eight cubes of ice on her forehead in a linen bag. But they took every drop of everything else. A serpent, that's what she is.'

'Mrs Fishbein?'

'Not Mrs Fishbein. That parlourmaid. That Vera Prebble. Just because I stopped her when she got to "boots, boots, boots, boots, marching over Africa" she ups and informs the police on me. And Mrs Fishbein with a hundred and eighty people coming tonight, including the ex-King of Ruritania!'

And, crossing the room, the speaker began to bang his head against a statue of Genius Inspiring the Motion-Picture Industry.

A good man is always appalled when he is forced to contemplate the depths to which human nature can sink, and Mr Schnellenhamer's initial reaction on hearing of this fresh outrage on the part of his late parlourmaid was a sort of sick horror. Then the brain which had built up the Colossal-Exquisite began to work once more.

'Well, the only thing for us to do,' he said, 'is to go round to Ben Zizzbaum and borrow some of his stock. How do you stand with Ben?'

'I stand fine with Ben,' said Mr Fishbein, cheering up. 'I heard something about him last week which I'll bet he wouldn't care to have known.'

'Where does he live?'

'Camden Drive.'

'Then tally-ho!' said Mr Schnellenhamer, who had once produced a drama in eight reels of two strong men battling for a woman's love in the English hunting district.

They were soon at Mr Zizzbaum's address. Entering the sitting-room, they were shocked to observe a form rolling in circles round the floor with its head between its hands. It was travelling quickly, but not so quickly that they were unable to recognise it as that of the chief executive of the Zizzbaum-Celluloid Corporation. Stopped as he was completing his eleventh lap and pressed for an explanation, Mr Zizzbaum revealed that a recent parlourmaid of his, Vera Prebble by name, piqued at having been dismissed for deliberate and calculated reciting of the works of Mrs Hemans, had informed the police of his stock of wines and spirits and that the latter had gone off with the whole collection not half an hour since.

'And don't speak so loud,' added the stricken man, 'or you'll wake Mrs Zizzbaum. She's in bed with ice on her head.'

'How many cubes?' asked Mr Fishbein.

'Six.'

'Mrs Fishbein needed eight,' said that lady's husband a little proudly.

The situation was one that might well have unmanned the

stoutest motion-picture executive and there were few motion-picture executives stouter than Jacob Schnellenhamer. But it was characteristic of this man that the tightest corner was always the one to bring out the full force of his intellect. He thought of Mrs Schnellenhamer waiting for him at home, and it was as if an electric shock of high voltage had passed through him.

'I've got it,' he said. 'We must go to Glutz of the Medulla-Oblongata. He's never been a real friend of mine, but if you loan him Stella Svelte and I loan him Orlando Byng and Fishbein loans him Oscar the Wonder-Poodle on his own terms, I think he'll consent to give us enough to see us through tonight. I'll get him on the phone.'

It was some moments before Mr Schnellenhamer returned from the telephone booth. When he did so, his associates were surprised to observe in his eyes a happy gleam.

'Boys,' he said, 'Glutz is away with his family over the weekend. The butler and the rest of the help are out joy-riding. There's only a parlourmaid in the house. I've been talking to her. So there won't be any need for us to give him those stars, after all. We'll just run across in the car with a few axes and help ourselves. It won't cost us above a hundred dollars to square this girl. She can tell him she was upstairs when the burglars broke in and didn't hear anything. And there we'll be, with all the stuff we need and not a cent to pay outside of overhead connected with the maid.'

There was an awed silence.

'Mrs Fishbein will be pleased.'

'Mrs Zizzbaum will be pleased.'

'And Mrs Schnellenhamer will be pleased,' said the leader of the expedition. 'Where do you keep your axes, Zizzbaum?'

'In the cellar.'

'Fetch 'em!' said Mr Schnellenhamer in the voice a Crusader might have used in giving the signal to start against the Paynim.

In the ornate residence of Sigismund Glutz, meanwhile, Vera Prebble, who had entered the service of the head of the Medulla-Oblongata that morning and was already under sentence of dismissal for having informed him with appropriate gestures that a bunch of the boys were whooping it up in the Malemute saloon, was engaged in writing on a sheet of paper a short list of names, one of which she proposed as a *nom de théâtre* as soon as her screen career should begin.

For this girl was essentially an optimist, and not even all the rebuffs which she had suffered had been sufficient to quench the fire of ambition in her.

Wiggling her tongue as she shaped the letters, she wrote:

Ursuline Delmaine
Theodora Trix
Uvula Gladwyn

None of them seemed to her quite what she wanted. She pondered. Possibly something a little more foreign and exotic . . .

Greta Garbo

No, that had been used . . .

And then suddenly inspiration descended upon her and, trembling a little with emotion, she inscribed on the paper the one name that was absolutely and indubitably right.

Minna Nordstrom

The more she looked at it, the better she liked it. And she was still regarding it proudly when there came the sound of a car stopping at the door and a few moments later in walked Mr Schnellenhamer, Mr Zizzbaum and Mr Fishbein. They all wore Homburg hats and carried axes.

Vera Prebble drew herself up.

'All goods must be delivered in the rear,' she had begun haughtily, when she recognised her former employers and paused, surprised.

The recognition was mutual. Mr Fishbein started. So did Mr Zizzbaum.

'Serpent!' said Mr Fishbein.

'Viper!' said Mr Zizzbaum.

Mr Schnellenhamer was more diplomatic. Though as deeply moved as his colleagues by the sight of this traitoress, he realised that this was no time for invective.

'Well, well, well,' he said, with a geniality which he strove to render frank and winning, 'I never dreamed it was you on the phone, my dear. Well, this certainly makes everything nice and smooth – us all being, as you might say, old friends.'

'Friends?' retorted Vera Prebble. 'Let me tell you . . .'

'I know, I know. Quite, quite. But listen. I've got to have some liquor tonight.'

'What do you mean, *you* have?' said Mr Fishbein.

'It's all right, it's all right,' said Mr Schnellenhamer soothingly. 'I was coming to that. I wasn't forgetting you. We're all in this together. The good old spirit of co-operation. You see, my dear,' he went on, 'that little joke you played on us . . . oh, I'm not blaming you. Nobody laughed more heartily than myself . . .'

'Yes, they did,' said Mr Fishbein, alive now to the fact that this girl before him must be conciliated. 'I did.'

'So did I,' said Mr Zizzbaum.

'We all laughed very heartily,' said Mr Schnellenhamer. 'You should have heard us. A girl of spirit, we said to ourselves. Still, the little pleasantry has left us in something of a difficulty, and it will be worth a hundred dollars to you, my dear, to go upstairs and put cotton wool in your ears while we get at Mr Glutz's cellar door with our axes.'

Vera Prebble raised her eyebrows.

'What do you want to break down the cellar door for? I know the combination of the lock.'

'You do?' said Mr Schnellenhamer joyfully.

'I withdraw that expression "Serpent",' said Mr Fishbein.

'When I used the term "Viper",' said Mr Zizzbaum, 'I was speaking thoughtlessly.'

'And I will tell it you,' said Vera Prebble, 'at a price.'

She drew back her head and extended an arm, twiddling the fingers at the end of it. She was plainly registering something, but they could not discern what it was.

'There is only one condition on which I will tell you the combination of Mr Glutz's cellar, and that is this. One of you has got to give me a starring contract for five years.'

The magnates started.

'Listen,' said Mr Zizzbaum, 'you don't want to star.'

'You wouldn't like it,' said Mr Fishbein.

'Of course you wouldn't,' said Mr Schnellenhamer. 'You would look silly, starring – an inexperienced girl like you. Now, if you had said a nice small part . . .'

'Star.'

'Or featured . . .'

'Star.'

The three men drew back a pace or two and put their heads together.

'She means it,' said Mr Fishbein.

'Her eyes,' said Mr Zizzbaum. 'Like stones.'

'A dozen times I could have dropped something heavy on that girl's head from an upper landing, and I didn't do it,' said Mr Schnellenhamer remorsefully.

Mr Fishbein threw up his hands.

'It's no use. I keep seeing that vision of Mrs Fishbein floating before me with eight cubes of ice on her head. I'm going to star this girl.'

'*You* are?' said Mr Zizzbaum. 'And get the stuff? And leave me to go home and tell Mrs Zizzbaum there won't be anything to drink at her party tonight for a hundred and eleven guests including the Vice-President of Switzerland? No, sir! *I* am going to star her.'

'I'll outbid you.'

'You won't outbid *me*. Not till they bring me word that Mrs Zizzbaum has lost the use of her vocal cords.'

'Listen,' said the other tensely. 'When it comes to using vocal cords, Mrs Fishbein begins where Mrs Zizzbaum leaves off.'

Mr Schnellenhamer, that cool head, saw the peril that loomed.

'Boys,' he said, 'if we once start bidding against one another, there'll be no limit. There's only one thing to be done. We must merge.'

His powerful personality carried the day. It was the President of the newly-formed Perfecto-Zizzbaum Corporation who a few moments later stepped forward and approached the girl.

'We agree.'

And, as he spoke, there came the sound of some heavy vehicle stopping in the road outside. Vera Prebble uttered a stricken exclamation.

'Well, of all the silly girls!' she cried distractedly. 'I've just remembered that an hour ago I telephoned the police, informing them of Mr Glutz's cellar. And here they are!'

Mr Fishbein uttered a cry, and began to look round for something to bang his head against. Mr Zizzbaum gave a short, sharp moan, and started to lower himself to the floor. But Mr Schnellenhamer was made of sterner stuff.

'Pull yourselves together, boys,' he begged them. 'Leave all this to me. Everything is going to be all right. Things have come to a pretty pass,' he said, with a dignity as impressive as it was simple, 'if a free-born American citizen cannot bribe the police of his native country.'

'True,' said Mr Fishbein, arresting his head when within an inch and a quarter of a handsome Oriental vase.

'True, true,' said Mr Zizzbaum, getting up and dusting his knees.

'Just let me handle the whole affair,' said Mr Schnellenhamer. 'Ah, boys!' he went on, genially.

Three policemen had entered the room – a sergeant, a patrolman, and another patrolman. Their faces wore a wooden, hard-boiled look.

'Mr Glutz?' said the sergeant.

'Mr Schnellenhamer,' corrected the great man. 'But Jacob to you, old friend.'

The sergeant seemed in no wise mollified by this amiability.

'Prebble, Vera?' he asked, addressing the girl.

'Nordstrom, Minna,' she replied.

'Got the name wrong, then. Anyway, it was you who phoned us that there was alcoholic liquor on the premises?'

Mr Schnellenhamer laughed amusedly.

'You mustn't believe everything that girl tells you, sergeant. She's a great kidder. Always was. If she said that, it was just one of her little jokes. I know Glutz. I know his views. And many is the time I have heard him say that the laws of his country are good enough for him and that he would scorn not to obey them. You will find nothing here, sergeant.'

'Well, we'll try,' said the other. 'Show us the way to the cellar,' he added, turning to Vera Prebble.

Mr Schnellenhamer smiled a winning smile.

'Now listen,' he said. 'I've just remembered I'm wrong. Silly mistake to make, and I don't know how I made it. There *is* a certain amount of the stuff in the house, but I'm sure you dear chaps don't want to cause any unpleasantness. You're broad-minded. Listen. Your name's Murphy, isn't it?'

'Donahue.'

'I thought so. Well, you'll laugh at this. Only this morning I was saying to Mrs Schnellenhamer that I must really slip down to headquarters and give my old friend Donahue that ten dollars I owed him.'

'What ten dollars?'

'I didn't say ten. I said a hundred. One hundred dollars, Donny, old man, and I'm not saying there mightn't be a little over for these two gentlemen here. How about it?'

The sergeant drew himself up. There was no sign of softening in his glance.

'Jacob Schnellenhamer,' he said coldly, 'you can't square me. When I tried for a job at the Colossal-Exquisite last spring I was turned down on account you said I had no sex appeal.'

The first patrolman, who had hitherto taken no part in the conversation, started.

'Is that so, Chief?'

'Yessir. No sex appeal.'

'Well, can you tie that!' said the first patrolman. 'When I tried to crash the Colossal-Exquisite, they said my voice wasn't right.'

'Me,' said the second patrolman, eyeing Mr Schnellenhamer sourly, 'they had the nerve to beef at my left profile. Lookut, boys,' he said, turning, 'can you see anything wrong with that profile?'

His companions studied him closely. The sergeant raised a hand and peered between his fingers with his head tilted back and his eyes half closed.

'Not a thing,' he said.

'Why, Basil, it's a lovely profile,' said the first patrolman.

'Well, that's how it goes,' said the second patrolman moodily.

The sergeant had returned to his own grievance.

'No sex appeal!' he said with a rasping laugh. 'And me that had specially taken sex appeal in the College of Eastern Iowa course of Motion Picture Acting.'

'Who says my voice ain't right?' demanded the first patrolman. 'Listen. Mi-mi-mi-mi-mi.'

'Swell,' said the sergeant.

'Like a nightingale or something,' said the second patrolman.

The sergeant flexed his muscles.

'Ready, boys?'

'Kayo, Chief.'

'Wait!' cried Mr Schnellenhamer. 'Wait! Give me one more
chance. I'm sure I can find parts for you all.'

The sergeant shook his head.

'No. It's too late. You've got us mad now. You don't appreciate
the sensitiveness of the artist. Does he, boys?'

'You're darned right he doesn't,' said the first patrolman.

'I wouldn't work for the Colossal-Exquisite now,' said the
second patrolman with a petulant twitch of his shoulder, 'not if
they wanted me to play Romeo opposite Jean Harlow.'

'Then let's go,' said the sergeant. 'Come along, lady, you show
us where this cellar is.'

For some moments after the officers of the Law, preceded by
Vera Prebble, had left, nothing was to be heard in the silent
sitting-room but the rhythmic beating of Mr Fishbein's head
against the wall and the rustling sound of Mr Zizzbaum rolling
round the floor. Mr Schnellenhamer sat brooding with his chin
in his hands, merely moving his legs slightly each time Mr
Zizzbaum came round. The failure of his diplomatic efforts had
stunned him.

A vision rose before his eyes of Mrs Schnellenhamer waiting
in their sunlit patio for his return. As clearly as if he had been
there now, he could see her, swooning, slipping into the goldfish
pond, and blowing bubbles with her head beneath the surface.
And he was asking himself whether in such an event it would
be better to raise her gently or just leave Nature to take its
course. She would, he knew, be extremely full of that stormy
emotion of which she had once been queen.

It was as he still debated this difficult point that a light step
caught his ear. Vera Prebble was standing in the doorway.

'Mr Schnellenhamer.'

The magnate waved a weary hand.

'Leave me,' he said. 'I am thinking.'

'I thought you would like to know,' said Vera Prebble, 'that I've just locked those cops in the coal cellar.'

As in the final reel of a super-super-film eyes brighten and faces light up at the entry of the United States Marines, so at these words did Mr Schnellenhamer, Mr Fishbein and Mr Zizzbaum perk up as if after a draught of some magic elixir.

'In the coal cellar?' gasped Mr Schnellenhamer.

'In the coal cellar.'

'Then if we work quick . . .'

Vera Prebble coughed.

'One moment,' she said. 'Just one moment. Before you go, I have drawn up a little letter covering our recent agreement. Perhaps you will all three just sign it.'

Mr Schnellenhamer clicked his tongue impatiently.

'No time for that now. Come to my office tomorrow. Where are you going?' he asked, as the girl started to withdraw.

'Just to the coal cellar,' said Vera Prebble. 'I think those fellows may want to come out.'

Mr Schnellenhamer sighed. It had been worth trying, of course, but he had never really had much hope.

'Gimme,' he said resignedly.

The girl watched as the three men attached their signatures. She took the document and folded it carefully.

'Would any of you like to hear me recite "The Bells", by Edgar Allan Poe?' she asked.

'No!' said Mr Fishbein.

'No!' said Mr Zizzbaum.

'No!' said Mr Schnellenhamer. 'We have no desire to hear you recite "The Bells", Miss Prebble.'

The girl's eyes flashed haughtily.

'Miss Nordstrom,' she corrected. 'And just for that you'll get "The Charge of the Light Brigade", and like it.'

GRAHAM GREENE

The Blue Film

'Other people enjoy themselves,' Mrs Carter said.

'Well,' her husband replied, 'we've seen . . .'

'The reclining Buddha, the emerald Buddha, the floating markets,' Mrs Carter said. 'We have dinner and then go home to bed.'

'Last night we went to Chez Eve . . .'

'If you weren't with *me*,' Mrs Carter said, 'you'd find . . . you know what I mean, Spots.'

It was true, Carter thought, eyeing his wife over the coffee-cups: her slave bangles chinked in time with her coffee-spoon: she had reached an age when the satisfied woman is at her most beautiful, but the lines of discontent had formed. When he looked at her neck he was reminded of how difficult it was to unstring a turkey. Is it my fault, he wondered, or hers – or was it the fault of her birth, some glandular deficiency, some inherited characteristic? It was sad how when one was young, one so often mistook the signs of frigidity for a kind of distinction.

'You promised we'd smoke opium,' Mrs Carter said.

'Not here, darling. In Saigon. Here it's "not done" to smoke.'

'How conventional you are.'

'There'd be only the dirtiest of coolie places. You'd be conspicuous. They'd stare at you.' He played his winning card. 'There'd be cockroaches.'

'I should be taken to plenty of Spots if I wasn't with a husband.'

He tried hopefully, 'The Japanese strip-teasers . . .' but she had heard all about them. 'Ugly women in bras,' she said. His irritation rose. He thought of the money he had spent to take his wife with him and to ease his conscience – he had been away too often without her, but there is no company more cheerless than that of a woman who is not desired. He tried to drink his coffee calmly: he wanted to bite the edge of the cup.

'You've spilt your coffee,' Mrs Carter said.

'I'm sorry.' He got up abruptly and said, 'All right, I'll fix something. Stay here.' He leant across the table. 'You'd better not be shocked,' he said. 'You've asked for it.'

'I don't think I'm usually the one who is shocked,' Mrs Carter said with a thin smile.

Carter left the hotel and walked up towards the New Road. A boy hung at his side and said, 'Young girl?'

'I've got a woman of my own,' Carter said gloomily.

'Boy?'

'No thanks.'

'French films?'

Carter paused. 'How much?'

They stood and haggled a while at the corner of the drab street. What with the taxi, the guide, the films, it was going to cost the best part of eight pounds, but it was worth it, Carter thought, if it closed her mouth for ever from demanding 'Spots'. He went back to fetch Mrs Carter.

They drove a long way and came to a halt by a bridge over a canal, a dingy lane overcast with indeterminate smells. The guide said, 'Follow me.'

Mrs Carter put a hand on Carter's arm. 'Is it safe?' she asked.

'How would I know?' he replied, stiffening under her hand.

They walked about fifty unlighted yards and halted by a bamboo fence. The guide knocked several times. When they were admitted it was to a tiny earth-floored yard and a wooden hut. Something – presumably human – was humped in the dark under a mosquito-net. The owner showed them into a tiny stuffy room with two chairs and a portrait of the King. The screen was about the size of a folio volume.

The first film was peculiarly unattractive and showed the rejuvenation of an elderly man at the hands of two blonde masseuses. From the style of the women's hairdressing the film must have been made in the late twenties. Carter and his wife sat in mutual embarrassment as the film whirled and clicked to a stop.

'Not a very good one,' Carter said, as though he were a connoisseur.

'So that's what they call a blue film,' Mrs Carter said. 'Ugly and not exciting.'

A second film started.

There was very little story in this. A young man – one couldn't see his face because of the period soft hat – picked up a girl in the street (her cloche hat extinguished her like a meat-cover) and accompanied her to her room. The actors were young: there was some charm and excitement in the picture. Carter thought, when the girl took off her hat, I know that face, and a memory which had been buried for more than a quarter of a century moved. A doll over a telephone, a pin-up girl of the period over the double bed. The girl undressed, folding her clothes very neatly: she leant over to adjust the bed, exposing herself to the camera's eye and to the young man: he kept his head turned from the camera. Afterwards, she helped him in turn to take off his clothes. It was only then he remembered – that particular playfulness confirmed by the birthmark on the man's shoulder.

Mrs Carter shifted on her chair. 'I wonder how they find the actors,' she said hoarsely.

'A prostitute,' he said. 'It's a bit raw, isn't it? Wouldn't you like to leave?' he urged her, waiting for the man to turn his head. The girl knelt on the bed and held the youth around the waist – she couldn't have been more than twenty. No, he made a calculation, twenty-one.

'We'll stay,' Mrs Carter said, 'we've paid.' She laid a dry hot hand on his knee.

'I'm sure we could find a better place than this.'

'No.'

The young man lay on his back and the girl for a moment left him. Briefly, as though by accident, he looked at the camera. Mrs Carter's hand shook on his knee. 'Good God,' she said, 'it's you.'

'It *was* me,' Carter said, 'thirty years ago.' The girl was climbing back on to the bed.

'It's revolting,' Mrs Carter replied.

'I don't remember it as revolting,' Carter replied.

'I suppose you went and gloated, both of you.'

'No, I never saw it.'

'Why did you do it? I can't look at you. It's shameful.'

'I asked you to come away.'

'Did they pay you?'

'They paid her. Fifty pounds. She needed the money badly.'

'And you had your fun for nothing?'

'Yes.'

'I'd never have married you if I'd known. Never.'

'That was a long time afterwards.'

'You still haven't said why. Haven't you any excuse?' She stopped. He knew she was watching, leaning forward, caught up herself in the heat of that climax more than a quarter of a century old.

Carter said, 'It was the only way I could help her. She'd never acted in one before. She wanted a friend.'

'A friend,' Mrs Carter said.

'I loved her.'

'You couldn't love a tart.'

'Oh yes, you can. Make no mistake about that.'

'You queued for her, I suppose.'

'You put it too crudely,' Carter said.

'What happened to her?'

'She disappeared. They always disappear.'

The girl leant over the young man's body and put out the light. It was the end of the film. 'I have new ones coming next week,' the Siamese said, bowing deeply. They followed their guide back down the dark lane to the taxi.

In the taxi Mrs Carter said, 'What was her name?'

'I don't remember.' A lie was easiest.

As they turned into the New Road she broke her bitter silence again. 'How could you have brought yourself . . .? It's so degrading. Suppose someone you knew – in business – recognised you.'

'People don't talk about seeing things like that. Anyway, I wasn't in business in those days.'

'Did it never worry you?'

'I don't believe I have thought of it once in thirty years.'

'How long did you know her?'

'Twelve months perhaps.'

'She must look pretty awful by now if she's alive. After all she was common even then.'

'I thought she looked lovely,' Carter said.

They went upstairs in silence. He went straight to the bathroom and locked the door. The mosquitoes gathered around the lamp and the great jar of water. As he undressed he caught glimpses of himself in the small mirror: thirty years had not been kind: he felt his thickness and his middle age. He thought: I hope to God she's dead. Please, God, he said, let her be dead. When I go back in there, the insults will start again.

But when he returned Mrs Carter was standing by the mirror. She had partly undressed. Her thin bare legs reminded him of a heron waiting for fish. She came and put her arms round him: a slave bangle joggled against his shoulder. She said, 'I'd forgotten how nice you looked.'

'I'm sorry. One changes.'

'I didn't mean that. I like you as you are.'

She was dry and hot and implacable in her desire. 'Go on,' she said, 'go on,' and then she screamed like an angry and hurt bird. Afterwards she said, 'It's years since that happened,' and continued to talk for what seemed a long half hour excitedly at his side. Carter lay in the dark silent, with a feeling of loneliness and guilt. It seemed to him that he had betrayed that night the only woman he loved.

J. G. BALLARD

The Screen Game

Every afternoon during the summer at Ciraquito we play the
screen game. After lunch today, when the arcades and café
terraces were empty and everyone was lying asleep indoors,
three of us drove out in Raymond Mayo's Lincoln along the
road to Vermilion Sands.

The season had ended, and already the desert had begun to
move in again for the summer, drifting against the yellowing
shutters of the cigarette kiosks, surrounding the town with
immense banks of luminous ash. Along the horizon the flat-
topped mesas rose into the sky like the painted cones of a
volcano jungle. The beachhouses had been empty for weeks,
and the abandoned sand-yachts stood in the centre of the lakes,
embalmed in the opaque heat. Only the highway showed any
signs of activity, the motion sculpture of concrete ribbon unfolding across the landscape.

Twenty miles from Ciraquito, where the highway forks to
Red Beach and Vermilion Sands, we turned on to the remains
of an old gravel track that ran away among the sand reefs. Only
a year earlier this had been a well-kept private road, but the
ornamental gateway lay collapsed to one side, and the guardhouse was a nesting place for scorpions and sand-rays.

Few people ever ventured far up the road. Continuous rock
slides disturbed the area, and large sections of the surface had
slipped away into the reefs. In addition a curious but unmistakable atmosphere of menace hung over the entire zone, marking
it off from the remainder of the desert. The hanging galleries of
the reefs were more convoluted and sinister, like the tortured
demons of medieval cathedrals. Massive towers of obsidian
reared over the roadway like stone gallows, their cornices

streaked with iron-red dust. The light seemed duller, unlike the rest of the desert, occasionally flaring into a sepulchral glow as if some subterranean fire-cloud had boiled to the surface of the rocks. The surrounding peaks and spires shut out the desert plain, and the only sounds were the echoes of the engine growling among the hills and the piercing cries of the sand-rays wheeling over the open mouths of the reefs like hieratic birds.

For half a mile we followed the road as it wound like a petrified snake above the reefs, and our conversation became more sporadic and fell away entirely, resuming only when we began our descent through a shallow valley. A few abstract sculptures stood by the roadside. Once these were sonic, responding to the slipstream of a passing car with a series of warning vibratos, but now the Lincoln passed them unrecognised.

Abruptly, around a steep bend, the reefs and peaks vanished, and the wide expanse of an inland sand-lake lay before us, the great summer-house of Lagoon West on its shore. Fragments of light haze hung over the dunes like untethered clouds. The tyres cut softly through the cerise sand, and soon we were overrunning what appeared to be the edge of an immense chessboard of black and white marble squares. More statues appeared, some buried to their heads, others toppled from their plinths by the drifting dunes.

Looking out at them this afternoon, I felt, not for the first time, that the whole landscape was compounded of illusion, the hulks of fabulous dreams drifting across it like derelict galleons. As we followed the road towards the lake, the huge wreck of Lagoon West passed us slowly on our left. Its terraces and balconies were deserted, and the once marble-white surface was streaked and lifeless. Staircases ended abruptly in midflight, and the floors hung like sagging marquees.

In the centre of the terrace the screens stood where we had left them the previous afternoon, their zodiacal emblems flashing like serpents. We walked across to them through the hot sunlight. For the next hour we played the screen game, pushing the screens along their intricate pathways, advancing and retreating across the smooth marble floor.

No one watched us, but once, fleetingly, I thought I saw a tall figure in a blue cape hidden in the shadows of a second-floor balcony.

'Emerelda!'

On a sudden impulse I shouted to her, but almost without moving she had vanished among the hibiscus and bougainvillaea. As her name echoed away among the dunes I knew that we had made our last attempt to lure her from the balcony.

'Paul.' Twenty yards away, Raymond and Tony had reached the car. 'Paul, we're leaving.'

Turning my back to them, I looked up at the great bleached bulk of Lagoon West leaning into the sunlight. Somewhere, along the shore of the sand-lake, music was playing faintly, echoing among the exposed quartz veins. A few isolated chords at first, the fragments hung on the afternoon air, the sustained tremolos suspended above my head like the humming of invisible insects.

As the phrases coalesced, I remembered when we had first played the screen game at Lagoon West. I remembered the last tragic battle with the jewelled insects, and I remembered Emerelda Garland . . .

I first saw Emerelda Garland the previous summer, shortly after the film company arrived in Ciraquito and was invited by Charles Van Stratten to use the locations at Lagoon West. The company, Orpheus Productions, Inc. – known to the aficionados of the café terraces such as Raymond Mayo and Tony Sapphire as the 'ebb tide of the new wave' – was one of those experimental units whose output is destined for a single rapturous showing at the Cannes Film Festival, and who rely for their financial backing on the generosity of the many millionaire dilettantes who apparently feel a compulsive need to cast themselves in the role of Lorenzo de Medici.

Not that there was anything amateurish about the equipment and technical resources of Orpheus Productions. The fleet of location trucks and recording studios which descended on Ciraquito on one of those empty August afternoons looked like the entire D-Day task force, and even the more conservative estimates of the budget for *Aphrodite 80*, the film we helped to make at Lagoon West, amounted to at least twice the gross national product of a Central American republic. What was amateurish was the indifference to normal commercial restraints, and the unswerving dedication to the highest aesthetic standards.

All this, of course, was made possible by the largesse of Charles Van Stratten. To begin with, when we were first co-opted into *Aphrodite 80*, some of us were inclined to be amused by Charles's naive attempts to produce a masterpiece, but later we all realised that there was something touching about Charles's earnestness. None of us, however, was aware of the private tragedy which drove him on through the heat and dust of that summer at Lagoon West, and the grim nemesis waiting behind the canvas floats and stage props.

At the time he became the sole owner of Orpheus Productions, Charles Van Stratten had recently celebrated his fortieth birthday, but to all intents he was still a quiet and serious undergraduate. A scion of one of the world's wealthiest banking families, in his early twenties he had twice been briefly married, first to a Neapolitan countess, and then to a Hollywood starlet, but the most influential figure in Charles's life was his mother. This domineering harridan, who sat like an immense ormolu spider in her sombre Edwardian mansion on Park Avenue, surrounded by dark galleries filled with Rubens and Rembrandt, had been widowed shortly after Charles's birth, and obviously regarded Charles as providence's substitute for her husband. Cunningly manipulating a web of trust funds and residuary legacies, she ruthlessly eliminated both Charles's wives (the second committed suicide in a Venetian gondola, the first eloped with his analyst), and then herself died in circumstances of some mystery at the summer-house at Lagoon West.

Despite the immense publicity attached to the Van Stratten family, little was ever known about the old dowager's death — officially she tripped over a second-floor balcony — and Charles retired completely from the limelight of international celebrity for the next five years. Now and then he would emerge briefly at the Venice Biennale, or serve as co-sponsor of some cultural foundation, but otherwise he retreated into the vacuum left by his mother's death. Rumour had it — at least in Ciraquito — that Charles himself had been responsible for her quietus, as if revenging (how long overdue!) the tragedy of Oedipus, when the dowager, scenting the prospect of a third liaison, had descended like Jocasta upon Lagoon West and caught Charles and his paramour *in flagrante*.

Much as I liked the story, the first glimpse of Charles Van Stratten dispelled the possibility. Five years after his mother's death, Charles still behaved as if she were watching his every movement through tripod-mounted opera glasses on some distant balcony. His youthful figure was a little more portly, but his handsome aristocratic face, its strong jaw belied by an indefinable weakness around the mouth, seemed somehow daunted and indecisive, as if he lacked complete conviction in his own identity.

Shortly after the arrival in Ciraquito of Orpheus Productions, the property manager visited the cafés in the artists' quarters, canvassing for scenic designers. Like most of the painters in Ciraquito and Vermilion Sands, I was passing through one of my longer creative pauses. I had stayed on in the town after the season ended, idling away the long, empty afternoons under the awning at the Café Fresco, and was already showing symptoms of beach fatigue – irreversible boredom and inertia. The prospect of actual work seemed almost a novelty.

'*Aphrodite 80*,' Raymond Mayo explained when he returned to our table after a kerb-side discussion. 'The whole thing reeks of integrity – they want local artists to paint the flats, large abstract designs for the desert backgrounds. They'll pay a dollar per square foot.'

'That's rather mean,' I commented.

'The property manager apologised, but Van Stratten is a millionaire – money means nothing to him. If it's any consolation, Raphael and Michelangelo were paid a smaller rate for the Sistine Chapel.'

'Van Stratten has a bigger budget,' Tony Sapphire reminded him. 'Besides, the modern painter is a more complex type, his integrity needs to be buttressed by substantial assurances. Is Paul a painter in the tradition of Leonardo and Larry Rivers, or a cut-price dauber?'

Moodily we watched the distant figure of the property manager move from café to café.

'How many square feet do they want?' I asked.
'About a million,' Raymond said.

Later that afternoon, as we turned off the Red Beach road and
were waved on past the guardhouse to Lagoon West, we could
hear the sonic sculptures high among the reefs echoing and
hooting to the cavalcade of cars speeding over the hills. Droves
of startled rays scattered in the air like clouds of exploding soot,
their frantic cries lost among the spires and reefs. Preoccupied
by the prospect of our vast fees – I had hastily sworn in Tony
and Raymond as my assistants – we barely noticed the strange
landscape we were crossing, the great gargoyles of red basalt
that uncoiled themselves into the air like the spirits of demented
cathedrals. From the Red beach – Vermilion Sands highway –
the hills seemed permanently veiled by the sand haze, and
Lagoon West, although given a brief notoriety by the death of
Mrs Van Stratten, remained isolated and unknown. From the
beach-houses on the southern shore of the sand-lake two miles
away, the distant terraces and tiered balconies of the summer-
house could just be seen across the fused sand, jutting into the
cerise evening sky like a stack of dominoes. There was no access
to the house along the beach. Quartz veins cut deep fissures
into the surface, the reefs of ragged sandstone reared into the
air like the rusting skeletons of forgotten ships.

The whole of Lagoon West was a continuous slide area.
Periodically a soft boom would disturb the morning silence as
one of the galleries of compacted sand, its intricate grottoes and
colonnades like an inverted baroque palace, would suddenly
dissolve and avalanche gently into the internal precipice below.
Most years Charles Van Stratten was away in Europe, and the
house was believed to be empty. The only sound the occupants
of the beach villas would hear was the faint music of the sonic
sculptures carried across the lake by the thermal rollers.

It was to this landscape, with its imperceptible transition
between the real and the superreal, that Charles Van Stratten
had brought the camera crews and location vans of Orpheus
Productions, Inc. As the Lincoln joined the column of cars
moving towards the summer-house, we could see the great
canvas hoardings, at least two hundred yards wide and thirty

feet high, which a team of construction workers was erecting among reefs a quarter of a mile from the house. Decorated with abstract symbols, these would serve as backdrops to the action, and form a fragmentary labyrinth winding in and out of the hills and dunes.

One of the large terraces below the summer-house served as a parking lot, and we made our way through the unloading crews to where a group of men in crocodile-skin slacks and raffia shirts – then the uniform of avant-garde film men – were gathered around a heavily jowled man like a perspiring bear who was holding a stack of script boards under one arm and gesticulating wildly with the other. This was Orson Kanin, director of *Aphrodite 80* and co-owner with Charles Van Stratten of Orpheus Productions. Sometime *enfant terrible* of the futurist cinema, but now a portly barrel-stomached fifty, Kanin had made his reputation some twenty years earlier with *Blind Orpheus*, a neo-Freudian, horror-film version of the Greek legend. According to Kanin's interpretation, Orpheus deliberately breaks the taboo and looks Eurydice in the face because he wants to be rid of her; in a famous nightmare sequence which projects his unconscious loathing, he becomes increasingly aware of something cold and strange about his resurrected wife, and finds that she is a disintegrating corpse.

As we joined the periphery of the group, a characteristic Kanin script conference was in full swing, a non-stop pantomime of dramatised incidents from the imaginary script, anecdotes, salary promises and bad puns, all delivered in a rich fruity baritone. Sitting on the balustrade beside Kanin was a handsome, youthful man with a sensitive face whom I recognised to be Charles Van Stratten. Now and then, *sotto voce*, he would interject some comment that would be noted by one of the secretaries and incorporated into Kanin's monologue.

As the conference proceeded I gathered that they would begin to shoot the film in some three weeks' time, and that it would be performed entirely without script. Kanin only seemed perturbed by the fact that no one had yet been found to play the Aphrodite of *Aphrodite 80* but Charles Van Stratten interposed here to assure Kanin that he himself would provide the actress.

At this eyebrows were raised knowingly. 'Of course,' Raymond murmured. *'Droit de seigneur*. I wonder who the next Mrs Van Stratten is?'

But Charles Van Stratten seemed unaware of these snide undertones. Catching sight of me, he excused himself and came over to us.

'Paul Golding?' He took my hand in a soft but warm grip. We had never met but I presumed he recognised me from the photographs in the art reviews. 'Kanin told me you'd agreed to do the scenery. It's wonderfully encouraging.' He spoke in a light, pleasant voice absolutely without affectation. 'There's so much confusion here it's a relief to know that at least the scenic designs will be first-class.' Before I could demur he took my arm and began to walk away along the terrace towards the hoardings in the distance. 'Let's get some air. Kanin will keep this up for a couple of hours at least.'

Leaving Raymond and Tony, I followed him across the huge marble squares.

'Kanin keeps worrying about his leading actress,' he went on. 'Kanin always marries his latest protégé – he claims it's the only way he can make them respond fully to his direction, but I suspect there's an old-fashioned puritan lurking within the cavalier. This time he's going to be disappointed, though not by the actress, may I add. The Aphrodite I have in mind will outshine Milos's.'

'The film sounds rather ambitious,' I commented, 'but I'm sure Kanin is equal to it.'

'Of course he is. He's very nearly a genius, and that should be good enough.' He paused for a moment, hands in the pockets of his dove-grey suit, before translating himself like a chess piece along a diagonal square. 'It's a fascinating subject, you know. The title is misleading, a box-office concession. The film is really Kanin's final examination of the Orpheus legend. The whole question of the illusions which exist in any relationship to make it workable, and of the barriers we willingly accept to hide ourselves from each other. How much reality can we stand?'

We reached one of the huge hoardings that stretched away among the reefs. Jutting upwards from the spires and grottoes, it seemed to shut off half the sky, and already I felt the atmosphere of shifting illusion and reality that enclosed the whole of Lagoon West, the subtle displacement of time and space. The great hoardings seemed to be both barriers and corridors. Leading away radially from the house and breaking up the landscape, of which they revealed sudden unrelated glimpses, they introduced a curiously appealing element of uncertainty into the placid afternoon, an impression reinforced by the emptiness and enigmatic presence of the summer-house.

Returning to Kanin's conference, we followed the edge of the terrace. Here the sand had drifted over the balustrade which divided the public sector of the grounds from the private. Looking up at the lines of balconies on the south face, I noticed someone standing in the shadows below one of the awnings.

Something flickered brightly from the ground at my feet. Momentarily reflecting the full disc of the sun, like a polished node of sapphire or quartz, the light flashed among the dust, then seemed to dart sideways below the balustrade.

'My God, a scorpion!' I pointed to the insect crouching away from us, the red scythe of its tail beckoning slowly. I assumed that the thickened chitin of the headpiece was reflecting the light, and then saw that a small faceted stone had been set into the skull. As it edged forward into the light, the jewel burned in the sun like an incandescent crystal.

Charles Van Stratten stepped past me. Almost pushing me aside, he glanced towards the shuttered balconies. He feinted deftly with one foot at the scorpion, and before the insect could recover had stamped it into the dust.

'Right, Paul,' he said in a firm voice. 'I think your suggested designs are excellent. You've caught the spirit of the whole thing exactly, as I knew you would.' Buttoning his jacket he made off towards the film unit, barely pausing to scrape the damp husk of the crushed carapace from his shoe.

I caught up with him. 'That scorpion was jewelled,' I said. 'There was a diamond, or zircon, inset in the head.'

He waved impatiently and then took a pair of large sunglasses from his breast pocket. Masked, his face seemed harder and more autocratic, reminding me of our true relationship.

'An illusion, Paul,' he said. 'Some of the insects here are

dangerous. You must be more careful.' His point made, he relaxed and flashed me his most winning smile.

Rejoining Tony and Raymond, I watched Charles Van Stratten walk off through the technicians and stores staff. His stride was noticeably more purposive, and he brushed aside an assistant producer without bothering to turn his head.

'Well, Paul.' Raymond greeted me expansively. 'There's no script, no star, no film in the cameras, and no one has the faintest idea what he's supposed to be doing. But there are a million square feet of murals waiting to be painted. It all seems perfectly straightforward.'

I looked back across the terrace to where we had seen the scorpion. 'I suppose it is,' I said.

Somewhere in the dust a jewel glittered brightly.

Two days later I saw another of the jewelled insects.

Supressing my doubts about Charles Van Stratten, I was busy preparing my designs for the hoardings. Although Raymond's first estimate of a million square feet was exaggerated – less than a tenth of this would be needed – the amount of work and materials required was substantial. In effect I was about to do nothing less than repaint the entire desert.

Each morning I went out to Lagoon West and worked among the reefs, adapting the designs to the contours and colours of the terrain. Most of the time I was alone in the hot sun. After the initial frenzy of activity Orpheus Productions had lost momentum. Kanin had gone off to a film festival at Red Beach and most of the assistant producers and writers had retired to the swimming pool at the Hotel Neptune in Vermilion Sands. Those who remained behind at Lagoon West were now sitting half asleep under the coloured umbrellas erected around the mobile cocktail bar.

The only sign of movement came from Charles Van Stratten, roving tirelessly in his white suit among the reefs and sand spires. Now and then I would hear one of the sonic sculptures on the upper balconies of the summer-house change its note, and turn to see him standing beside it. His sonic profile evoked a strange, soft sequence of chords, interwoven by sharper, almost plaintive notes that drifted away across the still afternoon

air towards the labyrinth of great hoardings that now surrounded the summer-house. All day he would wander among
them, pacing out the perimeters and diagonals as if trying to
square the circle of some private enigma, the director of a
Wagnerian psychodrama that would involve us all in its cathar-
tic unfolding.

Shortly after noon, when an intense pall of yellow light lay
over the desert, dissolving the colours in its glazed mantle, I sat
down on the balustrade, waiting for the meridian to pass. The
sand-lake shimmered in the thermal gradients like an immense
pool of sluggish wax. A few yards away something flickered in
the bright sand, a familiar flare of light. Shielding my eyes, I
found the source, the diminutive Promethean bearer of this
brilliant corona. The spider, a Black Widow, approached on its
stilted legs, a blaze of staccato signals pouring from its crown. It
stopped and pivoted, revealing the large sapphire inset into its
head.

More points of light flickered. Within a moment the entire
terrace sparked with jewelled light. Quickly I counted a score of
the insects – turquoised scorpions, a purple mantis with a giant
topaz like a tiered crown, and more than a dozen spiders,
pinpoints of emerald and sapphire light lancing from their
heads.

Above them, hidden in the shadows among the bougainvillaea on her balcony, a tall white-faced figure in a blue gown
looked down at me.

I stepped over the balustrade, carefully avoiding the motionless insects. Separated from the remainder of the terrace by the
west wing of the summer-house, I had entered a new zone,
where the bonelike pillars of the loggia, the glimmering surface
of the sand-lake, and the jewelled insects enclosed me in a
sudden empty limbo.

For a few moments I stood below the balcony from which the
insects had emerged, still watched by this strange sybilline figure
presiding over her private world. I felt that I had strayed across
the margins of a dream, on to an internal landscape of the
psyche projected upon the sun-filled terraces around me.

But before I could call to her, footsteps grated softly in the
loggia. A dark-haired man of about fifty, with a closed,

expressionless face, stood among the columns, his black suit neatly buttoned. He looked down at me with the impassive eyes of a funeral director.

The shutters withdrew upon the balcony, and the jewelled insects returned from their foray. Surrounding me, their brilliant crowns glittered with diamond hardness.

Each afternoon, as I returned from the reefs with my sketch pad, I would see the jewelled insects moving in the sunlight beside the lake, while their blue-robed mistress, the haunted Venus of Lagoon West, watched them from her balcony. Despite the frequency of her appearance, Charles Van Stratten made no attempt to explain her presence. His elaborate preparations for the filming of *Aphrodite 80* almost complete, he became more and more preoccupied.

An outline scenario had been agreed on. To my surprise the first scene was to be played on the lake terrace, and would take the form of a shadow ballet, for which I painted a series of screens to be moved about like chess pieces. Each was about twelve feet high, a large canvas mounted on a wooden trestle, representing one of the zodiac signs. Like the protagonist of *The Cabinet of Dr Caligari*, trapped in a labyrinth of tilting walls, the Orphic hero of *Aphrodite 80* would appear searching for his lost Eurydice among the shifting time stations.

So the screen game, which we were to play tirelessly on so many occasions, made its appearance. As I completed the last of the screens and watched a group of extras perform the first movement of the game under Charles Van Stratten's directions, I began to realise the extent to which we were all supporting players in a gigantic charade of Charles's devising.

Its real object soon became apparent.

The summer-house was deserted when I drove out to Lagoon West the next weekend, an immense canopy of silence hanging over the lake and the surrounding hills. The twelve screens stood on the terrace above the beach, their vivid, heraldic designs melting into blurred pools of turquoise and carmine which bled away in horizontal layers across the air. Someone had rearranged the screens to form a narrow spiral corridor. As

I straightened them, the train of a white gown disappeared with a startled flourish among the shadows within.

Guessing the probable identity of this pale and nervous intruder, I stepped quietly into the corridor. I pushed back one of the screens, a large Scorpio in royal purple, and suddenly found myself in the centre of the maze, little more than an arm's length from the strange figure I had seen on the balcony. For a moment she failed to notice me. Her exquisite white face, like a marble mask, veined by a faint shadow of violet that seemed like a delicate interior rosework, was raised to the canopy of sunlight which cut across the upper edges of the screens. She wore a long beach-robe, with a flared hood that enclosed her head like a protective bower.

One of the jewelled insects nestled on a fold above her neck. There was a curious glacé immobility about her face, investing the white skin with an almost sepulchral quality, the soft down which covered it like grave's dust.

'Who – ?' Startled, she stepped back. The insects scattered at her feet, winking on the floor like a jewelled carpet. She stared at me in surprise, drawing the hood of her gown around her face like an exotic flower withdrawing into its foliage. Conscious of the protective circle of insects, she lifted her chin and composed herself.

'I'm sorry to interrupt you,' I said. 'I didn't realise there was anyone here. I'm flattered that you like the screen.'

The autocratic chin lowered fractionally, and her head, with its swirl of blue hair, emerged from the hood. '*You* painted these?' she confirmed. 'I thought they were Dr Gruber's . . .' She broke off, tired or bored by the effort of translating her thoughts into speech.

'They're for Charles Van Stratten's film,' I explained. '*Aphrodite 80*. The film about Orpheus he's making here.' I added: 'You must ask him to give you a part. You'd be a great adornment.'

'A film?' Her voice cut across mine. 'Listen. Are you sure they are for this film? It's important that I know – '

'Quite sure.' Already I was beginning to find her exhausting. Talking to her was like walking across a floor composed of blocks of varying heights, an analogy reinforced by the squares of the terrace, into which her presence had let another random dimension. 'They're going to film one of the scenes here. Of course,' I volunteered when she greeted this news with a frown, 'you're free to play with the screens. In fact, if you like, I'll paint some for you.'

'Will you?' From the speed of the response I could see that I had at last penetrated to the centre of her attention. 'Can you start today? Paint as many as you can, just like these. Don't change the designs.' She gazed around at the zodiacal symbols looming from the shadows like the murals painted in dust and blood on the walls of a Toltec funeral corridor. 'They're wonderfully alive, sometimes I think they're even more real than Dr Gruber. Though – ' here she faltered ' – I don't know how I'll pay you. You see, they don't give me any money.' She smiled at me like an anxious child, then brightened suddenly. She knelt down and picked one of the jewelled scorpions from the floor. 'Would you like one of these?' The flickering insect, with its brilliant ruby crown, tottered unsteadily on her white palm.

Footsteps approached, the firm rap of leather on marble. 'They may be rehearsing today,' I said. 'Why don't you watch? I'll take you on a tour of the sets.'

As I started to pull back the screens I felt the long fingers of her hand on my arm. A mood of acute agitation had come over her.

'Relax,' I said. 'I'll tell them to go away. Don't worry, they won't spoil your game.'

'No! Listen, please!' The insects scattered and darted as the outer circle of screens was pulled back. In a few seconds the whole world of illusion was dismantled and exposed to the hot sunlight.

Behind the Scorpio appeared the watchful face of the dark-suited man. A smile played like a snake on his lips.

'Ah, Miss Emerelda,' he greeted her in a purring voice. 'I think you should come indoors. The afternoon heat is intense and you tire very easily.'

The insects retreated from his black patent shoes. Looking into his eyes, I caught a glimpse of deep reserves of patience, like that of an experienced nurse used to the fractious moods and uncertainties of a chronic invalid.

'Not now,' Emerelda insisted. 'I'll come in a few moments.'

'I've just been describing the screens,' I explained.

'So I gather, Mr Golding,' he rejoined evenly. 'Miss Emerelda,' he called.

For a moment they appeared to have reached deadlock. Emerelda, the jewelled insects at her feet, stood beside me, her hand on my arm, while her guardian waited, the same thin smile on his lips. More footsteps approached. The remaining screens were pushed back and the plump, well-talcumed figure of Charles Van Stratten appeared, his urbane voice raised in greeting.

'What's this – a story conference?' he asked jocularly. He broke off when he saw Emerelda and her guardian. 'Dr Gruber? What's going – Emerelda my dear?'

Smoothly, Dr Gruber interjected. 'Good afternoon, sir. Miss Garland is about to return to her room.'

'Good, good,' Charles exclaimed. For the first time I had known him he seemed unsure of himself. He made a tentative approach to Emerelda, who was staring at him fixedly. She drew her robe around her and stepped quickly through the screens. Charles moved forwards, uncertain whether to follow her.

'Thank you, doctor,' he muttered. There was a flash of patent leather heels, and Charles and I were alone among the screens. On the floor at our feet was a single jewelled mantis. Without thinking, Charles bent down to pick it up, but the insect snapped at him. He withdrew his fingers with a wan smile, as if accepting the finality of Emerelda's departure.

Recognising me with an effort, Charles pulled himself together. 'Well, Paul, I'm glad you and Emerelda were getting on so well. I knew you'd make an excellent job of the screens.'

We walked out into the sunlight. After a pause he said. 'That is Emerelda Garland; she's lived here since mother died. It was a tragic experience. Dr Gruber thinks she may never recover.'

'He's her doctor?'

Charles nodded. 'One of the best I could find. For some reason Emerelda feels herself responsible for mother's death. She's refused to leave here.'

I pointed to the screens. 'Do you think they help?'

'Of course. Why do you suppose we're here at all?' He lowered his voice, although Lagoon West was deserted. 'Don't tell Kanin yet, but you've just met the star of *Aphrodite 80*.'

'What?' Incredulously, I stopped. 'Emerelda? Do you mean that she's going to play – ?'

'Eurydice.' Charles nodded. 'Who better?'

'But Charles, she's . . .' I searched for a discreet term.

'That's exactly the point. Believe me, Paul,' – here Charles smiled at me with an expression of surprising canniness – 'this film is not as abstract as Kanin thinks. In fact, its sole purpose is therapeutic. You see, Emerelda was once a minor film actress, I'm convinced the camera crews and sets will help to carry her back to the past, to the period before her appalling shock. It's the only way left, a sort of total psychodrama. The choice of theme, the Orpheus legend and its associations, fit the situation exactly – I see myself as a latter-day Orpheus trying to rescue my Eurydice from Dr Gruber's hell.' He smiled bleakly, as if aware of the slenderness of the analogy and its faint hopes. 'Emerelda's withdrawn completely into her private world, spends all her time inlaying these insects with her jewels. With luck the screens will lead her out into the rest of this synthetic landscape. After all, if she knows that everything around her is unreal she'll cease to fear it.'

'But can't you simply move her physically from Lagoon West?' I asked. 'Perhaps Gruber is the wrong doctor for her. I can't understand why you've kept her here all these years.'

'I haven't kept her, Paul,' he smiled earnestly. 'She's clung to this place and its nightmare memories. Now she even refuses to let me come near her.'

We parted and he walked away among the deserted dunes. In the background the great hoardings I had designed shut out the distant reefs and mesas. Huge blocks of colour had been sprayed on to the designs, superimposing a new landscape upon the desert. The geometric forms loomed and wavered in the haze, like the shifting symbols of a beckoning dream.

As I watched Charles disappear, I felt a sudden sense of pity for his subtle but naive determination. Wondering whether to warn him of his almost certain failure, I rubbed the raw bruises on my arm. While she stared at him, Emerelda's fingers had clasped my arm with unmistakable fierceness, her sharp nails locked together like a clamp of daggers.

So, each afternoon, we began to play the screen game, moving the zodiacal emblems to and fro across the terrace. As I sat on the balustrade and watched Emerelda Garland's first tentative approaches, I wondered how far all of us were becoming ensnared by Charles Van Stratten, by the painted desert and the sculpture singing from the aerial terraces of the summer-house. Into all this Emerelda Garland had now emerged, like a beautiful but nervous wraith. First she would slip among the screens as they gathered below her balcony, and then, hidden behind the large Virgo at their centre, would move across the floor towards the lake, enclosed by the shifting pattern of screens.

Once I left my seat beside Charles and joined the game. Gradually I manoeuvred my screen, a small Sagittarius, into the centre of the maze where I found Emerelda in a narrow shifting cubicle, swaying from side to side as if entranced by the rhythm of the game, the insects scattered at her feet. When I approached she clasped my hand and ran away down a corridor, her gown falling loosely around her bare shoulders. As the screens once more reached the summer-house, she gathered her train in one hand and disappeared among the columns of the loggia.

Walking back to Charles, I found a jewelled mantis nestling like a brooch on the lapel of my jacket, its crown of amethyst melting in the fading sunlight.

'She's coming out, Paul,' Charles said. 'Already she's accepted the screens, soon she'll be able to leave them.' He frowned at the jewelled mantis on my palm. 'A present from Emerelda. Rather two-edged, I think, those stings are dangerous. Still, she's grateful to you, Paul, as I am. Now I know that only the artist can create an absolute reality. Perhaps you should paint a few more screens.'

'Gladly, Charles, if you're sure that . . .'

But Charles merely nodded to himself and walked away towards the film crew.

*

During the next days I painted several new screens, duplicating the zodiacal emblems, so that each afternoon the game became progressively slower and more intricate, the thirty screens forming a multiple labyrinth. For a few minutes, at the climax of the game, I would find Emerelda in the dark centre with the screens jostling and tilting around her, the sculpture on the roof hooting in the narrow interval of open sky.

'Why don't you join the game?' I asked Charles. After his earlier elation he was becoming impatient. Each evening as he drove back to Ciraquito the plume of dust behind his speeding Maserati would rise progressively higher into the pale air. He had lost interest in *Aphrodite 80*. Fortunately Kanin had found that the painted desert of Lagoon West could not be reproduced by an existing colour process, and the film was now being shot from models in a rented studio at Red Beach. 'Perhaps if Emerelda saw you in the maze . . .'

'No, no.' Charles shook his head categorically, then stood up and paced about. 'Paul, I'm less sure of this now.'

Unknown to him, I had painted a dozen more screens. Early that morning I had hidden them among the others on the terrace.

Three nights later, tired of conducting my courtship of Emerelda Garland within a painted maze, I drove out to Lagoon West, climbing through the darkened hills whose contorted forms reared in the swinging headlamps like the smoke clouds of some sunken hell. In the distance, beside the lake, the angular terraces of the summer-house hung in the grey opaque air, as if suspended by invisible wires from the indigo clouds which stretched like velvet towards the few faint lights along the beach two miles away.

The sculptures on the upper balconies were almost silent, and I moved past them carefully, drawing only a few muted chords from them, the faint sounds carried from one statue to the next to the roof of the summer-house and then lost on the midnight air.

From the loggia I looked down at the labyrinth of screens, and at the jewelled insects scattered across the terrace, sparkling on the dark marble like the reflection of a star field.

I found Emerelda Garland among the screens, her white face an oval halo in the shadows, almost naked in a silk gown like a veil of moonlight. She was leaning against a huge Taurus with her pale arms outstretched at her sides, like Europa supplicant before the bull, the luminous spectres of the zodiac guard surrounding her. Without moving her head, she watched me approach and take her hands. Her blue hair swirled in the dark wind as we moved through the screens and crossed the staircase into the summer-house. The expression on her face, whose porcelain planes reflected the torquoise light of her eyes, was one of almost terrifying calm, as if she were moving through some inner dreamscape of the psyche with the confidence of a sleepwalker. My arm around her waist, I guided her up the steps to her suite, realising that I was less her lover than the architect of her fantasies. For a moment the ambiguous nature of my role, and the questionable morality of abducting a beautiful but insane woman, made me hesitate.

We had reached the inner balcony which ringed the central hall of the summer-house. Below us a large sonic-sculpture emitted a tense nervous pulse, as if roused from its midnight silence by my hesitant step.

'Wait!' I pulled Emerelda back from the next flight of stairs, rousing her from her self-hypnotic torpor. 'Up there!'

A silent figure in a dark suit stood at the rail outside the door of Emerelda's suite, the downward inclination of his head clearly perceptible.

'Oh, my God!' With both hands Emerelda clung tightly to my arm, her smooth face seized by a rictus of horror and antici-pation. 'She's there . . . for heaven's sake, Paul, take me – '

'It's Gruber!' I snapped. 'Dr Gruber! Emerelda!'

As we recrossed the entrance the train of Emerelda's gown drew a discordant wail from the statue. In the moonlight the insects still flickered like a carpet of diamonds. I held her shoulders, trying to revive her.

'Emerelda! We'll leave here – take you away from Lagoon West and this insane place.' I pointed to my car, parked by the beach among the dunes. 'We'll go to Vermilion Sands or Red Beach, you'll be able to forget Dr Gruber for ever.'

We hurried towards the car, Emerelda's gown gathering up the insects as we swept past them. I heard her short cry in the moonlight and she tore away from me. I stumbled among the flickering insects. From my knees I saw her disappear into the screens.

For the next ten minutes, as I watched from the darkness by the beach, the jewelled insects moved towards her across the terrace, their last light fading like a vanishing night river.

I walked back to my car, and a quiet, white-suited figure appeared among the dunes and waited for me in the cool amber air, hands deep in his jacket pockets.

'You're a better painter than you know,' Charles said when I took my seat behind the wheel. 'On the last two nights she has made the same escape from me.'

He stared reflectively from the window as we drove back to Ciraquito, the sculptures in the canyon keening behind us like banshees.

The next afternoon, as I guessed, Charles Van Stratten at last played the screen game. He arrived shortly after the game had begun, walking through the throng of extras and cameramen near the car park, hands still thrust deep into the pockets of his white suit as if his sudden appearance among the dunes the previous night and his present arrival were continuous in time. He stopped by the balustrade on the opposite side of the terrace, where I sat with Tony Sapphire and Raymond Mayo, and stared pensively at the slow shuttling movements of the game, his grey eyes hidden below their blond brows.

By now there were so many screens in the game – over forty (I had secretly added more in an attempt to save Emerelda) – that most of the movement was confined to the centre of the group, as if emphasising the self-immolated nature of the ritual. What had begun as a pleasant divertimento, a picturesque introduction to *Aphrodite 80*, had degenerated into a macabre charade, transforming the terrace into the exercise area of a nightmare.

Discouraged or bored by the slowness of the game, one by one the extras taking part began to drop out, sitting down on the balustrade beside Charles. Eventually only Emerelda was left – in my mind I could see her gliding in and out of the nexus of corridors, protected by the zodiacal deities I had painted – and now and then one of the screens in the centre would tilt slightly.

'You've designed a wonderful trap for her, Paul,' Raymond Mayo mused. 'A cardboard asylum.'

'It was Van Stratten's suggestion. We thought they might help her.'

Somewhere, down by the beach, a sculpture had begun to play, and its plaintive voice echoed over our heads. Several of the older sculptures whose sonic cores had corroded had been broken up and left on the beach, where they had taken root again. When the heat gradients roused them to life they would emit a brief strangled music, fractured parodies of their former song.

'Paul!' Tony Sapphire pointed across the terrace. 'What's going on? There's something – '

Fifty yards from us, Charles Van Stratten had stepped over the balustrade, and now stood out on one of the black marble squares, hands loosely at his sides, like a single chess piece opposing the massed array of the screens. Everyone else had gone, and the three of us were now alone with Charles and the hidden occupant of the screens.

The harsh song of the rogue sculptures still pierced the air. Two miles away, through the haze which partly obscured the distant shore, the beach-houses jutted among the dunes, and the fused surface of the lake, in which so many objects were embedded, seams of jade and obsidian, was like a segment of embalmed time, from which the music of the sculpture was a slowly expiring leak. The heat over the vermilion surface was like molten quartz, stirring sluggishly to reveal the distant mesas and reefs.

The haze cleared and the spires of the sand reefs seemed to loom forward, their red barbs clawing towards us through the air. The light drove through the opaque surface of the lake, illuminating its fossilised veins, and the threnody of the dying sculpture lifted to a climax.

'Emerelda!'

As we stood up, roused by his shout, Charles Van Stratten was running across the terrace. 'Emerelda!'

Before we could move he began to pull back the screens, toppling them backwards on to the ground. Within a few moments the terrace was a mêlée of tearing canvas and collapsing trestles, the huge emblems flung left and right out of his path like disintegrating floats at the end of a carnival.

Only when the original nucleus of half a dozen screens was left did he pause, hands on hips.

'Emerelda!' he shouted thickly.

Raymond turned to me. 'Paul, stop him, for heaven's sake!'

Striding forward, Charles pulled back the last of the screens. We had a sudden glimpse of Emerelda Garland retreating from the inrush of sunlight, her white gown flared around her like the broken wings of some enormous bird. Then, with an explosive flash, a brilliant vortex of light erupted from the floor at Emerelda's feet, a cloud of jewelled spiders and scorpions rose through the air and engulfed Charles Van Stratten.

Hands raised helplessly to shield his head, he raced across the terrace, the armada of jewelled insects pursuing him, spinning and diving on to his head. Just before he disappeared among the dunes by the beach, we saw him for a last terrifying moment, clawing helplessly at the jewelled helmet stitched into his face and shoulders. His voice rang out, a sustained cry on the note of the dying sculptures, lost on the stinging flight of the insects.

We found him among the sculptures, face downwards in the hot sand, the fabric of his white suit lacerated by a hundred punctures. Around him were scattered the jewels and crushed bodies of the insects he had killed, their knotted legs and mandibles like abstract ideograms, the sapphires and zircons dissolving in the light.

His swollen hands were filled with the jewels. The cloud of insects returned to the summer-house, where Dr Gruber's black-suited figure was silhouetted against the sky, poised on the white ledge like some minatory bird of nightmare. The only sounds came from the sculptures, which had picked up Charles

Van Stratten's last cry and incorporated it into their own self-requiem.

'. . ."*she . . . killed*". . .' Raymond stopped, shaking his head in amazement. 'Paul, can you hear them, the words are unmistakable.'

Stepping through the metal barbs of the sculpture, I knelt beside Charles, watching as one of the jewelled scorpions crawled from below his chin and scuttled away across the sand.

'Not him,' I said. 'What he was shouting was "*She killed – Mrs Van Stratten.*" The old dowager, his mother. That's the real clue to this fantastic menage. Last night, when we saw Gruber by the rail outside her room – I realise now that was where the old harridan was standing when Emerelda pushed her. For years Charles kept her alone with her guilt here, probably afraid that he might be incriminated if the truth emerged – perhaps he was more responsible than we imagine. What he failed to realise was that Emerelda had lived so long with her guilt that she'd confused it with the person of Charles himself. Killing him was her only release – '

I broke off to find that Raymond and Tony had gone and were already half-way back to the terrace. There was the distant sound of raised voices as members of the film company approached, and whistles shrilled above the exhaust of cars.

The bulky figure of Kanin came through the dunes, flanked by a trio of assistant producers. Their incredulous faces gaped at the prostrate body. The voices of the sculptures faded for the last time, carrying with them into the depths of the fossil lake the final plaintive cry of Charles Van Stratten.

A year later, after Orpheus Productions had left Lagoon West and the scandal surrounding Charles's death had subsided, we drove out again to the summer-house. It was one of those dull featureless afternoons when the desert is without lustre, the distant hills illuminated by brief flashes of light, and the great summer-house seemed drab and lifeless. The servants and Dr Gruber had left, and the estate was beginning to run down. Sand covered long stretches of the roadway, and the dunes rolled across the open terraces, toppling the sculptures. These were silent now, and the sepulchral emptiness was only broken by the hidden presence of Emerelda Garland.

We found the screens where they had been left, and on an impulse spent the first afternoon digging them out of the sand. Those that had rotted in the sunlight we burned in a pyre on the beach, and perhaps the ascending plumes of purple and carmine smoke first brought our presence to Emerelda. The next afternoon, as we played the screen game, I was conscious of her watching us, and saw a gleam of her blue gown among the shadows.

However, although we played each afternoon throughout the summer, she never joined us, despite the new screens I painted and added to the group. Only on the night I visited Lagoon West alone did she come down, but I could hear the voices of the sculptures calling again and fled at the sight of her white face.

By some acoustic freak, the dead sculptures along the beach had revived themselves, and once again I heard the faint haunted echoes of Charles Van Stratten's last cry before he was killed by the jewelled insects. All over the deserted summer-house the low refrain was taken up by the statues, echoing through the empty galleries and across the moonlit terraces, carried away to the mouths of the sand reefs, the last dark music of the painted night.

ALBERTO MORAVIA

The Film Test

Serafino and I are friends although our work has taken us far apart from one another; he is chauffeur to an industrialist and I am a film cameraman and photographer. We are quite different in physical appearance too: he has fair, curly hair and a pink, child-like face, and his eyes, of a staring blue, are set flush with his face; whereas I am swarthy, with the serious face of an adult man, and deep-set, dark eyes. But the real difference lies in our characters: Serafino is a born liar, whereas I am quite unable to tell lies. Well, one Sunday Serafino let me know that he needed me: from his tone I suspected some sort of embarrassment, for Serafino constantly gets into trouble through his mania for cutting a dash. I went to keep the appointment at a café in the Piazza Colonna; and a moment later, there he was, arriving with Lie no. 1 – the very expensive, 'special model' car belonging to his employer, whom I knew to be away from Rome. He waved his hand to me from some distance off, in a slightly conceited way, just as though the car had been his own, and then went and parked it. I looked at him as he came towards me: he was dressed in a foppish kind of way, in short, narrow trousers of yellow corduroy, a jacket with a slit at the back, and a coloured handkerchief round his neck. A feeling of distaste came over me, for some reason, and, as he sat down, I remarked somewhat acidly: 'You look like a millionaire.'

He answered emphatically: 'Today I *am* a millionaire'; and I did not at once understand what he meant. 'What about the car?' I persisted. 'Have you won a football pool?'

'It's the boss's new car,' he answered indifferently. For a moment he sat thinking, and then went on: 'Listen, Mario, two young ladies are coming here shortly . . . as you see, I thought of you too . . . one for each of us . . . They're girls of good family, the daughters of a railway engineer . . . You're a film producer – is that understood? Don't give me away.'

'And you – what are you?'

'I've already told you – a millionaire.'

I said nothing, but rose to my feet. 'What are you doing? Are you going away?' he said in alarm.

'Yes, I'm going,' I replied; 'you know I don't like lies . . . Goodbye . . . enjoy yourself.'

'Wait, wait . . . you'll spoil my plan.'

'Don't worry, I won't spoil anything.'

'Wait a moment; these girls want to meet you.'

'But I don't want to meet them.'

In short, we argued for some time, he sitting down and I standing in front of him. In the end, since I am a good friend, I agreed to stay. However, I warned him: 'I don't guarantee to play this game of yours to the bitter end.' But he was paying no further attention to me. Beaming with pleasure, he said: 'Here they are.'

At first I could see nothing but hair. It looked as though they each of them had on their heads a large ball made of thick, frizzy, puffed-out hair. Then with some difficulty I caught sight, under these two vast masses, of their faces, peaked and thin, like two little birds peeping out of a nest. In figure, they were both of them supple and full of curves, all hips and bosom, with tiny wasp waists that could have gone through a napkin-ring. I thought they must be twins because they were dressed in the same way: tartan skirts, black jumpers, red shoes and bags. Serafino rose ceremoniously and performed the introductions: 'My friend Mario, the film producer; Signorina Iris, Signorina Mimosa.'

I could see them better, now that they were sitting down. From the careful attention he showed her, I realised that Serafino had reserved Iris for himself, leaving me Mimosa. They were not twins: Mimosa, who was clearly over thirty, had a more hungry-looking face, a longer nose, a bigger mouth and a more pronounced chin than Iris, and she was, in fact, almost ugly. Iris, on the other hand, must have been about twenty and was charming. I noticed, moreover, that they both had red, chapped hands – more like working women than young ladies. In the meantime Serafino, who with their arrival seemed to have become quite silly, was making conversation: what a pleasure it was to see them, how brown they were, where had they been for the summer? . . .

Mimosa began: 'At Ven – ' But by that time Iris had answered: 'At Viareggio.' Then they looked at each other and started laughing. Serafino asked: 'What are you laughing at?'

'Don't take any notice,' said Mimosa; 'my sister is silly . . . We were first at Venice, in an hotel, and then at Viareggio, in a little villa we have there.'

I knew she was lying because she lowered her eyes as she spoke. She was like me: I can't tell lies when I am looking someone in the face. Then she went on, coolly: 'Signor Mario, you're a film producer . . . Serafino told us you would give us a film test.'

I was disconcerted; I looked at Serafino, but he turned away his head. 'Well, you know, Signorina,' I said, 'a film test is like a little film, it's not a thing that can be done at a moment's notice . . . It needs a director, a cameraman, a studio . . . Serafino doesn't quite understand . . . But certainly, one of these days . . .'

'One of these days means never.'

'No, no, Signorina, I assure you . . .'

'Come on, be a good, kind man, do give us a test.' She was wriggling all over now, and had taken my arm and was pressing up against me. I realised that Serafino had turned her head with this story about a film test, and I tried again to explain to her that a film test was not a thing that could be done in a moment, there and then. Gradually she came, at length, to understand this; and she relaxed her hold on my arm. Then she said to her sister, who was chattering to Serafino: 'I told you it was just a story . . . Well, what shall we do? Shall we go home?'

Iris, who was not expecting this, was ill at ease. She said, with some embarrassment: 'We might stay with them . . . until this evening.'

'Yes,' urged Serafino, 'let's all stay together . . . Let's go out in the car.'

'You've got a car?' enquired Mimosa, almost reconciled.

'Yes, there it is.'

She followed the movement of his hand, saw the car and immediately changed her tone. 'Let's go, then . . . Sitting in a café bores me.' We all four rose to our feet. Iris went in front with Serafino; and Mimosa walked beside me, saying: 'You're not offended, are you? But you know, we're sick and tired of promises . . . Now, you *will* give me the test, won't you?'

So all my explanations had served no purpose at all: she still wanted the test. I made no answer, but got into the car and sat down beside her, at the back, while Serafino and Iris sat in front. 'Where shall we go?' asked Serafino.

Mimosa had now seized hold of my arm again, and had taken my hand in hers and was squeezing it. In a low voice, she tried to coax me: 'Come on, do be kind; tell him to go to the studio and we'll do the test.' For a momemt, from sheer anger, I sat silent; and she took advantage of this to add, still in a low voice: 'Look, if you give me a test, I'll give you a kiss.'

I had a sudden inspiration, and suggested: 'Let's go to Serafino's house . . . He has a lovely big house . . . Then I'll be able to take a better look at you both, and I'll tell you if there's a chance of giving you this test.'

I noticed that Serafino threw me a look of reproach: he might pass off his employer's car as his own; but he had not yet had the courage to bring anyone into the house. He tried, in fact, to make objections: 'Wouldn't it be better to go for a nice drive?'; but the girls, Mimosa especially, insisted: they didn't want a drive, they wanted to discuss the question of the film test. So he resigned himself and we went off at full speed towards the Parioli district, where the house was. All the way there, Mimosa continued to press up against me, talking to me in a low, insinuating, caressing voice. I did not listen to her; but every now and then I caught that oft-repeated word, which she reiterated like a hammer striking a nail: 'The test . . . You'll give me a test? . . . If we do the test . . .'

We reached the Parioli district, with its empty streets between rows of expensive houses, all balcony and window. We reached the residence of Serafino's employer, with its black marble entrance-hall and its glass and mahogany lift. We went up to the third floor and, on entering, found ourselves in the dark, with a smell of naphthalene and stuffiness everywhere. 'I'm sorry, but I've been away,' Serafino informed us; 'the flat's all upside down.' We went into the sitting-room; Serafino threw open the windows; we sat down on a divan upholstered in grey cloth, in front of a piano covered in dust-sheets which were fastened with safety-pins. Then, putting my plan into action, I said: 'We two are going to take a look at you now; you must just walk up and down the room for a bit . . . Then I shall be able to get an idea for the test.'

'Are we to show our legs?' asked Mimosa.

'No, no, not your legs . . . just walk about, that's enough.'

Obediently they started walking up and down in front of us, on the wax-polished wooden floor. No one could say they were not graceful, with those two big heads of hair, and their well-developed hips and busts and their thin waists. But I noticed that they had large, ugly feet as well as hands. And their legs were slightly crooked, stiff and clumsy in shape. They were, in fact, the sort of girls to whom film-producers do not give even a walking-on part. In the meantime they went on walking up and down, and each time they met in the middle of the room, they started laughing. All at once I called out: 'Halt! That's enough. Sit down!'

They went and sat down and looked at me with anxious faces. 'I'm sorry,' I said drily, 'but you won't do.'

'Why?'

'I'll tell you why, at once,' I explained seriously. 'For my films, I don't need refined, well-educated, distinguished ladylike girls such as you . . . What I need is working-class girls — girls who can even, if required, speak a few ugly words, girls who move in a provoking way, girls who are, in fact, awkward, ill-bred, unpolished . . . You, on the other hand, are the daughters of an engineer, you come of a good family . . . You're not what I'm looking for.'

I looked at Serafino: he had sunk back on the divan and appeared stupefied. 'But what d'you mean?' persisted Mimosa. 'We can surely pretend to be working-class girls, can't we?'

'No, you can't. There are some things that no one can do who isn't born to them.'

A short silence ensued. I had cast my hook and I was sure the fish would swallow it. And indeed, a moment later, Mimosa rose and went and whispered in her sister's ear. The latter did not appear pleased, but finally she made a gesture of consent. Then Mimosa placed her hands on her hips and swayed across to me; she gave me a punch in the chest and said: 'Come on, old sport, who d'you think you're talking to?'

If I were to say that she was transformed, it would be saying too much. In actual fact, it was herself, her own natural self. I replied, laughing: 'To the daughters of a railway engineer.'

'On the contrary, we're exactly what you want – two ordinary working-class girls . . . Iris is in service, and I'm a nurse . . .'

'And how about the villa at Viareggio?'

'There isn't one. We got our little bit of sunburn at Ostia.'

'But why did you tell so many lies?'

Iris said naively: 'I didn't want to . . . but Mimosa says you have to throw dust in people's eyes.'

'Anyhow, if we hadn't told lies,' Mimosa remarked flatly, 'Signor Serafino wouldn't have introduced us to you . . . so it served its purpose . . . Well, now, what about that film test?'

'We've done it already,' I replied, laughing, 'and it served to show that you're a couple of nice working-class girls . . . Besides, lie for lie: I'm not a film producer but an ordinary cameraman and photographer . . . and Serafino here, he's not the grand gentleman he pretends to be: he's a chauffeur.'

I must admit that Mimosa took the blow magnificently. 'Well, well, I was half expecting this,' she said sadly; 'we're unlucky . . . and if we meet a man with a car, of course he turns out to be a chauffeur . . . Come on, Iris.'

At last Serafino roused himself. 'Wait a moment,' he said. 'Where are you going?'

'We're going away, Mr Liar.'

All of a sudden I felt sorry for them, especially for Iris, who was so pretty and who seemed mortified and had tears in her eyes. I made a suggestion. 'Listen to me,' I said. 'We've all four of us told lies . . . but I propose that we let bygones be bygones and all go to the pictures together . . . What about it?'

A discussion followed. Iris wanted to accept; Mimosa, who was still offended, did not; Serafino, crestfallen, hadn't the courage to speak. But I persuaded Mimosa by saying finally:

'I'm a cameraman, not a producer . . . but I can introduce Iris to an assistant director that I know . . . It won't be a great recommendation, but it's better than nothing. It's no good for you, I'm afraid, but possibly something might be done about Iris.'

So off we went to the pictures; but in a bus, not in the car. And Iris, in the cinema, pressed close up against Serafino, whom she liked in spite of his being both a liar and a chauffeur. Mimosa, on the other hand, kept to herself. And during an interval she said to me: 'I'm more or less of a mother to Iris . . . She *is* a pretty girl, isn't she? Now remember you made a promise and you must keep it . . . there'll be the devil to pay if you don't.'

'It's only cowards who make promises and keep them,' I said jokingly.

'You made a promise and you're going to keep it,' said she; 'Iris is to have her film test, and have it she shall.'

Translated by Angus Davidson

RUDYARD KIPLING

Mrs Bathurst

The day that I chose to visit HMS *Peridot* in Simon's Bay was the day that the Admiral had chosen to send her up the coast. She was just steaming out to sea as my train came in, and since the rest of the Fleet were either coaling or busy at the rifle-ranges a thousand feet up the hill, I found myself stranded, lunchless, on the sea-front with no hope of return to Cape Town before 5 p.m. At this crisis I had the luck to come across my friend Inspector Hooper, Cape Government Railways, in command of an engine and a brake-van chalked for repair.

'If you get something to eat,' he said, 'I'll run you down to Glengariff siding till the goods comes along. It's cooler there than here, you see.'

I got food and drink from the Greeks who sell all things at a price, and the engine trotted us a couple of miles up the line to a bay of drifted sand and a plank-platform half buried in sand not a hundred yards from the edge of the surf. Moulded dunes, whiter than any snow, rolled far inland up a brown and purple valley of splintered rocks and dry scrub. A crowd of Malays hauled at a net beside two blue and green boats on the beach; a picnic party danced and shouted barefoot where a tiny river trickled across the flat, and a circle of dry hills, whose feet were set in sands of silver, locked us in against a seven-coloured sea. At either horn of the bay the railway line, just above high-water mark, ran round a shoulder of piled rocks, and disappeared.

'You see, there's always a breeze here,' said Hooper, opening the door as the engine left us in the siding on the sand, and the strong south-east buffeting under Elsie's Peak dusted sand into our tickey beer. Presently he sat down to a file full of spiked documents. He had returned from a long trip up-country, where he had been reporting on damaged rolling-stock, as far away as Rhodesia. The weight of the bland wind on my eyelids; the song of it under the car-roof, and high up among the rocks; the drift of fine grains chasing each other musically ashore; the tramp of the surf; the voices of the picnickers; the rustle of Hooper's file, and the presence of the assured sun, joined with the beer to cast me into magical slumber. The hills of False Bay were just dissolving into those of fairyland when I heard footsteps on the sand outside, and the clink of our couplings.

'Stop that!' snapped Hooper, without raising his head from his work. 'It's those dirtly little Malay boys, you see: they're always playing with the trucks . . .'

'Don't be hard on 'em. The railway's a general refuge in Africa,' I replied.

''Tis – up-country at any rate. That reminds me,' he felt in his waistcoat-pocket, 'I've got a curiosity for you from Wankies – beyond Bulawayo. It's more of a souvenir perhaps than – '

'The old hotel's inhabited,' cried a voice. 'White men, from the language. Marines to the front! Come on, Pritch. Here's your Belmont. Wha – i – i!'

The last word dragged like a rope as Mr Pyecroft ran round to the open door, and stook looking up into my face. Behind him an enormous Sergeant of Marines trailed a stalk of dried seaweed, and dusted the sand nervously from his fingers.

'What are you doing here?' I asked. 'I thought the *Hierophant* was down the coast?'

'We came in last Tuesday – from Tristan da Cunha – for overhaul, and we shall be in dockyard 'ands for two months, with boiler-seatings.'

'Come and sit down.' Hooper put away the file.

'This is Mr Hooper of the Railway,' I explained, as Pyecroft turned to haul up the black-moustached sergeant.

'This is Sergeant Pritchard, of the *Agaric*, an old shipmate,' said he. 'We were strollin' on the beach.' The monster blushed and nodded. He filled up one side of the van when he sat down.

'And this is my friend, Mr Pyecroft,' I added to Hooper, already busy with the extra beer which my prophetic soul had bought from the Greeks.

'*Moi aussi,*' quoth Pyecroft, and drew out beneath his coat a labelled quart bottle.

'Why, it's Bass!' cried Hooper.

'It was Pritchard,' said Pyecroft. 'They can't resist him.'

'That's not so,' said Pritchard mildly.

'Not *verbatim* per'aps, but the look in the eye came to the same thing.'

'Where was it?' I demanded.

'Just on beyond here – at Kalk Bay. She was slappin' a rug in a back verandah. Pritch 'adn't more than brought his batteries to bear, before she stepped indoors an' sent it flyin' over the wall.'

Pyecroft patted the warm bottle.

'It was all a mistake,' said Pritchard. 'I shouldn't wonder if she mistook me for Maclean. We're about of a size.'

I had heard householders of Muizenberg, St James, and Kalk Bay complain of the difficulty of keeping beer or good servants at the seaside, and I began to see the reason. None the less, it was excellent Bass, and I too drank to the health of the large-minded maid.

'It's the uniform that fetches 'em, an' they fetch it,' said Pyecroft. 'My simple navy blue is respectable, but not fascinatin'. Now Pritch in 'is Number One rig is always "purr Mary, on the terrace" – *ex officio* as you might say.'

'She took me for Maclean, I tell you,' Pritchard insisted. 'Why – why – to listen to him you wouldn't think that only yesterday – '

'Pritch,' said Pyecroft, 'be warned in time. If we begin tellin' what we know about each other we'll be turned out of the pub. Not to mention aggravated desertion on several occasions – '

'Never anything more than absence without leaf – I defy you to prove it,' said the Sergeant hotly. 'An' if it comes to that, how about Vancouver in '87?'

'How about it? Who pulled bow in the gig going ashore? Who told Boy Niven . . .?'

'Surely you were court-martialled for that?' I said. The story of Boy Niven who lured seven or eight able-bodied seamen and marines into the woods of British Columbia used to be a legend of the Fleet.

'Yes, we were court-martialled to rights,' said Pritchard, 'but we should have been tried for murder if Boy Niven 'adn't been unusually tough. He told us he had an uncle 'oo'd give us land to farm. 'E said he was born at the back o' Vancouver Island, and *all* the time the beggar was a balmy Barnardo orphan!'

'*But* we believed him,' said Pyecroft. 'I did – you did – Paterson did – an' 'oo was the Marine that married the coconut woman afterwards – him with the mouth?'

'Oh, Jones, Spit-Kid Jones. I 'aven't thought of 'im in years,' said Pritchard. 'Yes, Spit-Kid believed it, an' George Anstey and Moon. We were very young an' very curious.'

'*But* lovin' an' trustful to a degree,' said Pyecroft.

'Remember when 'e told us to walk in single file for fear o' bears? Remember, Pye, when 'e 'opped about in that bog full o' ferns an' sniffed an' said 'e could smell the smoke of 'is uncle's farm? An' *all* the time it was a dirty little outlyin' uninhabited island. We walked round it in a day, an' come back to our boat lyin' on the beach. A whole day Boy Niven kept us walkin' in circles lookin' for 'is uncle's farm! He said his uncle was compelled by the law of the land to give us a farm!'

'Don't get hot, Pritch. We believed,' said Pyecroft.

'He'd been readin' books. He only did it to get a run ashore an' have himself talked of. A day an' a night – eight of us – followin' Boy Niven round an uninhabited island in the Vancouver archipelago! Then the picket came for us an' a nice pack o' idiots we looked!'

'What did you get for it?' Hooper asked.

'Heavy thunder with continuous lightning for two hours. Thereafter sleet-squalls, a confused sea, and cold, unfriendly weather till conclusion o' cruise,' said Pyecroft. 'It was only what we expected, but what we felt – an' I assure you, Mr Hooper, even a sailor-man has a heart to break – was bein' told that we able seamen an' promisin' marines 'ad misled Boy Niven. Yes, we poor back-to-the-landers was supposed to 'ave misled him! He rounded on us, o' course, an' got off easy.'

'Excep' for what we gave him in the steerin'-flat when we came out o' cells. 'Eard anything of 'im lately, Pye?'

'Signal Boatswain in the Channel Fleet, I believe – Mr L. L. Niven is.'

'An' Anstey died o' fever in Benin,' Pritchard mused. 'What come to Moon? Spit-Kid we know about.'

'Moon – Moon! Now where did I last . . .? Oh yes, when I was in the *Palladium*. I met Quigley at Buncrana Station. He told me Moon 'ad run when the *Astrild* sloop was cruising among the South Seas three years back. He always showed signs o' bein' a Mormonastic beggar. Yes, he slipped off quietly an' they 'adn't time to chase 'im round the islands even if the navigatin' officer 'ad been equal to the job.'

'Wasn't he?' said Hooper.

'Not so. Accordin' to Quigley the *Astrild* spent half her commission rompin' up the beach like a she-turtle, an' the other half hatching turtles' eggs on the top o' numerous reefs. When she was docked at Sydney her copper looked like Aunt Maria's washing on the line – an' her 'midship frames was sprung. The commander swore the dockyard 'ad done it haulin' the pore thing on to the slips. They *do* do strange things at sea, Mr Hooper.'

'Ah! I'm not a taxpayer,' said Hooper, and opened a fresh bottle. The Sergeant seemed to be one who had a difficulty in dropping subjects.

'How it all comes back, don't it?' he said. 'Why, Moon must 'ave 'ad sixteen years' service before he ran.'

'It takes 'em at all ages. Look at – you know,' said Pyecroft.

'Who?' I asked.

'A service man within eighteen months of his pension is the party you're thinkin' of,' said Pritchard. 'A warrant 'oo's name begins with a V, isn't it?'

'But, in a way o' puttin' it, we can't say that he actually did desert,' Pyecroft suggested.

'Oh no,' said Pritchard. 'It was only permanent absence up-country without leaf. That was all.'

'Up-country?' said Hooper. 'Did they circulate his description?'

'What for?' said Pritchard, most impolitely.

'Because deserters are like columns in the war. They don't move away from the line, you see. I've known a chap caught at Salisbury that way tryin' to get to Nyassa. They tell me, but o' course I don't know, that they don't ask questions on the Nyassa

Lake Flotilla up there. I've heared of a P & O quartermaster in full command of an armed launch there.'

'Do you think Click 'ud ha' gone up that way?' Pritchard asked.

'There's no saying. He was sent up to Bloemfontein to take over some Navy ammunition left in the fort. We know he took it over and saw it into the trucks. Then there was no more Click – then or thereafter. Four months ago it transpired, and thus the *casus belli* stands at present,' said Pyecroft.

'What were his marks?' said Hooper again.

'Does the Railway get a reward for returnin' 'em then?' said Pritchard.

'If I did d'you suppose I'd talk about it?' Hooper retorted angrily.

'You seemed so very interested,' said Pritchard with equal crispness.

'Why was he called Click?' I asked, to tide over an uneasy little break in the conversation. The two men were staring at each other very fixedly.

'Because of an ammunition hoist carryin' away,' said Pyecroft. 'And it carried away four of 'is teeth – on the lower port side, wasn't it, Pritch? The substitutes which he bought weren't screwed home, in a manner o' sayin'. When he talked fast they used to lift a little on the bedplate. 'Ence, "Click". They called 'im a superior man, which is what we'd call a long, black-'aired, genteelly-speakin', 'alf-bred beggar on the lower deck.'

'Four false teeth in the lower left jaw,' said Hooper, his hand in his waistcoat-pocket. 'What tattoo marks?'

'Look here,' began Pritchard, half rising. 'I'm sure we're very grateful to you as a gentleman for your 'orspitality, but per'aps we may 'ave made an error in – '

I looked at Pyecroft for aid – Hopper was crimsoning rapidly.

'If the fat marine now occupying the foc'-sle will kindly bring 'is *status quo* to an anchor yet once more, we may be able to talk like gentlemen – not to say friends,' said Pyecroft. 'He regards you, Mr Hooper, as a emissary of the Law.'

'I only wish to observe that when a gentleman exhibits such a peculiar, or I should rather say, such a *bloomin'* curiosity in identification marks as our friend here – '

'Mr Pritchard,' I interposed, 'I'll take all the responsibility for Mr Hooper.'

'An' *you'll* apologise all round,' said Pyecroft. 'You're a rude little man, Pritch.'

'But how was I – ' he began, wavering.

'I don't know an' I don't care. Apologise!'

The giant looked round bewildered and took our little hands into his vast grip, one by one.

'I was wrong,' he said meekly as a sheep. 'My suspicions was unfounded. Mr Hooper, I apologise.'

'You did quite right to look out for your own end o' the line,' said Hooper. 'I'd ha' done the same with a gentleman I didn't know, you see. If you don't mind I'd like to hear a little more o' your Mr Vickery. It's safe with me, you see.'

'Why did Vickery run?' I began, but Pyecroft's smile made me turn my question to 'Who was she?'

'She kep' a little hotel at Hauraki – near Auckland,' said Pyecroft.

'By Gawd!' roared Pritchard, slapping his hand on his leg. 'Not Mrs Bathurst!'

Pyecroft nodded slowly, and the Sergeant called all the powers of darkness to witness his bewilderment.

'So far as I could get at it, Mrs B. was the lady in question.'

'But Click was married,' cried Pritchard.

'An' 'ad a fifteen-year-old daughter. 'E's shown me her photograph. Settin' that aside, so to say, 'ave you ever found these little things make – much difference? Because I haven't.'

'Good Lord Alive an' Watchin'! . . . Mrs Bathurst . . .' Then with another roar: 'You can say what you please, Pye, but you don't make me believe it was any of 'er fault. She wasn't *that*!'

'If I was going to say what I please, I'd begin by callin' you a silly ox an' work up to the higher pressures at leisure. I'm trying to say solely what transpired. M'rover, for once you're right. It wasn't her fault.'

'You couldn't 'aven't made me believe it if it 'ad been,' was the answer.

Such faith in a Sergeant of Marines interested me greatly. 'Never mind about that,' I cried. 'Tell me what she was like.'

'She was a widow,' said Pyecroft. 'Left so very young and

never re-spliced. She kep' a little hotel for warrants and non-coms close to Auckland, an' she always wore black silk, and 'er neck – '

'You ask what she was like,' Pritchard broke in. 'Let me give you an instance. I was at Auckland first in '97, at the end o' the *Marroquin*'s commission, an' as I'd been promoted I went up with the others. She used to look after us all, an' she never lost by it – not a penny! "Pay me now," she'd say, "or settle later. I know you won't let me suffer. Send the money from home if you like." Why, gentlemen all, I tell you I've see that lady take her own gold watch an' chain off her neck in the bar an' pass it to a bosun 'oo'd come ashore without 'is ticker an' 'ad to catch the last boat. "I don't know your name," she said, "but when you've done with it, you'll find plenty that know me on the front. Send it back by one o' them." And it was worth thirty pounds if it was worth 'arf-a-crown. The little gold watch, Pye, with the blue monogram at the back. But, as was sayin', in those days she kep' a beer that agreed with me – Slits it was called. One way an' another I must 'ave punished a good few bottles of it while we was in the bay – comin' ashore every night or so. Chaffin' across the bar like, once when we were alone, "Mrs B.," I said, "when next I call I want you to remember that this is my particular – just as you're my particular." (She'd let you go *that* far!) "Just as you're my particular," I said. "Oh, thank you, Sergeant Pritchard," she says, an' put 'er hand up to the curl be'ind 'er ear. Remember that way she had, Pye?'

'I think so,' said the sailor.

'Yes, "Thank you, Sergeant Pritchard," she says. "The least I can do is to mark it for you in case you change your mind. There's no great demand for it in the Fleet," she says, "but to make sure I'll put it at the back o' the shelf," an' she snipped off a piece of her hair ribbon with that old dolphin cigar-cutter on the bar – remember it, Pye? – an' she tied a bow round what was left – just four bottles. That was '97 no, '96. In '98 I was in the *Resilient* – China Station – full commission. In Nineteen One, mark you, I was in the *Carthusian*, back in Auckland Bay again. Of course I went up to Mrs B.'s with the rest of us to see how things were goin'. They were the same as ever. (Remember the big tree on the pavement by the side-bar, Pye?) I never said anythin' in special (there was too many of us talkin' to her), but she saw me at once.'

'That wasn't difficult?' I ventured.

'Ah, but wait. I was comin' up to the bar, when, "Ada," she says to her niece, "get me Sergeant Pritchard's particular," and, gentlemen all, I tell you before I could shake 'ands with the lady, there were those four bottles o' Slits, with 'er 'air-ribbon in a bow round each o' their necks, set down in front o' me, an' as she drew the cork she looked at me under her eyebrows in that blindish way she had o' lookin', an', "Sergeant Pritchard," she says, "I do 'ope you 'aven't changed your mind about your particulars." That's the kind o' woman she was – after five years!'

'I don't *see* her yet somehow,' said Hooper, but with sympathy.

'She – she never scrupled to feed a lame duck or set 'er foot on a scorpion at any time of 'er life,' Pritchard added valiantly.

'That don't help me either. My mother's like that for one.'

The giant heaved inside his uniform and rolled his eyes at the car-roof. Said Pyecroft suddenly:

'How many women have you been intimate with all over the world, Pritch?'

Pritchard blushed plum-colour to the short hairs of his seventeen-inch neck.

''Undreds,' said Pyecroft. 'So've I. How many of 'em can you remember in your own mind, settin' aside the first – an' per'aps the last – *and one more*?'

'Few, wonderful few, now I tax myself,' said Sergeant Pritchard relievedly. 'An' how many times might you 'ave been at Auckland?'

'One – two,' he began – 'why, I can't make it more than three times in ten years. But I can remember every time that I ever saw Mrs B.'

'So can I – an' I've only been to Auckland twice – how she stood an' what she was sayin' an' what she looked like. That's the secret. 'Tisn't beauty, so to speak, nor good talk necessarily. It's just It. Some women'll stay in a man's memory if they once walk down a street, but most of 'em you can live with a month on end, an' next commission you'd be put to it to certify whether they talked in their sleep or not, as one might say.'

'Ah!' said Hooper. 'That's more the idea. I've known just two women of that nature.'

'An' it was no fault o' theirs?' asked Pritchard.

'None whatever. I know *that*!'

'An' if a man gets struck with that kind o' woman, Mr Hooper?' Pritchard went on.

'He goes crazy – or just saves himself,' was the slow answer.

'You've hit it,' said the Sergeant. 'You've seen an' known somethin' in the course o' your life, Mr Hooper. I'm lookin' at you!' He set down his bottle.

'And how often had Vickery seen her?' I asked.

'That's the dark an' bloody mystery,' Pyecroft answered. 'I'd never come across him till I come out in the *Hierophant* just now, an' there wasn't any one in the ship who knew much about him. You see, he was what you call a superior man. 'E spoke to me once or twice about Auckland and Mrs B. on the voyage out. I called that to mind subsequently. There must 'ave been a good deal between 'em, to my way o' thinkin'. Mind you, I'm only giving you my *résumé* of it all, because all I know is second-hand so to speak, or rather I should say more than second-'and.'

'How?' said Hooper peremptorily. 'You must have seen it or heard it.'

'Ye-es,' said Pyecroft. 'I used to think seein' and hearin' was the only regulation aids to ascertainin' facts, but as we get older we get more accommodatin'. The cylinders work easier, I suppose ... Were you in Cape Town last December when Phyllis's Circus came?'

'No – up country,' said Hooper, a little nettled at the change of venue.

'I ask because they had a new turn of a scientific nature called "Home and Friends for a Tickey".'

'Oh, you mean the cinematograph – the pictures of prize-fights and steamers. I've seen 'em up-country.'

'Biograph or cinematograph was what I was alludin' to. London Bridge with the omnibuses – a troopship goin' to war –

marines on parade at Portsmouth, an' the Plymouth Express arrivin' at Paddin'ton.'

'Seen 'em all. Seen 'em all,' said Hooper impatiently.

'We *Hierophants* came in just before Christmas week an' leaf was easy.'

'I think a man gets fed up with Cape Town quicker than anywhere else on the station. Why, even Durban's more like Nature. We was there for Christmas,' Pritchard put in.

'Not bein' a devotee of Indian *peeris*, as our Doctor said to the Pusser, I can't exactly say. Phyllis's was good enough after musketry practice at Mozambique. I couldn't get off the first two or three nights on account of what you might call an inbroglio with our Torpedo Lieutenant in the submerged flat, where some pride of the West Country had sugared up a gyroscope; but I remember Vickery went ashore with our Carpenter Rigdon – old Crocus we called him. As a general rule Crocus never left 'is ship unless an' until he was 'oisted out with a winch, but *when* 'e went 'e would return noddin' like a lily gemmed with dew. We smothered him down below that night, but the things 'e said about Vickery as a fittin' playmate for a Warrant Officer of 'is cubic capacity, before we got him quiet, was that I should call pointed.'

'I've been with Crocus – in the *Redoubtable*,' said the Sergeant. 'He's a character if there is one.'

'Next night I went into Cape Town with Dawson and Pratt; but just at the door of the Circus I came across Vickery. "Oh!" he says, "you're the man I'm looking for. Come and sit next me. This way to the shillin' places!" I went astern at once, protestin' because tickey seats better suited my so-called finances. "Come on," says Vickery, "I'm payin'." Naturally I abandoned Pratt and Dawson in anticipation o' drinks to match the seats. "No," he says, when this was 'inted – "not now. Not now. As many as you please afterwards, but I want you sober for the occasion." I caught 'is face under a lamp just then, an' the appearance of it quite cured me of my thirst. Don't mistake. It didn't frighten me. It made me anxious. I can't tell you what it was like, but that was the effect which it 'ad on me. If you want to know, it reminded me of those things in bottles in those herbalistic shops at Plymouth – preserved in spirits of wine. White an' crumply things – previous to birth as you might say.'

'You 'ave a bestial mind, Pye,' said the Sergeant, relighting his pipe.

'Perhaps. We were in the front row, an' "Home an' Friends" came on early. Vickery touched me on the knee when the number went up. "If you see anything that strikes you," he says, "drop me a hint"; then he went on clicking. We saw London Bridge an' so forth an' so on, an' it was most interestin'. I'd never seen it before. You 'eard a little dynamo like buzzin', but the pictures were the real thing – alive an' movin'.'

'I've seen 'em,' said Hooper. 'Of course they are taken from the very thing itself – you see.'

'Then the Western Mail came in to Paddin'ton on the big magic-lantern sheet. First we saw the platform empty an' the porters standin' by. Then the engine come in, head on, an' the women in the front row jumped: she headed so straight. Then the doors opened and the passengers came out and the porters got the luggage – just like life. Only – only when any one came down too far towards us that was watchin', they walked right out o' the picture, so to speak. I was 'ighly interested, I can tell you. So were all of us. I watched an old man with a rug 'oo'd dropped a book an' was tryin' to pick it up, when quite slowly, from be'ind two porters – carrying a little reticule an' lookin' from side to side – comes our Mrs Bathurst. There was no mistakin' the walk in a hundred thousand. She come forward – right forward – she looked out straight at us with that blindish look which Pritch alluded to. She walked on and on till she melted out of the picture – like – like a shadow jumpin' over a candle, an' as she went I 'eard Dawson in the tickey seats be'ind sing out: "Christ! there's Mrs B.!"'

Hooper swallowed his spittle and leaned forward intently.

'Vickery touched me on the knee again. He was clickin' his four false teeth with his jaw down like an enteric at the last kick. "Are you sure?" he says. "Sure," I says, "didn't you 'ear Dawson give tongue? Why, it's the woman herself." "I was sure before," he says, "but I brought you to make sure. Will you come again with me tomorrow?"

' "Willingly," I says, "it's like meetin' old friends."

' "Yes," he says, openin' his watch, "very like. It will be four-and-twenty hours less four minutes before I see her again. Come and have drink," he says. "It may amuse you, but it's no sort of earthly use to me." He went out shaking his head an' stumblin' over people's feet as if he was drunk already. I anticipated a swift drink an' a speedy return, because I wanted to see the performin' elephants. Instead o' which Vickery began to navigate the town at the rate o' lookin' in at a bar every three minutes approximate Greenwich time. I'm not a drinkin' man, though there are those present' – he cocked his unforgettable eye at me – 'who may have seen me more or less imbued with the fragrant spirit. None the less when I drink I like to do it at anchor an' not at an average speed of eighteen knots on the measured mile. There's a tank as you might say at the back o' that big hotel up the hill – what do they call it?'

'The Molteno Reservoir,' I suggested, and Hooper nodded.

'That was his limit o' drift. We walked there an' we come down through the Gardens – there was a South-Easter blowin' – an' we finished up by the Docks. Then we bore up the road to Salt River, and wherever there was a pub Vickery put in sweatin'. He didn't look at what he drunk – he didn't look at the change. He walked an' he drunk an' he perspired rivers. I understood why old Crocus 'ad came back in the condition 'e did, because Vickery an' I 'ad two an' a half hours o' this gipsy manoeuvre, an' when we got back to the station there wasn't a dry atom on or in me.'

'Did he say anything?' Pritchard asked.

'The sum total of 'is conversation from 7.45 p.m. till 11.15 p.m. was "Let's have another". Thus the mornin' an' the evenin' were the first day, as Scripture says . . . To abbreviate a lengthy narrative, I went into Cape Town for five consecutive nights with Master Vickery, and in that time I must 'ave logged about fifty knots over the ground an' taken in two gallon o' all the worst spirits south the Equator. The evolution never varied. Two shilling seats for us two; five minutes o' the pictures, an' perhaps forty-five seconds o' Mrs B. walking down towards us with that blindish look in her eyes an' the reticule in her hand. Then out – walk – and drink till train time.'

'What did you think?' said Hooper, his hand fingering his waistcoat-pocket.

'Several things,' said Pyecroft. 'To tell you the truth, I aren't quite done thinkin' about it yet. Mad? The man was a dumb lunatic – must 'ave been for months – years p'raps. I know somethin' o' maniacs, as every man in the Service must. I've been shipmates with a mad skipper – an' a lunatic Number One, but never both together, I thank 'Eaven. I could give you the names o' three captains now 'oo ought to be in an asylum, but you don't find me interferin' with the mentally afflicted till they begin to lay about 'em with rammers an' winch-handles. Only once I crept up a little into the wind towards Master Vickery. "I wonder what she's doin' in England," I says. "Don't it seem to you she's lookin' for somebody?" That was in the Gardens again, with the South-Easter blowin' as we were makin' our desperate round. "She's lookin' for me," he says, stoppin' dead under a lamp an' clickin'. When he wasn't drinkin', in which case all 'is teeth clicked on the glass, 'e was clickin' 'is four false teeth like a Marconi ticker. "Yes! lookin' for me," he said, an' he went on very softly an' as you might say affectionately. "*But*," he went on, "in future, Mr Pyecroft, I should take it kindly of you if you'd confine your remarks to the drinks set before you. Otherwise," he says, "with the best will in the world towards you, I may find myself guilty of murder! Do you understand?" he says. "Perfectly," I says, "but would it at all soothe you to know that in such a case the chances o' your being killed are precisely equivalent to the chances o' me being outed." "Why, no," he said, "I'm almost afraid that 'ud be a temptation." Then I said – we was right under the lamp by that arch at the end o' the Gardens where the trams come round – "Assumin' murder was done – or attempted murder – I put it to you that you would still be left so badly crippled, as one might say, that your subsequent capture by the police – to 'oom you would 'ave to explain – would be largely inevitable." "That's better," 'e says, passin' 'is hands over his forehead. "That's much better, because," he says, "do you know, as I am now, Pye, I'm not so sure if I could explain anything much." Those were the only particular words I had with 'im in our walks as I remember.'

'What walks!' said Hooper. 'Oh my soul, what walks!'

'They were chronic,' said Pyecroft gravely, 'but I didn't anticipate any danger till the Circus left. Then I anticipated that, bein' deprived of 'is stimulant, he might react on me, so to say, with a hatchet. Consequently, after the final performance an' the ensuin' wet walk, I kep' myself aloof from my superior officer on board in the execution of 'is duty, as you might put it. Consequently, I was interested when the sentry informs me while I was passin' on my lawful occasions that Click had asked to see the captain. As a general rule warrant-officers don't dissipate much of the owner's time, but Click put in an hour and more be'ind that door. My duties kep' me within eyeshot to it. Vickery came out first, an' 'e actually nodded at me an' smiled. This knocked me out o' the boat, because, havin' seen 'is face for five consecutive nights, I didn't anticipate any change there more than a condenser in hell, so to speak. The owner emerged later. His face didn't read off at all, so I fell back on his cox, 'oo'd been eight years with him and knew him better than boat signals. Lamson — that was the cox's name — crossed 'is bows once or twice at low speeds an' dropped down to me visibly concerned. "He's shipped 'is court-martial face," says Lamson. "Some one's goin' to be 'ung. I've never seen that look but once before, when they chucked the gun-sights overboard in the *Fantastic*." Throwin' gun-sights overboard, Mr Hooper, is the equivalent for mutiny in these degenerate days. It's done to attract the notice of the authorities an' the *Western Mornin' News* — generally by a stoker. Naturally, word went round the lower deck an' we had a private over'aul of our little con- sciences. But, barrin' a shirt which a second-class stoker said 'ad walked into 'is bag from the marines' flat by itself, nothin' vital transpired. The owner went about flyin' the signal for "attend public execution", so to say, but there was no corpse at the yard-arm. 'E lunched on the beach an' 'e returned with 'is regulation harbour-routine face about 3 p.m. Thus Lamson lost prestige for raising false alarms. The only person 'oo might 'ave connected the epicycloidal gears correctly was one Pyecroft, when he was told that Mr Vickery would go up-country that same evening to take over certain naval ammunition left after the war in Bloemfontein Fort. No details was ordered to

accompany Master Vickery. He was told off first person singular
– as a unit – by himself.'

The marine whistled penetratingly.

'That's what I thought,' said Pyecroft. 'I went ashore with
him in the cutter an' 'e asked me to walk through the station.
He was clickin' audibly, but otherwise seemed happy-ish.

' "You might like to know," he says, stoppin' just opposite the
Admiral's front gate, "that Phyllis's Circus will be performin' at
Worcester tomorrow night. So I shall see 'er yet once again.
You've been very patient with me," he says.

' "Look here, Vickery," I said, "this thing's come to be just as
much as I can stand. Consume your own smoke. I don't want
to know any more."

' "You!" he said. "What have you got to complain of? – you've
only 'ad to watch. I'm *it*," he says, "but that's neither here nor
there," he says. "I've one thing to say before shakin' 'ands.
Remember," 'e says – we were just by the Admiral's garden-
gate then – "remember that I am *not* a murderer, because my
lawful wife died in childbed six weeks after I came out. That
much at least I am clear of," 'e says.

' "Then what have you done that signifies?" I said. "What's
the rest of it?"

' "The rest," 'e says, "is silence," an' he shook 'ands and went
clickin' into Simonstown station.'

'Did he stop to see Mrs Bathurst at Worcester?' I asked.

'It's not known. He reported at Bloemfontein, saw the ammunition into the trucks, and then 'e disappeared. Went out –
deserted, if you care to put it so – within eighteen months of his
pension, an' if what 'e said about 'is wife was true he was a free
man as 'e then stood. How do you read it off?'

'Poor devil!' said Hooper. 'To see her that way every night! I
wonder what it was.'

'I've made my 'ead ache in that direction many a long night.'

'But I'll swear Mrs B. 'ad no 'and in it,' said the Sergeant,
unshaken.

'No, whatever the wrong or deceit was, he did it, I'm sure o'
that. I 'ad to look at 'is face for five consecutive nights. I'm not
so fond o' navigatin' about Cape Town with a South-Easter
blowin' these days. I can hear those teeth click, so to say.'

'Ah, those teeth,' said Hooper, and his hand went to his waistcoat-pocket once more. 'Permanent things false teeth are. You read about 'em in all the murder trials.'

'What d'you suppose the captain knew – or did?' I asked.

'I've never turned my searchlight that way,' Pyecroft answered unblushingly.

We all reflected together, and drummed on empty beer bottles as the picnic-party, sunburned, wet, and sandy, passed our door singing 'The Honeysuckle and the Bee'.

'Pretty girl under that kapje,' said Pyecroft.

'They never circulated his description?' said Pritchard.

'I was askin' you before these gentlemen came,' said Hooper to me, 'whether you knew Wankies – on the way to the Zambesi – beyond Bulawayo?'

'Would he pass there – tryin' get to that Lake what's 'is name?' said Pritchard.

Hooper shook his head and went on: 'There's a curious bit o' line there, you see. It runs through solid teak forest – a sort o' mahogany really – seventy-two miles without a curve. I've had a train derailed there twenty-three times in forty miles. I was up there a month ago relievin' a sick inspector, you see. He told me to look out for a couple of tramps in the teak.'

'Two?' Pyecroft said. 'I don't envy that other man if – '

'We get heaps of tramps up there since the war. The inspector told me I'd find 'em at M'Bindwe siding waiting to go North. He'd given 'em some grub and quinine, you see. I went up on a construction train. I looked out for 'em. I saw them miles ahead along the straight, waiting in the teak. One of 'em was standin' up by the dead-end of the siding an' the other was squattin' down lookin' up at 'im, you see.'

'What did you do for 'em?' said Pritchard.

'There wasn't much I could do, except bury 'em. There'd been a bit of a thunderstorm in the teak, you see, and they were both stone dead and as black as charcoal. That's what they really were, you see – charcoal. They fell to bits when we tried to shift 'em. The man who was standin' up had the false teeth. I saw 'em shining against the black. Fell to bits he did too, like his mate squatting down an' watchin' him, both of 'em all wet in the rain. Both burned to charcoal, you see. And – that's what made me ask about marks just now – the false-toother was tattooed on the arms and chest – a crown and foul anchor with M.V. above.'

'I've seen that,' said Pyecroft quickly. 'It was so.'

'But if he was all charcoal-like?' said Pritchard, shuddering.

'You know how writing shows up white on a burned letter? Well, it was like that, you see. We buried 'em in the teak and I kept . . . But he was a friend of you two gentlemen, you see.'

Mr Hooper brought his hand away from his waistcoat-pocket – empty.

Pritchard covered his face with his hands for a moment, like a child shutting out an ugliness.

'And to think of her at Hauraki!' he murmured – 'with 'er 'air-ribbon on my beer. "Ada," she said to her niece . . . Oh, my Gawd!' . . .

'On a summer afternoon, when the honeysuckle blooms,
    And all Nature seems at rest,
Underneath the bower, 'mid the perfume of the flower,
    Sat a maiden with the one she loves the best – '

sang the picnic-party waiting for their train at Glengariff.

'Well, I don't know how you feel about it,' said Pyecroft, 'but 'avin' seen 'is face for five consecutive nights on end, I'm inclined to finish what's left of the beer an' thank Gawd he's dead!'

JOHN O'HARA

Malibu from the Sky

In the hills above Malibu she stopped her car for a look at the not too distant sea, her first real look at the waters of the Pacific. And though she had driven out from Hollywood with no other purpose than to be able to say she had seen the Pacific, it seemed a waste of time not to stay a few minutes and find out what thoughts came to her on this occasion. The thoughts began to come, and she did not like them much. She was here, she had come all the way, with too many stops along the way, and now that she was here, what the hell of it?

Down there was Malibu Beach, where the big shots had their beach houses, which they pretended were mere cottages, nothing at all, really. But she knew enough about those big shots to know that they had not started life with anything so grand as those mere cottages. Back where she had started her own life the biggest house in the whole town could not hold a candle to most of those beach cottages, in size or luxury. She knew. She had been to the biggest house in her old home town, and she had been to a couple of those beach cottages, so-called. In her home town the biggest house was owned by a rich Irish doctor, Dr Kelly, who practically owned the local hospital and was said to own most of the stock in the larger of the two town banks, and out in the country he owned a farm where he had four or five trotting horses. She had never been to the farm, but she had been invited often to children's parties at the house in town – until, that is, she stopped being a child and started wearing high heels and a brassière. Then the invitations stopped, although for a while there she was seeing more of Dr Kelly's eldest son when he was home on vacations from Georgetown Prep. She well knew who had stopped the invitations to the

Kelly house – Mrs Kelly, Kevin's mother. 'It's funny I never get invited to your house any more,' she said to Kevin one night. She did not think it was very funny, but she wanted to see what Kevin would say. He fooled her. 'You want to know why you're not invited any more?' he said. 'I can give you two reasons.' And he pressed his hand over each of her breasts. He was a wild one, not safe for a decent girl to go out with, everyone said. More money than was good for him, they said. Started drinking too early, others said. Spoiled by both his parents and chased after by everything in skirts, including a couple of married women who had husbands working in the mines. She had had some very anxious moments because of Kevin, especially those first two weeks after he was killed in an auto accident and she thought she might be having a baby. She would never have been able to go to Dr and Mrs Kelly for help, help of any kind. But after that narrow escape she left town, with sixty-five dollars her father gave her and thirty-five dollars from her mother. 'Get work quick,' said her father. 'That's the last you can expect from us.'

'I'll pay you back, every cent,' she said.

'All right, if you can. We'll accept your kind offer,' said her father. 'But don't send home for any more, because there's none to give you. You only got this much because we won't be supporting you and there'll be that much saved.' Her father worked in the mines, made good money in good times, but ever since the big strike, work in the mines was anything but steady. The car went, the washing machine was repossessed, the food on the table was enough to live on but not a pleasure to eat. The only time she saw steak was when Kevin would take her out in his car and they would stop for a sandwich on the way home.

The work she got in Philadelphia was not hard, even if it did not pay well, but with only two years of high school she was lucky to get anything that was easy and in pleasant surroundings and did not take much brains. It was clerking in a candy store near the Reading Terminal, eighteen dollars a week. It did not take her long to figure out why they hired her. Philadelphians eat a lot of candy, and a lot of it is bought by men. The commuters who took the Chestnut Hill local every afternoon

liked her looks, as well they might, and pretty soon they were
asking her to go out with them. One of them began to get pretty
serious. She had no intention of letting him give up his wife
and two kids, but she took money from him so that she could
dress better and attract men who did not offer matrimony but
might help her on her way to Hollywood.

It had always been Hollywood, Hollywood for itself and
because it was the great chance for girls like herself. Some of
the biggest stars had never had any acting experience, could not
sing or dance. The important thing was to get there under
contract to some studio, not to go there in the hope of finding a
pleasant job in a candy store. A girl would be making a big
mistake to go to Hollywood without a contract, and that was
one mistake she was not going to make. She had even read
about one girl who was *born* in Hollywood and went to school
there, but had been smart enough to go to New York to be
discovered. They did not think much of you out there unless
you had a contract. And so the idea of a contract had always
been in her mind.

One of the men she attracted in Philadelphia had a connection
with a big movie company. That is, he worked in an office that
distributed films. He never got to the Coast, although he often
went to the New York office and had met the big stars. He had
a lot of inside gossip on the stars and their peculiarities. It was
quite a letdown to learn from him that one of her favorites did
not like girls at all. How did he mean he did not like girls? 'He
likes boys,' said her friend, Sid. That was her first personal
disillusionment about Hollywood, and she did not like Sid for
telling her such a thing. However, she went out with Sid and a
couple of times she went to New York with him, and through
Sid she met the man who persuaded her to come to New York.
New York was New York, and she did not feel so strongly that
you could not go there without a contract. The new man did
not offer her a contract or even a job, but he paid her rent in an
apartment just off Fifth Avenue in the West Fifties, and she got
work modeling lingerie and hosiery and managed to get along
rather well. Arthur, the man who paid her rent, was more
important in the film business than Sid. He was in the theater
end, with a title that she never could get straight – eastern

district something, advertising, publicity, and exploitation. When he took her out to restaurants and speakeasies he was always saying hello to the newspaper fellows, and more or less as a gag one of the fellows that wrote a column put her name in print for the first time: 'Model Mary-Lou Lloyd being screen-tested?' The comparatively few people who knew her were very impressed and took the item very seriously. A couple of nights later she was actually introduced as Mary-Lou Lloyd, who was being screen-tested. 'Who by?' said the man to whom she was being introduced.

'Oh, there's nothing to that,' said Mary-Lou.

'Don't be cagey,' said the man. 'Give, *give*.'

'No, there isn't anything to it,' she said.

'When are they making the test?' said the man.

'That was just something in one of the columns,' she said.

'Listen, if you're not signed up, I might be able to arrange a test for you. If you're not signed up. If you already signed, skip it.'

'I haven't signed a thing,' she said.

'She really hasn't,' said Arthur.

'Arthur, I wouldn't believe you under oath,' said the man. 'Young lady, come to my office eleven o'clock tomorrow morning and we'll have a conversation.' The man's name was Lew Linger, and he had a job similar to Arthur's at another studio. 'Will you be there? Eleven a.m.?'

'Tomorrow I can't, but thanks for the invitation,' she said.

'Then when can you?' said Lew Linger. 'The next day?'

'All right, the day after tomorrow,' she said.

That night Arthur was greatly disturbed. 'He means it, Lew Linger.'

'Well, that's great,' she said.

'Yeah, but where does it put me if *his* company makes a test of my girl? I'm making with the rent and Lew Linger steals her right out from under me. I'll be the laughing-stock. I *could* lose my god-damn job. Supposing Lew's company makes a test and they sign you? I heard of guys getting fired for a lot less than that.'

'Well, you get me a test with your company.'

'I don't have the authority. Those tests cost money, and

anyway that's not my department. Who the hell does Lew Linger think he is?'

'I don't know, but he can get me a screen test, and if he's that inarrested . . .'

'Oh, personally he is, all right. Lew Linger is a regular wolf.'

'If he can get me a screen test he can take a bite out of me – where it won't show.'

'Don't *say* that,' said Arthur.

'I will say it. Sixty dollars a month rent doesn't mean you own me. You're getting off pretty light, considering. You don't think I don't get other offers? Listen, there isn't a day goes by without I get some kind of a proposition. And a lot better than sixty a month rent. As far as that goes I could pay my own rent.'

'Sixty dollars? You think that's all you cost me? I'm always giving you presents. Who gave you the silver fox, two hundred and seventy-five dollars and worth twice that retail? How much do you think I spent taking you to the cafés?'

'Is it worth it, or isn't it? That's the main question. You're not doing it for charity, Arthur. You make me mad, throwing that up at me how much you spend on me. Big-hearted Otis, sure. Well, listen, Big-hearted Otis, go on back to that dumpy wife of yours in Fort Washington – '

'Port Washington, and I never said she was dumpy,' said Arthur. 'I said she was zaftig, which doesn't mean the same thing.'

'That's your way. You always try to change the subject, but you're not getting away with it this time. I'm mad, see? So either you get me a screen test or don't call me up any more. You can go home right this minute, for all I care.'

'At ha' past two in the morning?' said Arthur.

Before the night was over he had agreed to try to get her a screen test, and before the day was over he had persuaded the studio to give her one. His argument was based on the fact that Lew Linger, who was a wolf but a cagey one, had shown so much interest on his very first meeting with her.

The test was made in a studio in Brooklyn, without sound, and consisted largely of Mary-Lou walking around in a silk bathing suit. It was hardly more than some footage of a young girl with an exceptionally good figure, and such tests were as often as not put away and forgotten. But Mary-Lou, who was learning fast, telephoned the fellow who had put her name in his column and thanked him for the mention. He in turn thanked her for thanking him and two days later she was in his column again. 'You saw it here,' he wrote. 'Lovely Model Mary-Lou Lloyd was slated for a screen test, we said. She made the test and execs of the Peerless Studio are readying an all-out campaign for their new discovery.'

When the item appeared she telephoned Lew Linger. 'Why you double-crossing little bitch,' he said.

'Maybe I am,' she said. 'But it would of been worse to double-cross Arthur. You know how it is with Arthur and I. Almost a year now.'

'Don't tell me you're in love with him,' said Lew Linger.

'I didn't *say* that, Mr Linger. But he's been awfully good to me.'

'Are you leveling?'

'He has been. If it wasn't for Arthur I never would of got to know all these people.'

'If you're leveling – you remind me of an old song. "I Found a Rose in the Devil's Garden." All right, no hard feelings. Maybe we have that talk some other time, wuddia say?'

'That's entirely up to you, Mr Linger,' she said.

'I get it. Well, how about this afternoon?'

'What time?' she said.

Lew Linger was a much more interesting man than Arthur, and not only because he was a wolf and Arthur was not. You went out with Lew Linger and people were always coming to *his* table, not a case of him always going to theirs as it was with Arthur. You never saw Arthur's name in the gossip columns, but Lew was in them all the time, either as the escort of some girl or as the originator of some wisecrack. To a certain extent he was a celebrity on his own, not the recognisable kind who was asked for his autograph, but a special kind that got a big hello from a lot of those who were asked for their autographs. More to the point was that when you went out with Lew Linger you often ended up at Reuben's in the company of some very famous people.

Nothing had come of the screen test that Arthur got for her and Arthur naturally stopped speaking to her when he found out that she had dated Lew. It went without saying that Arthur would stop making with the rent money, but Mary-Lou, after an anxious week or two, adopted the habit of borrowing money. She would say to a man, 'How would you like to lend me a hundred bucks?'

'What the hell for?' the man would say.

'Well, I might be able to pay you back *some* way,' she would say.

'That's a new approach,' the man would say. But it was remarkable how often it worked, and putting it on a loan basis made it a different transaction from that of a hustler and a john. She always paid the man back, and not in money, and usually within twenty-four hours. Some of the men were repeaters, and she had a pretty good winter, borrowing from some and going out with Lew Linger, but Lew said no more about a screen test for his company. One movie star invited her to accompany him on the train ride back to the Coast, but she told him she would never go to Hollywood without a contract. 'You're not so dumb,' said the movie star.

'Who said I was?' said Mary-Lou.

However, she was beginning to get a bit worried about the summer, when a lot of the men would be going away and things would be slack, as her father always said about work at the mines. Lew Linger was planning a trip to Europe with some company executives. 'I wish you'd take me, but it'd be like carrying coals to Newcastle,' she said.

'Yeah, or taking a broad to Hollywood,' said Lew. 'I understand a certain movie star offered you a ride out to the Coast.'

'I wouldn't leave *you*, Lew,' she said.

'The hell you wouldn't. Don't try to con me, baby. I went for that act once, but not twice.'

'Well, you tried to con me, too, you know. That stuff about the screen test.'

'You want to know something? That wasn't altogether a con,' said Lew.

'Well, you can still get me one,' said Mary-Lou.

'You don't want a screen test, you want a term contract.'

'All right, so I do. So get me one.'

'You want one of those seventy-five a week for the first six

months and options up to seven years? You wouldn't want one
of those. You're doing better right here in New York City,
putting the arm on guys.'

'I want to go to Hollywood,' she said.

'Baby, you'll be out there six months and they won't take up
your first option.'

'I don't care, just so I have a contract. Let me worry about the
option. Do this for me, Lew, and I'll never ask you for another
thing.'

'You wouldn't get another thing.'

'Listen, I know if I go out there under contract I'll stay. Once
I'm in pictures I'm all set. And even if I don't get to be a star, a
big star, I'll manage all right. There's none of them are better
built than I am, and who says you have to act?'

'Nobody,' said Lew.

'I just want to be in pictures, Lew. I got a fixation on it, a real
fixation. Since I was ten years old, going to the matinees on
Saturday afternoon. That was where I wanted to be, up there
on that screen.'

'Yeah? Who was your favorite movie star?'

'I didn't have any. It was me I wanted to be up there. I didn't
go around imitating other people, or wishing I was Clara Bow. I
never saw a one of them that I didn't think I was prettier than,
and better built.'

'I was thinking more of the male stars. Who were your
favorites among them?'

'You know the only one I ever sent away for his picture? Eric
Von Stroheim. I never got it, either,' she said, and paused.

'If I ever got in a picture with him I'd fall away in a dead
faint,' she went on. 'The handsome ones never thrilled me,
except one I found out later was a queer.'

'Who was that?'

'I'd be ashamed to tell you. Everybody knows he's queer,
everybody in picture business. You'd laugh at me if I told you.
The first time I ever heard it was in Philly, a fellow I knew in
the distributing end. I wanted to hit him. But that's me. The
only male stars I ever went for, the big heavy and a panseroo.
Get me a contract, Lew. Even if it's only one of those seventy-
five a week ones.'

'That's all it would be, too,' he said. 'All right, I'll speak to Jack Marlborough.'

'Who's he?'

'Nobody very big, I assure you. But big enough to get you that kind of contract. You might say he's vice-president in charge of starlets, only he's not a vice-president. He's assistant to the casting director, and if *he* signs you it's the kiss of death, because everybody'll know he's doing somebody a favor. In this case, me.'

They gave her a contract, and it was for seventy-five a week for six months, a hundred a week for the second six months, and so on for five years until she might be earning five hundred a week if all her options were taken up. They paid her fare to Los Angeles, in a lower berth on less famous trains, and she was not at the studio two weeks before she realised that she was never going to be a star in motion pictures. They had her posing for stills – fan magazine art – but the only time she appeared before a movie camera was as a cigarette girl in a gangster film. She was not given lines to read, not even 'Cigars, cigarettes.' She took a one-room apartment in the Rossmore section and bought a Ford V-8 roadster on the instalment plan at a used car lot on Vine Street. She slept with the head cameraman who shot the gangster picture and he put her name in his little black book. Jack Marlborough introduced her to a couple of agents who showed no interest in furthering her professional career, but one of them invited her to a party at Malibu Beach which turned out to be a celebration of the twenty-first birthday of the son of a movie producer. She and the four other girls at the party were required to take off their clothes for the men at the party, who consisted of the birthday boy, the agent, and two college classmates of the birthday boy. It was the messiest party Mary-Lou had ever been to and it lasted two days. It came to an end when the birthday boy's uncle arrived and compelled the agent to take the girls back to Hollywood.

Her next visit to Malibu Beach was hardly more profitable but somewhat less messy. An English novelist, who had been singularly unsuccessful in his efforts to get the big stars to go to bed with him, was the house guest of an ageing character actress who had a cottage at Malibu. He complained to her that he simply could not go back to England with his virtue intact, and she told him that he must lower his sights; that he might be a very popular author throughout the United Kingdom, but to the glamor girls of Hollywood he was just another Englishman with ants in his pants and no studio connection. 'I'll see what I can do,' she said, and Mary-Lou Lloyd got a surprise invitation to dinner from Cecilia Ranleigh, whom she had never met. Jack Marlborough, who had suggested Mary-Lou to the old lady, said that it would be a good chance for her to meet a different class of people.

'What's the gimmick? Why me?' said Mary-Lou.

'You'll find out when you get there. Miss Ranleigh is sending her car for you.'

The car, a ten-year-old Rolls-Royce, was reassuring, but when Mary-Lou was greeted by her hostess and introduced to the other guests she knew immediately why she had been invited. The eager smile of the man with the missing molars gave him away. The dinner guests were ten in number, English writers with their husbands or wives, and with the exception of Cecilia Ranleigh, no one Mary-Lou had ever seen before. She had a hard time understanding what they said, but what got through was some juicy gossip about absent members of the British colony. The gossip was not particularly new, but they all enjoyed retelling it. The only man who did not join in was the writer on Mary-Lou's left, and he hung back because he was waiting to be asked to do his spessiality, his collection of Goldwynisms. On Mary-Lou's right was Geoffrey Graves, the man with the missing molars, who was so eager to be pleasing. He emphasised several conversational points with pats on Mary-Lou's knee under the table and she let him get away with it temporarily. Her mood, however, was not jovial. Jack Marlborough had practically ordered her to go to this party, despite the fact that he would not discuss her soon-due option. He was going to get all he could out of her before telling her that the ax was about to fall. In the second place, she was having a lousy time with these people, who managed to make her feel that they all knew she was there to entertain Geoffrey Graves. In the third place, she was not even repelled by Geoffrey Graves. He was a slightly lecherous schoolboy, and neither a Kevin Kelly, a

Lew Linger nor an Eric Von Stroheim. In the fourth place, she did not like being made to feel like a foreigner when she was the only person there who was not one. Accordingly, at the dessert, when Mr Graves let his hand linger on her knee, she looked deep into his eyes and smiled and burnt his hand with her cigarette. All present guessed what had happened, and laughed. But though they were laughing at him, they made it seem that the laugh was on her.

'Could have happened to anyone, you know,' said the man who had done the Goldwynisms. 'Imeantosay.'

It was a great, great joke. 'Serves you jolly well right, Geoffrey,' one of the women said, but without in the least being on Mary-Lou's side.

Furious, Mary-Lou got up and said, 'If you don't mind, I'm going home.'

'Oh, my dear, you've been embarrassed and you mustn't be,' said Cecilia Ranleigh. 'Really you mustn't.'

'Puts old Geoffrey in the spot, I mustsay,' said the Goldwynist.

'I'm most dreadfully sorry,' said Geoffrey Graves, but he divided his apology between Mary-Lou and Cecilia Ranleigh.

'Skip it,' said Mary-Lou. 'If you don't want me to take your car, call me a taxi. But I'm getting out of here.'

'Well – if you won't change your mind,' said Cecilia Ranleigh. She spoke to the butler-chauffeur. 'Bring the car around for Miss Lloyd, please.'

Mary-Lou left the dining-room and waited in the hall. No one bothered to wait with her, and she could hear a lot of laughter from the dining-room. They were having a lot of fun at the expense of Geoffrey Graves, but at hers too. On the ride back to Hollywood the chauffeur said nothing until they got past Beverly Hills and were in the Sunset Strip with the lights of the Trocadero and other restaurants. It was not yet ten o'clock. 'It's early, Miss,' said the chauffeur. 'Would you care to stop for a drink?'

'With you?'

'That's what I had in mind,' he said.

'Don't you have to be back there right away?'

'They could do without me. I could have a flat tire.'

'Well, why not?' said Mary-Lou. Without his chauffeur's cap

his livery made him look like a middle-aged man in a dark suit. 'Not the Troc, though. Let's go to some place quiet.'

The place they picked was quiet in that it did not have an orchestra. Otherwise it was lively. The customers were finishing their dinner and settling down to their drinking. It was a youngish crowd, and Mary-Lou recognised some of them. 'Strange people,' said the chauffeur, when they were seated.

'Who? These?'

'I was thinking of those we left. The dinner party. By the way, my name is Jack.'

'You're not a real butler, are you?'

'Not a real butler, but a real chauffeur. I buttle when I have to but only for money. There aren't so many jobs for chauffeur only.' He was bald and probably close to fifty, but the moment he lit a cigarette he abandoned the servant manner. 'Welsh, aren't you. With the name Lloyd.'

'My father was Welsh descent. My mother was Irish.'

'Quite a combination, isn't it? Produce quite a temper. Well, he deserved it. I've watched him making his passes and getting nowhere, Mr Geoffrey Graves. He's not a very personable chap, but I suppose at home he trades on his reputation. Here, so few ever heard of him.' He talked on and they had two or three drinks until he looked at his watch. 'Oh, dear. Time I fixed that flat tire. The bill, waiter, please.'

They went back to the car. 'I'm going to sit in front,' said Mary-Lou.

'Very well,' said Jack. 'I get Thursdays off and every other Sunday. Could I have your phone number? I'd like to take you out to dinner.'

'You would?'

'Yes. You like me, don't you?'

'Yes.'

'Do you like flying?'

'You mean in an aeroplane? I've never been up in one,' she said.

'Never? You must let me take you up. I was in the RFC, and I've kept up. Chap out in Glendale lets me fly his Moth. Will you go up with me one day soon?'

'Maybe I might. Not if I think about it, but I might.'

'You'd love it. I know you would.'

'How do you know?'

'Oh – one knows.'

'What else does one know?'

'Well – one knows that you stood up to those hyenas single-handed. Miss Cecilia Ranleigh is a formidable woman, and the others are not bad individually. But en masse they can be very cruel.'

'I hated them,' said Mary-Lou.

'Of course you did. Then you'll let me take you up?'

'Yes,' she said.

'You might like it enough to learn.'

'Let's not rush things,' she said.

He never telephoned her, but as it happened he had only two weeks left in which he might have. An item in a chatter column said: 'British colony saddened to hear Cecilia Ranleigh's butler, John Motley, killed in plane crash at Glendale.' That was all he got in the press, and it was probably too late to send flowers . . .

Down there was Malibu Beach, and now Mary-Lou could honestly say, when she went back to New York, that she had seen the Pacific Ocean. She had almost been able to say she had seen it from the sky.

R. K. NARAYAN

The Antidote

His director was already at work on the set – the interior of an office with a large table in the middle and a revolving chair beyond it. Gopal, dressed as decreed in bushcoat and corduroy trousers and with his face painted, went up and did obeisance to the director. The director said, 'Go up and take your position four paces from the chair; let us have a couple of rehearsals while the lights are being fixed.'

'Yes, sir,' said Gopal, going to his spot. He had no idea what he was expected to do or why. This director was not in the habit of narrating the story to anyone. He took his actors shot by shot, just indicating to them their portion of work for the moment. If they put questions to him, he said, 'Just do what I am telling you now, and don't get too curious.' It was unnecessary for a puppet to do its own thinking.

Now this superman gently pushed Gopal towards the chair. 'Sit down and . . . rest your right elbow on the table . . . that is right . . . look happy because you have just been through a satisfactory business deal . . .' He surveyed Gopal's posture critically and said, 'When that telephone rings, pick it up with your left hand and say . . . remember that you are not to clutch the telephone so desperately, hold it gently, and don't pay any attention to it until it has given three clear rings. A habitual telephone-user will never be in a hurry to take the receiver.'

'Yes, sir, I understand,' said Gopal.

'You will say into the telephone, "Ramnarayan speaking. Oh! . . . Hallo . . . Is that so!" in a tone of great astonishment and shock.'

'Then do I put down the telephone?' asked the actor.

'That you will know later . . . This is all for this shot. Don't rush through your lines, speak naturally.'

The telephone rang thrice. Gopal acted his part. It was rehearsed a dozen times before a microphone dangling from a cross-arm and moving up and down like the proverbial carrot before a donkey. Gopal delivered his lines with measured precision, yet something always seemed to go wrong. The sound recordist's assistant peeped in at the doorway and repeatedly implored, 'Don't swallow the last syllable. Keep the level. Another monitor, if you don't mind.' They didn't believe in recording a voice when it was fresh. They always liked it to go husky and inaudible with repetition.

Gopal went through his action and words again and again till he lost all sense of what he was saying or doing. Amidst cries of 'Ready,' 'Start,' 'Cut,' and 'Another monitor, please,' in various keys, the shot was at last taken. The director was satisfied and grudgingly admitted, 'That is the best one can get out of you, I suppose.' He added, 'Don't shift your position. We are continuing the scene.' He ordered the lights to be moved. He viewed the actor through the camera and said, 'Don't let go the telephone receiver but you may relax your right arm a bit. Don't be so wooden. Be natural.' He came away from the camera, stood before the table, looked critically at Gopal, and said, 'Yes, now you have got it right. Only action, no dialogue for this shot.'

The microphone on the cross-arm moved away. Gopal felt relieved. Thank God, no speech. I can go home early, I suppose. The director said, 'Listen carefully to this. You remember your last dialogue line was "Hallo . . . Is that so!" It is to be continued in action. You will pause for a tenth of a second, let the telephone drop from your hand, fall back in your chair, and let your head roll to the side ever so lightly.'

'Why? Why, sir?' Gopal asked anxiously. This was the first time he was questioning the director's proposal. The director replied, 'Because you have just heard shocking news on the phone.'

'What is it, sir?' Gopal asked. 'Don't bother about it. Don't waste your energy in putting unnecessary questions.'

'This bad news makes me swoon?' Gopal asked, his heart

palpitating with faint hope. 'No,' said the director emphatically. 'You die on hearing it.' He then went on to elaborate the details: how the telephone should slip down, where Gopal's head should strike, how much his arm should convulse, and so on. He approached Gopal's person and gently tapped his forehead. He treated him as lumber; he pushed his head back and rolled it side to side. 'Why! You don't look happy!' the director remarked. Gopal hesitated to reply.

The director paused for a moment. Gopal hoped that he would read his thoughts. The director began, 'Or would you rather . . .' Gopal waited on his words hopefully. This man was after all going to relent. The director completed his sentence with: '. . . fall on your face and spread out your arms?'

'In a swoon?' Gopal asked again. 'No, completely dead. Your heart fails on hearing the bad news,' said the director.

Gopal's hand involuntarily strayed near the region of his heart. It was still beating. He looked up at the director. The man stood over him ruthlessly, waiting for an answer. This fellow looks like Yama, Gopal thought. He will choke me if I don't die at his bidding. What a bother!

He asked pathetically, 'Can't you change the story, sir?' There was a big lamp directly in front of him, scorching his face. Beyond that was a region of shadow in which a group of persons was assembled, watching him – executives, technicians, and light-shifters.

The director was aghast at his suggestion. 'What do you mean? You just do what you are told.'

'Certainly, sir. But this, this . . . I don't like.'

'Who are you to say what you like or dislike?' asked the director haughtily. This man was ruthless as fate. Even hostile planets might relent occasionally, but this man with the kerchief around his throat was unbudging. He would throttle a baby for effect.

He asked, 'What is the matter with you, Gopal? Why are you talking absurd things today?'

'This is my birthday, sir,' Gopal explained timidly.

'Wish you many happy returns,' said the director promptly, and added, 'What if it is your birthday?'

'Rather a peculiar birthday,' explained Gopal. 'This is my

forty-ninth birthday. Astrologers have often told me that I might not see this birthday, and if I lived to see this day I should have nothing more to worry about . . . I have lived in secret terror of this day all my life. Whenever I saw my wife and children I used to be racked with the thought that I should probably be leaving them orphans. I came late today because we held some propitiatory rites at home for the planets, and we celebrated my survival this day with a feast. My astrologer has suggested that I do nothing unpleasant today, sir. I wish to treat it as a very auspicious day, sir.'

The director was impressed. He turned to his assistant, who always shadowed him, carrying a portfolio under his arm, and commanded, 'Fetch the story-writer.' Presently the story-writer arrived, his lips red with the chewing of betel leaves. He was a successful story-writer who made a lot of money by dashing off plots for film producers. He laughed aloud on hearing of the problem created by the actor. He was not the angry type to feel upset at contrary suggestions. He declared, 'Impossible to change the story. How can he refuse to die? I am busy.'

He turned on his heel and started out. At the door he stopped to add, 'Anyway, send for our boss and tell him about it.'

The boss came running into the scene. He asked anxiously, 'What is the trouble? What is it all about?'

Gopal sat in his chair unmoving; he was not allowed to shift his position even slightly; continuity would be spoilt otherwise. He felt stuffy. The big lamp scorched his face. They all stood around and looked at him as if he were a freak. Their faces were blurred beyond the shadows. All of them are my Yamas, Gopal thought. They are bent upon seeing me dead.

The boss came over to his table and asked, 'Are you in your senses?' Gopal thought he might appeal to the other's box-office sentiment. He said, 'People generally like to see happy things on the screen, sir. I have seen the public turn away from pictures which present scenes of death.'

'Oh!' exclaimed the boss. He remained thoughtful and said, 'You are wrong.' He turned to the director and said, 'Formerly no doubt the public liked to see only happy stuff. Today is different. I have statistics. Pictures with tragic accidents have grossed thirty per cent more than happy stories, if you take the figures of the last six months. It shows that the public likes to exercise sentiments of sympathy and pity . . . No, I will not have the story tampered with on any account.'

The director patted Gopal's back affectionately and said, 'This is a brief shot. I won't take much time. Do make up your mind to co-operate.' He adopted a mollifying tone. He was cajoling. But what did it matter? What was the use of cajoling if it was only to persuade a man to die co-operatively? Gopal felt that he was about to lose his job and see his family in the streets. He was wasting precious studio hours. More crowds had gathered to watch the sensational happening today.

The director asked softly, 'Will you be prepared to go through this scene tomorrow at least?'

'Certainly, sir,' Gopal said with relief. 'I shall do whatever you may order tomorrow – even the funeral.'

At this the assistant with a portfolio under his arm dashed forward and cried, 'We have to finish this scene today. We are not getting this floor tomorrow. The other unit wants it for the palace set. They are only waiting for you to complete the scene in order to dismantle this set. They are already grumbling that we have delayed too long. They are already behind their schedule.'

'This puny fellow with the portfolio holds my life in his hand. He won't even hear of a postponement of execution.'

The director retreated for a while into the outer darkness where the technicians were gathered. He spoke to them in whispers.

He stirred them again into activity. Now he advanced towards Gopal with an air of one who had examined all aspects of the case and come to a decision. As he saw him come up, Gopal felt that the man's picture would be complete if he put on a black cap and carried a halter in his hand. Gopal knew that he was a condemned man. The jury had given its verdict. Even before the director opened his mouth to say anything, Gopal said, 'All right, sir. I will die.'

Lights were on. The camera was ready to shoot. The director howled, 'Action.' Gopal dropped the telephone. His head fell back and rolled slightly to the side. Scores of persons were gazing on his dying with satisfaction. But before the director cried, 'Cut,' Gopal did something which he hoped would pass unnoticed. Though he was supposed to be dead, he shook his head slightly, opened his right eye, and winked at the camera, which he hoped would act as an antidote to the inauspicious role he was doing.

The director, however, shouted: 'No good. Repeat action. Retake . . .'

F. SCOTT FITZGERALD

Magnetism

I

The pleasant, ostentatious boulevard was lined at prosperous intervals with New England Colonial houses – without ship models in the hall. When the inhabitants moved out here the ship models had at last been given to the children. The next street was a complete exhibit of the Spanish-bungalow phase of West Coast architecture: while two streets over, the cylindrical windows and round towers of 1897 – melancholy antiques which sheltered swamis, yogis, fortune tellers, dressmakers, dancing teachers, art academies and chiropractors – looked down now upon brisk buses and trolley cars. A little walk around the block could, if you were feeling old that day, be a discouraging affair.

On the green flanks of the modern boulevard children, with their knees marked by the red stains of the mercurochrome era, played with toys with a purpose – beams that taught engineering, soldiers that taught manliness, and dolls that taught motherhood. When the dolls were so banged up that they stopped looking like real babies and began to look like dolls, the children developed affection for them. Everything in the vicinity – even the March sunlight – was new, fresh, hopeful and thin, as you would expect in a city that had tripled its population in fifteen years.

Among the very few domestics in sight that morning was a handsome young maid sweeping the steps of the biggest house on the street. She was a large, simple Mexican girl with the large, simple ambitions of the time and the locality, and she was already conscious of being a luxury – she received one hundred dollars a month in return for her personal liberty. Sweeping, Dolores kept an eye on the stairs inside, for Mr Hannaford's car was waiting and he would soon be coming down to breakfast. The problem came first this morning, however – the problem as to whether it was a duty or a favour when she helped the English nurse down the steps with the perambulator. The English nurse always said 'Please', and 'Thanks very much', but Dolores hated her and would have liked, without any special excitement, to beat her insensible. Like most Latins under the stimulus of American life, she had irresistible impulses towards violence.

The nurse escaped, however. Her blue cape faded haughtily into the distance just as Mr Hannaford, who had come quietly downstairs, stepped into the space of the front door.

'Good morning.' He smiled at Dolores; he was young and extraordinarily handsome. Dolores tripped on the broom and fell off the stoop. George Hannaford hurried down the steps, reached her as she was getting to her feet cursing volubly in Mexican, just touched her arm with a helpful gesture and said, 'I hope you didn't hurt yourself.'

'Oh, no.'

'I'm afraid it was my fault; I'm afraid I startled you, coming out like that.'

His voice had real regret in it; his brow was knit with solicitude.

'Are you sure you're all right?'

'Aw, sure.'

'Didn't turn your ankle?'

'Aw, no.'

'I'm terribly sorry about it.'

'Aw, it wasn't your fault.'

He was still frowning as she went inside, and Dolores, who was not hurt and thought quickly, suddenly contemplated having a love affair with him. She looked at herself several times in the pantry mirror and stood close to him as she poured his coffee, but he read the paper and she saw that that was all for the morning.

Hannaford entered his car and drove to Jules Rennard's house. Jules was French Canadian by birth, and George Hannaford's best friend; they were fond of each other and spent much time together. Both of them were simple and dignified in their tastes and in their way of thinking, instinctively gentle, and in a world of the volatile and the bizarre found in each other a certain quiet solidity.

He found Jules at breakfast.

'I want to fish for barracuda,' said George abruptly. 'When will you be free? I want to take the boat and go down to Lower California.'

Jules had dark circles under his eyes. Yesterday he had closed out the greatest problem of his life by settling with his ex-wife for two hundred thousand dollars. He had married too young, and the former slavey from the Quebec slums had taken to drugs upon her failure to rise with him. Yesterday, in the presence of lawyers, her final gesture had been to smash his finger with the base of a telephone. He was tired of women for a while and welcomed the suggestion of a fishing trip.

'How's the baby?' he asked.

'The baby's fine.'

'And Kay?'

'Kay's not herself, but I don't pay any attention. What did you do to your hand?'

'I'll tell you another time. What's the matter with Kay, George?'

'Jealous.'

'Of who?'

'Helen Avery. It's nothing. She's not herself, that's all.' He got up. 'I'm late,' he said. 'Let me know as soon as you're free. Any time after Monday will suit me.'

George left and drove out by an interminable boulevard which narrowed into a long, winding concrete road and rose into the hilly country behind. Somewhere in the vast emptiness a group of buildings appeared, a barnlike structure, a row of offices, a large but quick restaurant and half a dozen small bungalows. The chauffeur dropped Hannaford at the main entrance. He went in and passed through various enclosures, each marked off by swinging gates and inhabited by a stenographer.

'Is anybody with Mr Schroeder?' he asked, in front of a door lettered with that name.

'No, Mr Hannaford.'

Simultaneously his eye fell on a young lady who was writing at a desk aside, and he lingered a moment.

'Hello, Margaret,' he said. 'How are you, darling?'

A delicate, pale beauty looked up, frowning a little, still abstracted in her work. It was Miss Donovan, the script girl, a friend of many years.

'Hello. Oh, George, I didn't see you come in. Mr Douglas wants to work on the book sequence this afternoon.'

'All right.'

'These are the changes we decided on Thursday night.' She smiled up at him and George wondered for the thousandth time why she had never gone into pictures.

'All right,' he said. 'Will initials do?'

'Your initials look like George Harris's.'

'Very well, darling.'

As he finished, Peter Schroeder opened his door and beckoned him. 'George, come here!' he said with an air of excitement. 'I want you to listen to someone on the phone.'

Hannaford went in.

'Pick up the phone and say "Hello",' directed Schroeder. 'Don't say who you are.'

'Hello,' said Hannaford obediently.

'Who is this?' asked a girl's voice.

Hannaford put his hand over the mouthpiece. 'What am I supposed to do?'

Schroeder snickered and Hannaford hesitated, smiling and suspicious.

'Who do you want to speak to?' he temporised into the phone.

'To George Hannaford, I want to speak to. Is this him?'

'Yes.'

'Oh, George; it's me.'

'Who?'

'Me – Gwen. I had an awful time finding you. They told me – '

'Gwen who?'

'Gwen – can't you hear? From San Francisco – last Thursday night.'

'I'm sorry,' objected George. 'Must be some mistake.'

'Is this George Hannaford?'

'Yes.'

The voice grew slightly tart: 'Well this is Gwen Becker you spent last Thursday evening with in San Francisco. There's no use pretending you don't know who I am, because you do.'

'Schroeder took the apparatus from George and hung up the receiver.

'Somebody has been doubling for me up in Frisco,' said Hannaford.

'So that's where you were Thursday night!'

'Those things aren't funny to me – not since that crazy Zeller girl. You can never convince them they've been sold because the man always looks something like you. What's new, Pete?'

'Let's go over to the stage and see.'

Together they walked out a back entrance along a muddy walk, and opening a little door in the big blank wall of the studio building entered into its half darkness.

Here and there figures spotted the dim twilight, figures that turned up white faces to George Hannaford, like souls in purgatory watching the passage of a half-god through. Here and there were whispers and soft voices and, apparently from afar, the gentle tremolo of a small organ. Turning the corner made by some flats, they came upon the white crackling glow of a stage with two people motionless upon it.

An actor in evening clothes, his shirt front, collar and cuffs tinted a brilliant pink, made as though to get chairs for them, but they shook their heads and stood watching. For a long while nothing happened on the stage – no one moved. A row of lights went off with a savage hiss, went on again. The plaintive tap of a hammer begged admission to nowhere in the distance; a blue face appeared among the blinding lights above and called something unintelligible into the upper blackness. Then the silence was broken by a low clear voice from the stage:

'If you want to know why I haven't got stockings on, look in my dressing-room. I spoiled four pairs yesterday and two already this morning . . . This dress weighs six pounds.'

A man stepped out of the group of observers and regarded the girl's brown legs; their lack of covering was scarcely distinguishable, but, in any event, her expression implied that she would do nothing about it. The lady was annoyed, and so intense was her personality that it had taken only a fractional flexing of her eyes to indicate the fact. She was a dark, pretty girl with a figure that would be full-blown sooner than she wished. She was just eighteen.

Had this been the week before, George Hannaford's heart would have stood still. Their relationship had been in just that stage. He hadn't said a word to Helen Avery that Kay could have objected to, but something had begun between them on the second day of this picture that Kay had felt in the air. Perhaps it had begun even earlier, for he had determined, when he saw Helen Avery's first release, that she should play opposite him. Helen Avery's voice and the dropping of her eyes when she finished speaking, like a sort of exercise in control, fascinated him. He had felt that they both tolerated something, that each knew half of some secret about people and life, and that if they rushed towards each other there would be a romantic communion of almost unbelievable intensity. It was this element of promise and possibility that had haunted him for a fortnight and was now dying away.

Hannaford was thirty, and he was a moving-picture actor only through a series of accidents. After a year in a small technical college he had taken a summer job with an electric company, and his first appearance in a studio was in the role of repairing a bank of Klieg lights. In an emergency he played a small part and made good, but for fully a year after that he thought of it as a purely transitory episode in his life. At first much of it had offended him – the almost hysterical egotism and excitability hidden under an extremely thin veil of elaborate good-fellowship. It was only recently, with the advent of such men as Jules Rennard into pictures, that he began to see the possibilities of a decent and secure private life, much as his would have been as a successful engineer. At last his success felt solid beneath his feet.

He met Kay Tompkins at the old Griffith Studios at Mamaroneck and their marriage was a fresh, personal affair, removed from most stage marriages. Afterwards they had possessed each other completely, had been pointed to: 'Look, there's one couple in pictures who manage to stay together.' It would have taken something out of many people's lives – people who enjoyed a vicarious security in the contemplation of their marriage – if they hadn't stayed together, and their love was fortified by a certain effort to live up to that.

He held women off by a polite simplicity that underneath was hard and watchful; when he felt a certain current being turned on he became emotionally stupid. Kay expected and took much more from men, but she, too, had a careful thermometer against her heart. Until the other night, when she reproached him for being interested in Helen Avery, there had been an absolute minimum of jealousy between them.

George Hannaford was still absorbed in the thought of Helen Avery as he left the studio and walked towards his bungalow over the way. There was in his mind, first, a horror that anyone should come between him and Kay, and second, a regret that he no longer carried that possibility in the forefront of his mind. It had given him a tremendous pleasure like the things that happened to him during his first big success, before he was so 'made' that there was scarcely anything better ahead; it was something to take out and look at – a new and still mysterious joy. It hadn't been love, for he was critical of Helen Avery as he had never been critical of Kay. But his feeling of last week had been sharply significant and memorable, and he was restless, now that it had passed.

Working that afternoon, they were seldom together, but he was conscious of her and he knew that she was conscious of him.

She stood a long time with her back to him at one point, and when she turned at length, their eyes swept past each other's, brushing like bird wings. Simultaneously he saw they had gone far, in their way; it was well that he had drawn back. He was glad that someone came for her when the work was almost over.

Dressed, he returned to the office wing, stopping in for a moment to see Schroeder. No one answered his knock, and, turning the knob, he went in. Helen Avery was there alone.

Hannaford shut the door and they stared at each other. Her face was young, frightened. In a moment in which neither of them spoke, it was decided that they would have some of this out now. Almost thankfully he felt the warm sap of emotion flow out of his heart and course through his body.

'Helen!'

She murmured 'What?' in an awed voice.

'I feel terrible about this.' His voice was shaking.

Suddenly she began to cry; painful, audible sobs shook her. 'Have you got a handkerchief?' she said.

He gave her a handkerchief. At that moment there were steps outside. George opened the door halfway just in time to keep Schroeder from entering on the spectacle of her tears.

'Nobody's in,' he said facetiously. For a moment longer he kept his shoulder against the door. Then he let it open slowly.

Outside in his limousine, he wondered how soon Jules would be ready to go fishing.

II

From the age of twelve Kay Tompkins had worn men like rings on every finger. Her face was round, young, pretty and strong; a strength accentuated by the responsive play of brows and lashes around her clear, glossy, hazel eyes. She was the daughter of a senator from a Western state and she hunted unsuccessfully for glamour through a small Western city until she was seventeen, when she ran away from home and went on the stage. She was one of those people who are famous far beyond their actual achievement.

There was that excitement about her that seemed to reflect the excitement of the world. While she was playing small parts in Ziegfeld shows she attended proms at Yale, and during a temporary venture into pictures she met George Hannaford, already a star of the new 'natural' type then just coming into vogue. In him she found what she had been seeking.

She was at present in what is known as a dangerous state. For six months she had been helpless and dependent entirely upon George, and now that her son was the property of a strict and possessive English nurse, Kay, free again, suddenly felt the need of proving herself attractive. She wanted things to be as they had been before the baby was thought of. Also she felt that lately George had taken her too much for granted; she had a strong instinct that he was interested in Helen Avery.

When George Hannaford came home that night he had minimised to himself their quarrel of the previous evening and was honestly surprised at her perfunctory greeting.

'What's the matter, Kay?' he asked after a minute. 'Is this going to be another night like last night?'

'Do you know we're going out tonight?' she said, avoiding an answer.

'Where?'

'To Katherine Davis'. I didn't know whether you'd want to go – '

'I'd like to go.'

'I didn't know whether you'd want to go. Arthur Busch said he'd stop for me.'

They dined in silence. Without any secret thoughts to dip into like a child into a jam jar, George felt restless, and at the same time was aware that the atmosphere was full of jealousy, suspicion and anger. Until recently they had preserved between them something precious that made their house one of the pleasantest in Hollywood to enter. Now suddenly it might be any house; he felt common and he felt unstable. He had come near to making something bright and precious into something cheap and unkind. With a sudden surge of emotion, he crossed the room and was about to put his arm around her when the doorbell rang. A moment later Dolores announced Mr Arthur Busch.

Busch was an ugly, popular little man, a continuity writer and lately a director. A few years ago they had been hero and heroine to him, and even now, when he was a person of some consequence in the picture world, he accepted with equanimity Kay's use of him for such purposes as tonight's. He had been in love with her for years, but, because his love seemed hopeless, it had never caused him much distress.

They went on to the party. It was a housewarming, with Hawaiian musicians in attendance, and the guests were largely of the old crowd. People who had been in the early Griffith pictures, even though they were scarcely thirty, were considered to be of the old crowd; they were different from those coming along now, and they were conscious of it. They had a dignity and straightforwardness about them from the fact that they had worked in pictures before pictures were bathed in a golden haze of success. They were still rather humble before their amazing triumph, and thus, unlike the new generation, who took it all for granted, they were constantly in touch with reality. Half a dozen or so of the women were especially aware of being unique. No one had come along to fill their places; here and there a pretty face had caught the public imagination for a year, but those of the old crowd were already legends, ageless and disembodied. With all this, they were still young enough to believe that they would go for ever.

George and Kay were greeted affectionately; people moved over and made place for them. The Hawaiians performed and the Duncan sisters sang at the piano. From the moment George saw who was here he guessed that Helen Avery would be here, too, and the fact annoyed him. It was not appropriate that she should be part of this gathering through which he and Kay had moved familiarly and tranquilly for years.

He saw her first when someone opened the swinging door to the kitchen, and when, a little later, she came out and their eyes met, he knew absolutely that he didn't love her. He went up to speak to her, and at her first words he saw something had happened to her, too, that had dissipated the mood of the afternoon. She had got a big part.

'I'm in a daze!' she cried happily. 'I didn't think there was a chance and I've thought of nothing else since I read the book a year ago.'

'It's wonderful. I'm awfully glad.'

He had the feeling, though, that he should look at her with a certain regret; one couldn't jump from such a scene as this afternoon to a plane of casual friendly interest. Suddenly she began to laugh.

'Oh, we're such actors, George – you and I.'

'What do you mean?'

'You know what I mean.'

'I don't.'

'Oh, yes, you do. You did this afternoon. It's a pity we didn't have a camera.'

Short of declaring then and there that he loved her, there was absolutely nothing more to say. He grinned acquiescently. A group formed around them and absorbed them, and George, feeling that the evening had settled something, began to think about going home. An excited and sentimental elderly lady – somebody's mother – came up and began telling him how much she believed in him, and he was polite and charming to her, as only he could be, for half an hour. Then he went to Kay, who had been sitting with Arthur Busch all evening, and suggested that they go.

She looked up unwillingly. She had had several highballs and the fact was mildly apparent. She did not want to go, but she got up after a mild argument and George went upstairs for his coat. When he came down Katherine Davis told him that Kay had already gone out to the car.

The crowd had increased; to avoid a general good-night he went out through the sun-parlour door to the lawn; less than twenty feet away from from him he saw the figures of Kay and Arthur Busch against a bright street lamp; they were standing close together and staring into each other's eyes. He saw that they were holding hands.

After the first start of surprise George instinctively turned about, retraced his steps, hurried through the room he had just left, and came noisily out the front door. But Kay and Arthur Busch were still standing close together, and it was lingeringly and with abstracted eyes that they turned around finally and saw him. Then both of them seemed to make an effort; they drew apart as if it was a physical ordeal. George said goodbye to Arthur Busch with a special cordiality, and in a moment he and Kay were driving homeward through the clear California night.

He said nothing, Kay said nothing. He was incredulous. He suspected that Kay had kissed a man here and there, but he had never seen it happen or given it any thought. This was different; there had been an element of tenderness in it and there was something veiled and remote in Kay's eyes that he had never seen there before.

Without having spoken, they entered the house; Kay stopped by the library door and looked in.

'There's someone there,' she said, and she added without interest: 'I'm going upstairs. Good night.'

As she ran up the stairs the person in the library stepped out into the hall.

'Mr Hannaford – '

He was a pale and hard young man; his face was vaguely familiar, but George didn't remember where he had seen it before.

'Mr Hannaford?' said the young man. 'I recognise you from your pictures.' He looked at George, obviously a little awed.

'What can I do for you?'

'Well, will you come in here?'

'What is it? I don't know who you are.'

'My name is Donovan. I'm Margaret Donovan's brother.' His face toughened a little.

'Is anything the matter?'

Donovan made a motion towards the door. 'Come in here.' His voice was confident now, almost threatening.

George hesitated, then he walked into the library. Donovan followed and stood across the table from him, his legs apart, his hands in his pockets.

'Hannaford,' he said, in the tone of a man trying to whip himself up to anger. 'Margaret wants fifty thousand dollars.'

'What the devil are you talking about?' exclaimed George incredulously.

'Margaret wants fifty thousand dollars,' repeated Donovan.

'You're Margaret Donovan's brother?'

'I am.'

'I don't believe it.' But he saw the resemblance now. 'Does Margaret know you're here?'

'She sent me here. She'll hand over those two letters for fifty thousand, and no questions asked.'

'What letters?' George chuckled irresistibly. 'This is some joke of Schroeder's, isn't it?'

'This ain't no joke, Hannaford. I mean the letters you signed your name to this afternoon.'

III

An hour later George went upstairs in a daze. The clumsiness of the affair was at once outrageous and astounding. That a friend of seven years should suddenly request his signature on papers that were not what they were purported to be made all his surroundings seem diaphanous and insecure. Even now the design engrossed him more than a defence against it, and he tried to re-create the steps by which Margaret had arrived at this act of recklessness or despair.

She had served as a script girl in various studios and for various directors for ten years; earning first twenty, now a hundred dollars a week. She was lovely-looking and she was intelligent; at any moment in those years she might have asked for a screen test, but some quality of initiative or ambition had been lacking. Not a few times had her opinion made or broken incipient careers. Still she waited at directors' elbows, increasingly aware that the years were slipping away.

That she had picked George as a victim amazed him most of all. Once, during the year before his marriage, there had been a momentary warmth; he had taken her to a Mayfair ball, and he remembered that he had kissed her going home that night in the car. The flirtation trailed along hesitantly for a week. Before it could develop into anything serious he had gone East and met Kay.

Young Donovan had shown him a carbon of the letters he had signed. They were written on the typewriter that he kept in his bungalow at the studio, and they were carefully and convincingly worded. They purported to be love letters, asserting that he was Margaret Donovan's lover, that he wanted to marry her, and that for that reason he was about to arrange a divorce. It was incredible. Someone must have seen him sign them that morning; someone must have heard her say: 'Your initials are like Mr Harris's.'

George was tired. He was training for a screen football game to be played next week, with the Southern California varsity as extras, and he was used to regular hours. In the middle of a confused and despairing sequence of thought about Margaret

Donovan and Kay, he suddenly yawned. Mechanically he went upstairs, undressed and got into bed.

Just before dawn Kay came to him in the garden. There was a river that flowed past it now, and boats faintly lit with green and yellow lights moved slowly, remotely by. A gentle starlight fell like rain upon the dark, sleeping face of the world, upon the black mysterious bosoms of the trees, the tranquil gleaming water and the farther shore.

The grass was damp, and Kay came to him on hurried feet; her thin slippers were drenched with dew. She stood upon his shoes, nestling close to him, and held up her face as one shows a book open at a page.

'Think how you love me,' she whispered. 'I don't ask you to love me always like this, but I ask you to remember.'

'You'll always be like this to me.'

'Oh no; but promise me you'll remember.' Her tears were falling. 'I'll be different, but somewhere lost inside me there'll always be the person I am tonight.'

The scene dissolved slowly but George struggled into consciousness. He sat up in bed; it was morning. In the yard outside he heard the nurse instructing his son in the niceties of behaviour for two-month-old babies. From the yard next door a small boy shouted mysteriously: 'Who let that barrier through on me?'

Still in his pyjamas, George went to the phone and called to his lawyers. Then he rang for his man, and while he was being shaved a certain order evolved from the chaos of the night before. First, he must deal with Margaret Donovan; second, he must keep the matter from Kay, who in her present state might believe anything; and third, he must fix things up with Kay. The last seemed the most important of all.

As he finished dressing he heard the phone ring downstairs and, with an instinct of danger, picked up the receiver.

'Hello . . . Oh, yes.' Looking up, he saw that both his doors were closed. 'Good morning, Helen . . . It's all right, Dolores. I'm taking it up here.' He waited till he heard the receiver click downstairs.

'How are you this morning, Helen?'

'George, I called up about last night. I can't tell you how sorry I am.'

'Sorry? Why are you sorry?'

'For treating you like that. I don't know what was in me, George. I didn't sleep all night thinking how terrible I'd been.'

A new disorder established itself in George's already littered mind.

'Don't be silly,' he said. To his despair he heard his own voice run on: 'For a minute I didn't understand, Helen. Then I thought it was better so.'

'Oh, George,' came her voice after a moment, very low.

Another silence. He began to put in a cuff button.

'I had to call up,' she said after a moment. 'I couldn't leave things like that.'

The cuff button dropped to the floor; he stooped to pick it up, and then said 'Helen!' urgently into the mouthpiece to cover the fact that he had momentarily been away.

'What, George?'

At this moment the hall door opened and Kay, radiating a faint distaste, came into the room. She hesitated.

'Are you busy?'

'It's all right.' He stared into the mouthpiece for a moment.

'Well, goodbye,' he muttered abruptly and hung up the receiver. He turned to Kay: 'Good morning.'

'I didn't mean to disturb you,' she said distantly.

'You didn't disturb me.' He hesitated. 'That was Helen Avery.'

'It doesn't concern me who it was. I came to ask you if we're going to the Coconut Grove tonight.'

'Sit down, Kay.'

'I don't want to talk.'

'Sit down a minute,' he said impatiently. She sat down. 'How long are you going to keep this up?' he demanded.

'I'm not keeping up anything. We're simply through, George, and you know it as well as I do.'

'That's absurd,' he said. 'Why, a week ago — '

'It doesn't matter. We've been getting nearer to this for months, and now it's over.'

'You mean you don't love me?' He was not particularly alarmed. They had been through scenes like this before.

'I don't know. I suppose I'll always love you in a way.'

Suddenly she began to sob. 'Oh, it's all so sad. He's cared for me for so long.'

George stared at her. Face to face with what was apparently a real emotion, he had no words of any kind. She was not angry, not threatening or pretending, not thinking about him at all, but concerned entirely with her emotions towards another man.

'What is it?' he cried. 'Are you trying to tell me you're in love with this man?'

'I don't know,' she said helplessly.

He took a step towards her, then went to the bed and lay down on it, staring in misery at the ceiling. After a while a maid knocked to say that Mr Busch and Mr Castle, George's lawyer, were below. The fact carried no meaning to him. Kay went into her room and he got up and followed her.

'Let's send word we're out,' he said. 'We can go somewhere and talk this over.'

'I don't want to go away.'

She was already away, growing more and more mysterious and remote with every minute. The things on her dressing-table were the property of a stranger.

He began to speak in a dry, hurried voice. 'If you're still thinking about Helen Avery, it's nonsense. I've never given a damn for anybody but you.'

They went downstairs and into the living-room. It was nearly noon – another bright emotionless California day. George saw that Arthur Busch's ugly face in the sunshine was wan and white; he took a step towards George and then stopped, as if he were waiting for something – a challenge, a reproach, a blow.

In a flash the scene that would presently take place ran itself off in George's mind. He saw himself moving through the scene, saw his part, an infinite choice of parts, but in every one of them Kay would be against him and with Arthur Busch. And suddenly he rejected them all.

'I hope you'll excuse me,' he said quickly to Mr Castle. 'I called you up because a script girl named Margaret Donovan wants fifty thousand dollars for some letters she claims I wrote her. Of course the whole thing is – ' He broke off. It didn't matter. 'I'll come and see you tomorrow.' He walked up to Kay and Arthur, so that only they could hear.

'I don't know about you two – what you want to do. But leave me out of it; you haven't any right to inflict any of it on me, for after all it's not my fault. I'm not going to be mixed up in your emotions.'

He turned and went out. His car was before the door and he said 'Go to Santa Monica' because it was the first name that popped into his head. The car drove off into the everlasting hazeless sunlight.

He rode for three hours, past Santa Monica and then along towards Long Beach by another road. As if it were something he saw out of the corner of his eye and with but a fragment of his attention, he imagined Kay and Arthur Busch progressing through the afternoon. Kay would cry a great deal and the situation would seem harsh and unexpected to them at first, but the tender closing of the day would draw them together. They would turn inevitably towards each other and he would slip more and more into the position of the enemy outside.

Kay had wanted him to get down in the dirt and dust of a scene and scramble for her. Not he; he hated scenes. Once he stooped to compete with Arthur Busch in pulling at Kay's heart, he would never be the same to himself. He would always be a little like Arthur Busch: they would always have that in common, like a shameful secret. There was little of the theatre about George; the millions before whose eyes the moods and changes of his face had flickered during ten years had not been deceived about that. From the moment when, as a boy of twenty, his handsome eyes had gazed off into the imaginary distance of a Griffith western, his audience had been really watching the progress of a straightforward, slow-thinking, romantic man through an accidentally glamorous life.

His fault was that he had felt safe too soon. He realised suddenly that the two Fairbankses, in sitting side by side at table, were not keeping up a pose. They were giving hostages to fate. This was perhaps the most bizarre community in the rich, wild, bored empire, and for a marriage to succeed here, you must expect nothing or you must be always together. For a moment his glance had wavered from Kay and he stumbled blindly into disaster.

As he was thinking this and wondering where he would go

and what he should do, he passed an apartment house that jolted his memory. It was on the outskirts of town, a pink horror built to represent something, somewhere, so cheaply and sketchily that whatever it copied the architect must have long since forgotten. And suddenly George remembered that he had once called for Margaret Donovan here the night of a Mayfair dance.

'Stop at this apartment!' he called through the speaking-tube.

He went in. The negro elevator boy stared open-mouthed at him as they rose in the cage. Margaret Donovan herself opened the door.

When she saw him she shrank away with a little cry. As he entered and closed the door she retreated before him into the front room. George followed.

It was twilight outside and the apartment was dusky and sad. The last light fell softly on the standardised furniture and the great gallery of signed photographs of moving-picture people that covered one wall. Her face was white, and as she stared at him she began nervously wringing her hands.

'What's this nonsense, Margaret?' George said, trying to keep any reproach out of his voice. 'Do you need money that bad?'

She shook her head vaguely. Her eyes were still fixed on him with a sort of terror; George looked at the floor.

'I suppose this was your brother's idea. At least I can't believe you'd be so stupid.' He looked up, trying to preserve the brusque masterly attitude of one talking to a naughty child, but at the sight of her face every emotion except pity left him. 'I'm a little tired. Do you mind if I sit down?'

'No.'

'I'm a little confused today,' said George after a minute. 'People seem to have got it in for me today.'

'Why, I thought' – her voice became ironic in mid-sentence – 'I thought everybody loved you, George.'

'They don't.'

'Only me?'

'Yes,' he said abstractedly.

'I wish it had been only me. But then, of course, you wouldn't have been you.'

Suddenly he realised that she meant what she was saying.

'That's just nonsense.'

'At least you're here,' Margaret went on. 'I suppose I ought to be glad of that. And I am. I most decidedly am. I've often thought of you sitting in that chair, just at this time when it was almost dark. I used to make up little one-act plays about what would happen then. Would you like to hear one of them? I'll have to begin by coming over and sitting on the floor at your feet.'

Annoyed and yet spellbound, George kept trying desperately to seize upon a word or mood that would turn the subject.

'I've seen you sitting there so often that you don't look a bit more real than your ghost. Except that your hat has squashed your beautiful hair down on one side and you've got dark circles or dirt under your eyes. You look white, too, George. Probably you were on a party last night.'

'I was. And I found your brother waiting for me when I got home.'

'He's a good waiter, George. He's just out of San Quentin prison, where he's been waiting the last six years.'

'Then it was his idea?'

'We cooked it up together. I was going to China on my share.'

'Why was I the victim?'

'That seemed to make it realer. Once I thought you were going to fall in love with me five years ago.'

The bravado suddenly melted out of her voice and it was still light enough to see that her mouth was quivering.

'I've loved you for years,' she said – 'since the first day you came West and walked into the old Realart Studio. You were so brave about people, George. Whoever it was, you walked right up to them and tore something aside as if it was in your way and began to know them. I tried to make love to you, just like the rest, but it was difficult. You drew people right up close to you and held them there, not able to move either way.'

'This is all entirely imaginary,' said George, frowning uncomfortably, 'and I can't control – '

'No, I know. You can't control charm. It's simply got to be used. You've got to keep your hand in if you have it, and go through life attaching people to you that you don't want. I don't blame you. If you only hadn't kissed me the night of the Mayfair dance. I suppose it was the champagne.'

George felt as if a band which had been playing for a long time in the distance had suddenly moved up and taken a station beneath his window. He had always been conscious that things like this were going on around him. Now that he thought of it, he had always been conscious that Margaret loved him, but the faint music of these emotions in his ear had seemed to bear no relation to actual life. They were phantoms that he had conjured up out of nothing; he had never imagined their actual incarnations. At his wish they should die inconsequently away.

'You can't imagine what it's been like,' Margaret continued after a minute. 'Things you've just said and forgotten. I've put myself asleep night after night remembering – trying to squeeze something more out of them. After that night you took me to the Mayfair other men didn't exist for me any more. And there were others, you know – lots of them. But I'd see you walking along somewhere about the lot, looking at the ground and smiling a little, as if something very amusing had just happened to you, the way you do. And I'd pass you and you'd look up and really smile; "Hello, darling!" "Hello, darling" and my heart would turn over. That would happen four times a day.'

George stood up and she, too, jumped up quickly.

'Oh, I've bored you,' she cried softly. 'I might have known I'd bore you. You want to go home. Let's see – is there anything else? Oh, yes; you might as well have those letters.'

Taking them out of a desk, she took them to a window and identified them by a rift of lamplight.

'They're really beautiful letters. They'd do you credit. I suppose it was pretty stupid, as you say, but it ought to teach you a lesson about – about signing things, or something.' She tore the letters small and threw them in the wastebasket: 'Now go on,' she said.

'Why must I go now?'

For the third time in twenty-four hours sad and uncontrollable tears confronted him.

'Please go!' she cried angrily – 'or stay if you like. I'm yours for the asking. You know it. You can have any woman you want in the world by just raising your hand. Would I amuse you?'

'Margaret – '

'Oh, go on then.' She sat down and turned her face away. 'After all you'll begin to look silly in a minute. You wouldn't like that, would you? So get out.'

George stood there helpless, trying to put himself in her place and say something that wouldn't be priggish, but nothing came.

He tried to force down his personal distress, his discomfort, his vague feeling of scorn, ignorant of the fact that she was watching him and understanding it all and loving the struggle in his face. Suddenly his own nerves gave way under the strain of the past twenty-four hours and he felt his eyes grow dim and his throat tighten. He shook his head helplessly. Then he turned away – still not knowing that she was watching him and loving him until she thought her heart would burst with it – and went out to the door.

IV

The car stopped before his house, dark save for small lights in the nursery and the lower hall. He heard the telephone ringing, but when he answered it, inside, there was no one on the line. For a few minutes he wandered about in the darkness, moving from chair to chair and going to the window to stare out into the opposite emptiness of the night.

It was strange to be alone, to feel alone. In his overwrought condition the fact was not unpleasant. As the trouble of last night had made Helen Avery infinitely remote, so his talk with Margaret had acted as a catharsis to his own personal misery. It would swing back upon him presently, he knew, but for a moment his mind was too tired to remember, to imagine or to care.

Half an hour passed. He saw Dolores issue from the kitchen, take the paper from the front steps and carry it back to the kitchen for a preliminary inspection. With a vague idea of packing his grip, he went upstairs. He opened the door of Kay's room and found her lying down.

For a moment he didn't speak, but moved around the bathroom between. Then he went into her room and switched on the lights.

'What's the matter?' he asked casually. 'Aren't you feeling well?'

'I've been trying to get some sleep,' she said. 'George, do you think that girl's gone crazy?'

'What girl?'

'Margaret Donovan. I've never heard of anything so terrible in my life.'

For a moment he thought that there had been some new development.

'Fifty thousand dollars!' she cried indignantly. 'Why, I wouldn't give it to her even if it were true. She ought to be sent to jail.'

'Oh, it's not so terrible as that,' he said. 'She has a brother who's a pretty bad egg and it was his idea.'

'She's capable of anything,' Kay said solemnly. 'And you're just a fool if you don't see it. I've never liked her. She has dirty hair.'

'Well, what of it?' he demanded impatiently, and added: 'Where's Arthur Busch?'

'He went home right after lunch. Or rather I sent him home.'

'You decided you were not in love with him?'

She looked up almost in surprise. 'In love with him? Oh, you mean this morning. I was just mad at you; you ought to have known that. I was a little sorry for him last night, but I guess it was the highballs.'

'Well, what did you mean when you – ' He broke off. Wherever he turned he found a muddle, and he resolutely determined not to think.

'My heavens!' exclaimed Kay. 'Fifty thousand dollars!'

'Oh, drop it. She tore up the letters – she wrote them herself – and everything's all right.'

'George.'

'Yes.'

'Of course Douglas will fire her right away.'

'Of course he won't. He won't know anything about it.'

'You mean to say you're not going to let her go? After this?'

He jumped up. 'Do you suppose she thought that?' he cried.
'Thought what?'

'That I'd have them let her go?'

'You certainly ought to.'

He looked hastily through the phone book for her name.

'Oxford – ' he called.

After an unusually long time the switchboard operator
answered: 'Bourbon Apartments.'

'Miss Margaret Donovan, please.'

'Why – ' The operator's voice broke off. 'If you'll just wait a
minute, please.' He held the line; the minute passed, then
another. Then the operator's voice: 'I couldn't talk to you then.
Miss Donovan has had an accident. She's shot herself. When
you called they were taking her through the lobby to St
Catherine's hospital.'

'Is she – is it serious?' George demanded frantically.

'They thought so at first, but now they think she'll be all
right. They're going to probe for the bullet.'

'Thank you.'

He got up and turned to Kay.

'She's tried to kill herself,' he said in a strained voice. 'I'll
have to go around to the hospital. I was pretty clumsy this
afternoon and I think I'm partly responsible for this.'

'George,' said Kay suddenly.

'What?'

'Don't you think it's sort of unwise to get mixed up in this?
People might say – '

'I don't give a damn what they say,' he answered roughly.

He went to his room and automatically began to prepare for
going out. Catching sight of his face in the mirror, he closed his
eyes with a sudden exclamation of distaste, and abandoned the
intention of brushing his hair.

'George,' Kay called from the next room, 'I love you.'

'I love you, too.'

'Jules Rennard called up. Something about barracuda fishing.
Don't you think it would be fun to get up a party? Men and
girls both?'

'Somehow the idea doesn't appeal to me. The whole idea of
barracuda fishing – '

The phone rang below and he started. Dolores was answering it.

It was a lady who had already called twice today.

'Is Mr Hannaford in?'

'No,' said Dolores promptly. She stuck out her tongue and hung up the phone just as George Hannaford came downstairs. She helped him into his coat, standing as close as she could to him, opened the door and followed a little way out on the porch.

'Meester Hannaford,' she said suddenly, 'that Miss Avery she call up five-six times today. I tell her you out and say nothing to missus.'

'What?' He stared at her, wondering how much she knew about his affairs.

'She call up just now and I say you out.'

'All right,' he said absently.

'Meester Hannaford.'

'Yes, Dolores.'

'I deedn't hurt myself thees morning when I fell off the porch.'

'That's fine. Good night, Dolores.'

'Good night, Meester Hannaford.'

George smiled at her, faintly, fleetingly, tearing a veil from between them, unconsciously promising her a possible admission to the thousand delights and wonders that only he knew and could command. Then he went to his waiting car and Dolores, sitting down on the stoop, rubbed her hands together in a gesture that might have expressed either ecstasy or strangulation, and watched the rising of the thin, pale California moon.

ROBERT COOVER

Intermission

The lights come up and a thin curtain covers the screen, but the sign behind it telling everyone to please visit the concession stands in the lobby while they're getting ready for the next feature can still be seen, and the ripply picture on it of a huge drippy banana split, which they don't even sell as far as she knows, makes her stomach rumble loud enough to give a zombie hiccups, so she decides to go out and see what she can find with less than six zillion calories in it. Her friend, who's flirting with some broken-nosed character a row back in a high school letter jacket and sweaty cowboy hat, turns and asks her jokingly to bring her back a salty dog – 'Straight up, mind!' – making the guy snort and heehaw and push his hands in his pockets.

In the lobby, there's a line for everything – candy, soft drinks, popcorn, cigarettes, ice cream, even the water fountain. The soft drinks line is the shortest so she gets in it, though the smells of minty chewing gum, chocolate, and hot butter are driving her crazy. She feels like she's caught in that Chinese torture movie where they locked this guy in a steel collar with his arms tied behind him and left his food two inches from his mouth until he finally strangled himself to death trying to get at it. Her unhappy tum complains again and she grabs a fistful and squeezes it just to remind herself why she's being so mean to it.

At almost the same moment, some creep behind her, as though to say and that ain't all, kid, grabs a handful of what her girlfriend calls her holey altar – 'You just kneel down and kiss it, honey!' she liked to say – numb from so much sitting, but not so numb she doesn't go lurching into the smart-alecky young schoolkids in front of her, setting off a lot of sniggering insults, mostly about her bosom, which is among more adult audiences usually her best feature. She turns to scowl at the masher behind her, but there's no one there. Instead, over by a movie poster advertising a sexy religious epic, there's this dazzling guy, all class and muscle, a real dreamboat, as they used to say in her favorite musicals, looking somehow heroic and vulnerable at the same time, and dressed in clothes they don't even sell in a town like this – and he's staring straight at her! She's almost sure she recognises him from somewhere, not from this dump of course, it would have to be from some movie – like possibly he was a private eye with a tragic past or a great explorer or an alcoholic or a happy-go-lucky guy who gave his life for the woman he loved, something like that. Maybe even a half-naked martyr from that religious opus behind him, a show, if so, she wouldn't want to miss, much as she admires his present wardrobe. She sucks in her tummy and takes a breath to lift her breasts a tad, just in case he might be interested (fat chance, she cautions herself, all too often a fool for love, she's famous for it) – and amazingly enough, he *is*! He fits a cigarette between his lips, curls his hands around it and lights it, never once taking his eyes off her, glancing appreciatively down at her breasts (her sudden gasp makes them quiver in her bra cups like sing-along bouncing balls, she can tell by the way his brows bob), then back up at her eyes once more. He smiles faintly, blows smoke, then holds up the pack as though offering her one.

When she walks over toward him, her heart's beating so hard she's sure it must be showing through her blouse like she's got something alive in there trying to get out, and she knows just what they've always meant when they say in the movies, 'I felt like I was walking on air.' Only it's a kind of bumpy air, like any minute something might catch her heels and make her fall on her face and turn the whole thing into some awful slapstick routine, the story of her crummy life. And sure enough, just when she gets close enough to pick up his smell (which is something between pepper steak, hot bathwater, and a Christmas tree – buttered popcorn can't touch it), her knees go all mushy, and she thinks, wobbling, oh boy, here we go again – but he reaches out and steadies her with just the lightest touch on her elbow, and then, as though there's some secret signal between them, they turn and (she checks to make sure she's still got her ticket stub, you never know, don't burn your britches, as her girlfriend likes to say) step out onto the street.

Her hands are trembling when she reaches for the cigarette he offers her, and there's a kind of fog swirling around (it makes her think of steamy train stations and damp farewells, though in fact she hasn't even said hello yet) or else she's going blind with mad passion, very likely, and she's just trying to think of something brainy yet romantic to say – like, 'Isn't destiny wonderful, I agree, but it's sometimes, you know, kind of weird, too, am I right?' or, 'When you looked at me in there, I felt like I was stumbling on air, me and my big feet,' or maybe just, 'How did you guess, yum, my favorite flavor,' wondering to tell the truth what kinds of cigarettes they sold nowadays, not having tried to smoke one of the things since way back before she became a cheerleader her third year in high school – when four guys step out of the shadows and grab her and start dragging her toward the curb. 'Hey!' she yelps, any language fancier than that escaping her as her feet leave the ground. She twists around toward her erstwhile lover-boy, hoping, if not for a heroic rescue, at least for a little sympathy, but he only smiles mysteriously, takes a drag on his butt, flips it away, and, trailing wisps of fog and cigarette smoke like a kind of end-of-reel tease, disappears back into the movie house.

A black unmarked car with thick windows pulls up and they push her into it, two of these blue-suited meatsacks squeezing in beside her in the back seat, another jumping up front with the driver who is hunched over the wheel in a cloth cap and a coat with the collar turned up around his ears, like something she has seen a thousand times, yet never seen before. The fourth guy flops a jump seat down in front of her and sits facing her with a machine gun pointed straight at her belly, which even in her present panic she realises is what has gotten her into all this trouble in the first place. Maybe he can even hear it growling because, as they roar away from the curb, he tells her to shut up even though she hasn't said a word and couldn't if she tried.

It's scary enough that she's jammed into this car with a bunch of muscle-bound maniacs who, if they aren't gangsters, sure act like it, a gun poked at her stomach and the car going about a hundred miles an hour through the thickest downtown traffic she's ever seen around this place, running lights and swerving around oncoming cars and generally scaring the pants off anybody who has time to see them coming (someone who looked a little bit like her mother just went leaping backwards through a plate glass window back there – this is no joke!), but she's also got the distinct impression that the driver, who should have his eyes on the road ('Yikes!' she yips as the side of a huge bus looms before them and the guy with the gun gives her a jab with it and says: 'I thought I told you to shut up!'), has them on her instead, staring darkly at her through his rearview mirror, like either he's got designs on her, evil or whatever, or he's trying to tell her something. 'There's somebody followin' us,' he snarls suddenly, as though to hide what he really wants to say.

The other guys whip out their weapons and roll the windows down. '*Step on it!*' the one with the gun on her yells and now they *really* get going, jumping curbs and racing the wrong way down one-way streets, taking corners on two wheels, tires screeching, crashing right through news-stands and flower carts, beating speeding engines to train crossings, leaping roadworks and gaping bridges, the gorillas beside her meanwhile leaning out of the windows and blasting away at whoever it is that's following them. No one's paying any attention to her now, if they weren't going a thousand miles an hour she could just open the door and step out and never be missed – no one, that is, except the driver, who is still eyeing her through the rearview mirror like he can't get enough of her. Is he crazy?

Then suddenly one of the bruisers beside her slumps to the floor with a big hole where an eye should be, making her clench her teeth and pull her lips back, and the guy in the jump seat, looking like somebody just yanked his plug and let all the blood run out, shoves her toward the empty window and yells in a high nervous voice: 'You think it's funny? You just stick *your* head out there for a while!' She shrinks back at the same moment that the gunman on the other side of her spasms and flops against her like a bag of dirty laundry (and where *are* they now? they seem to be racing along the edge of some *cliff!*), and she tries her best to erase the grimace, but the squeaky guy just screams and pokes her with his machine gun again. His finger is jittery on the trigger, his eyes rolling around like he's about to lose his taffy, and the driver, squinting at her in the mirror, gives her a little go-ahead nod as if he might have something in mind, so what else can she do?

They're going so fast her eyes tear when she sticks her head out and she can't see a thing, but she can hear the squealing tires and howling sirens and the bullets ricocheting off the side of the car. As for those two hours in the beauty parlor this afternoon, forget it, it's a good thing it's her own hair or it'd all be gone by now. Whenever she tries to pull back inside, she can feel that fruitcake behind her prodding at her fundamentals with the pointy end of his tommy gun, pushing her further and further out the window like he might be trying to unload ballast, as her girlfriend likes to say when she has to go to the ladies'. Then amazingly, amid the roar of rushing wind and gunfire and speeding wheels, she seems to hear someone whisper, '*Jump!*' right in her ear. What? She catches just a glimpse through her windblown lashes (*those* aren't her own, and − *zip!* − they're gone) of the brim of his cloth cap, leaning out of the window toward her. '*Now!*'

The car seems to swerve and the next thing she knows she's all alone out in midair some place (out of the corner of her eye she sees the gangsters' car leave the cliff edge and go somersaulting explosively far below), and then she's falling. She doesn't know how long she keeps falling, maybe she passes out for a second, because it seems like almost the next day when she hits the water − which is cold as ice and churning like an old washing machine and wakes her up right away if in fact she was asleep before. She flounders in the swirling waves, wishing now she hadn't always been so self-conscious in a swimming suit and had at least gone to the pool enough to learn something about how you stay on top of this stuff and keep from swallowing so much of it. What's worse, when for a moment she does manage to get her head above the surface, she can see she's being swept toward some kind of rapidly approaching horizon, which even she in her landlocked innocence knows can only be the edge of a waterfall: the roar is deafening and she can see spume rising from below like the mist they use in those films about dying and going to the other world. Well, out of the frying pan and down the drain, as her friend would say: she holds her nose and gets ready for the plunge.

But, just as the current starts to pick up speed and propel her over the edge, along comes this empty barrel, tumbling and rolling in the waves, and sort of scoops her up, head first – and there she is, halfway inside, her head banging around on the bottom, her backside up in the air and feet kicking, when she feels the whole apparatus tip, pause, and then drop. It is not a pleasant ride. The half of her left outside feels very airy and vulnerable the whole way down, not unlike the way it felt when she got sent to the principal's office for a paddling in the fourth grade, while the half on the inside gets shaken around like the churning balls in a lucky numbers barrel. *Ow!* It hurts worse than the time she went rollerskating and got thrown off the tail end of a snakeline. Or the night her friends shoved some cotton candy and a double-dip ice-cream cone in her two hands and pushed her down the collapsing ramp of a carnival fun house, with a thousand people standing out front watching and laughing their fat heads off.

It seems to take centuries to get to the bottom, that's how it is when you think each second is going to be your last, but finally the whirling and pounding is over and she finds herself dizzily afloat, her head at the dark smelly end of the barrel, her legs dangling in the water, which does not seem so cold now. She knows the barrel's starting to fill up and sink, she has to do something soon, but her head hurts too much to think, and besides, it feels good just lying there like in a bathtub, all alone, the cool water swirling gently around her as though to kiss away the hurt. She remembers a movie she saw once in which this queen was taking her bubble bath when some gorgeous guy she'd never seen before came running in, being chased by the heavies and desperately needing some place to hide, so she gave him a kind of regal smile and let him duck into her bathwater. You couldn't see anything, the only way you could tell what was going on down there while the yoyos after him were clanking around grumpily stabbing at the curtains was by the majestic expression on the queen's face as she clawed at the edge of the tub. Just thinking about that movie makes her head hurt a little less.

A kind of chilly current passes under her and something tickles her thighs, giving her the shivers, so, somewhat reluctantly, she slides out of the barrel at last and, holding on to its rim, gazes dreamily around her. She seems to have been cast far out to sea: nothing but water in all directions. And then she sees them: fins slicing through the water! Sharks! *Hundreds* of them! She scrambles back into the barrel, kicking frantically, and by throwing her weight at the bottom tips it upright, even as those huge slimy things come streaking by, whumping and thumping against it, as though trying to tip it over again.

She squats down, peering over the edge at them, her heart in her throat (why is everything in this world so *hungry* all the time?), safe for the moment, but not for long: the barrel is more than half full of water, it's nearly up to her nibbles, as her girlfriend would say, and more is lapping in over the rim every minute. She tries to scoop it out with her hands, but it's too slow. Her shoe doesn't work much better. She makes a kind of bag out of her blouse, but it's too torn up to hold anything. She feels like she's in one of those slow-motion sequences in which the more you run the more you don't go anywhere. Finally what works best is her bra, always the friend closest to her heart, as the ads say. She develops a kind of fast jack-in-the-box motion, collapsing her hands together underwater, filling both cups at once, then quickly spreading them apart as she snaps the bra upward – splash! *whoosh!* splash! *whoosh!* – over and over again, like she might be trying to fill up the ocean.

Eventually the bra snaps – that much action it was never made for – but she has won the battle. She bails the rest out with her one remaining shoe. She notices the sharks have gone. Probably it just got too weird for them. Not that her problems are over of course. She's adrift in a leaky barrel on an endless ocean, no food, no water, not even a cough drop. Boy, isn't that the way it always is? The one time she's worked off enough calories to really let herself go, and they take away the concessions. She pulls what's left of her blouse back on, loosens the buttons at the waist of her skirt, and slumps once again into a cramped-up squat at the puddly bottom of the barrel, feeling empty and bloated at the same time. She'd chew on the ticket stub she's still clinging to if it weren't all soggy with sea brine.

Days pass; weeks maybe, she loses count. She gets lonely, exhilarated, depressed, raving mad, horny. Then one day, on the distant horizon, she sees smoke. Right away, of course, she thinks of somebody roasting hotdogs or marshmallows and starts paddling frantically toward it with her bare hands. This is not very effective. She makes a sail out of her skirt and holds it up between her arms, which works better. The smoke, she sees, is coming out of the top of a mountain. It's all a lot farther away than she'd thought. The sharks come back and she has to beat them off with her shoe, temporarily losing the use of her masts, as they might be called, but still, slowly, progress is made.

As she bobs, at last, toward the shore, her arms feeling like they're about twenty feet long and made of waterlogged lead, she sees that a welcoming party – a bunch of natives with long spears and flowery necklaces – has come out to meet her. Her skirt has shrunk so much she can't get it up past her knees, but her underpants have little purple and green hearts on them (ever a wishful thinker) and might easily be mistaken for a swimsuit, especially by foreigners who aren't wearing all that much themselves. She's not sure what you say to natives on occasions like this, but finally decides the best thing is just to wave and say hi. This doesn't work as well as she might have hoped. They grab her, tie her hands and feet to long poles, and start lugging her on their shoulders up the mountainside. 'Volcano god much hungry,' one of them explains, stroking his belly, and it's true she can hear its insides rumbling even worse than her own. 'But, hey, I haven't eaten for weeks; shouldn't you at least fatten me up first?' she shouts back hopefully as he walks on ahead, but he doesn't hear her, or pretends not to.

At the lip of the volcano, just as they're about to heave her in – she can already feel the heat on her backside, smell the sulphur coiling around, it's a desperate situation, but what more can she do? she's never been good at languages – an argument breaks out. There's some little fellow there, who looks a lot like the driver of the gangsters' car but now with burnt cork smeared on his face, leaping about hysterically and screaming something about 'Medicine man! Medicine man!' This sets off a lot of squawking and hallooing and spear rattling, but at last they untie her and send her off down the mountainside with kicks and spear-swats, snatching up her rescuer and tossing him in instead. She can hear his fading yell for what seems like hours as she runs away down the trail they've sent her.

The trail leads to a small hut in a clearing, where a man stands waiting for her. It's the same guy she saw in the theater lobby, except his chest is bare and bronzed now and his shorts are so thin you can almost see through them. 'The plan worked!' he exclaims, taking her in his arms. 'We're alone at last!' Listen, there were probably easier ways, she might have said if she weren't so out of breath, but by now he is peeling back her blouse shreds and gazing pop-eyed at her best act, so what the heck. Don't step on them, as her friend would say.

He fills his hands with them, rolling them round and round, pinching the nipples between his fingers, having all kinds of fun, then leans down to give them a little lick with his tongue, which might be a lot more exciting if it didn't remind her how ravenous she is. That shoulder under her nose is about the most delicious thing she's seen since the invention of peanut butter. He gapes his mouth and is just about to take one of them in whole, when everything gets shaken by a tremendous explosion and suddenly a bunch of trees that were there aren't there anymore. He looks up anxiously, holding her close, and then another one whistles and hits, knocking them off their feet. '*Invasion!*' he cries and grabs her hand, dragging her, both of them scrambling on all fours, toward the jungle cover.

His hut gets hit next and it sends plumes of flame soaring miles into the sky, debris bombing out everywhere: they've gotten away from it in the nick of time! What was he doing, running a dynamite factory in there? 'My precious experiments!' he explains, gasping, as he pulls her, his pained face scratched and soot-streaked, on into the jungle. He leads her along a treacherous path through snarling panthers, shrieking birds, swamps full of crocodiles and mosquitoes, until they reach a row of bunkers down near the beach, where a handful of exhausted soldiers are holding out against wave after wave of enemy invaders. He dumps a couple of bodies aside, grabs up their rifles, hands her one, and throws himself down into the bunker just as a dozen bullets ricochet off the lip of it. He pops up, guns down four or five invaders, ducks down again, the bullets pinging and whizzing around his ears, jeepers, he's something amazing. I'm in love! she thinks, unable to deny it any longer, I'm cuckoo, I'm on fire, I'm over the harvest moon! *'Get down!'* he yells at her. Oh yeah, right. Cripes! she's almost too excited to think straight!

She knuckles down beside him and he shows her how to use the rifle. He's such a cutiepie, she wishes he'd take another quick lap at what her friend calls her honey-dewzies, dangling ripely in front of him – or at anything else for that matter, she's open to suggestions – but, no, he's too busy jumping up and shooting at these other bozos, it's like some kind of obsession with him. Well, she'll try anything once, in spite of all the trouble that dubious principle has got her into in the past, she must be a slow learner. She picks out a gangly guy just splashing in at the shoreline, shooting dopily in all directions, gets him in her sights, and jerks the trigger. Wow, it nearly takes her arm right off at the shoulder! But it's fun watching him go down: he kind of spread-eagles and goes up in the air about six inches, falling flat on his back in the wave rolling in. She braces herself and takes another shot: it doesn't hurt as much as before, and this time the enemy soldier does a kind of pirouette, spinning on one foot and bouncing a little before flopping to the beach. She pops one in the face, propelling him into a backwards somersault, hits another in the knees and then in his cowlick when his hat comes off as he crumples toward her, gets this one in the belly button (misery loves company, she thinks, suffering an evil burbling and gargling behind her own) and that one in the ear, spins them around and doubles them over with shots in their ribs and finishes them off with bullets up their booboos, lines them up in her sights and blasts them two, three at a time, aims down their own barrels so their guns blow up in their faces. This is great! She never knew guys had so much fun!

But it's too good to last, as she might have known. She feels a tugging on the seat of her drawers and looks down: it's the sport she came with, lying wounded at her feet, a bloody bandage around his head, hands still clenching his smoking rifle, the knuckles raw, his eyes red with pain and fever. He seems to be trying to whisper something. She leans close. She can hear the enemy whooping and squealing as they scramble impetuously up the hill toward them like little kids on an Easter egg hunt. 'There aren't many of us left!' he gasps. 'You've got to go for help!' She starts to protest – where's the kick in that? – but he cuts her off with a sad endearing smile: 'We're depending on you, sweetheart!' he wheezes, giving her a weak slap on her fanny like one pal to another, so what can she do?

She hurries back through the jungle, knocking off crocs and tigers as she goes, having pretty much got the hang of this shooting thing, but somehow, maybe because she can't get her lover off her mind (she thinks of him now as her lover, such intimacies as they've shared being no big deal for some people maybe, naming no names, but all histories, like they say, are relative), she takes a wrong turn and ends up in the desert. She tries to circle back round to the jungle, which she can still see on the horizon, but after plowing up and down a couple of dunes in her bare feet, she can't see it anymore, just acres and acres of endless sand. She tries to trace her footprints backwards, but after five or six steps, they disappear.

She thinks maybe it's about time to sit down and have a good cry, but while she's still only thinking about it, some guys in turbans, pyjamas, and silky boots with curled toes come galloping along and snatch her up. 'Hey, fellas, you wouldn't happen to have a cracker or something?' she asks hopefully, but they only heave her over the back end of the horse, her little hearts aloft, and go thundering off to some sheik's palace in an oasis.

So OK, she's had a few surprises since the night she stepped into that movie lobby back in her old hometown all those years ago, but the biggest one is yet to come. This sheik is the very same guy who was standing under the poster and who she just left battling impossible odds back in that bunker, only now here he is with what is obviously a very phony moustache pasted on his lip, and she's made to understand that she's his new favorite and is to be his bride. Tonight. Of course, there are a lot of brides, the palace is full of veiled ladies sneaking about, there's a couple of dozen of them here in his bedroom alone, but she considers herself a gregarious person and doesn't mind company. She winks at the sheik to let him know she's in on whatever he's got in mind, but he only scowls darkly and bellows something about 'stinking pig' and 'prepare her for bridal sacrament.' OK, let him play it his way.

She's handed over to some eunuchs and serving girls who lead her down to a kind of shallow swimming pool full of bareass ladies and peel her rags off her. She pats her belly and points into her open mouth with her bunched fingers, but they don't get it. Oh well, it's a wedding, isn't it, probably there's going to be a banquet, she tells herself, ever the cheery optimist. She's just got her toe in the water, testing how hot it is, when up comes that driver of the gangsters' car again. The last couple of times she's seen him, he was crashing down a cliff in an exploding car and getting thrown into the maw of a smoking volcano, yet here he is again, disguised this time as a naked eunuch, and insisting to everybody that before her bath she has to be taken down to what he calls the 'virginorium' for a health check.

Before she or anyone else can protest, he is hauling her at full pelt down a mirrored hall, her bare feet slapping boisterously on the marble floor, the rest of her all aquiver and goose-bumpy and no doubt rosy pink under all the grime. Her birthday suit, unfortunately, even as starved as she is, could still use a few tucks here and there, a fact that has probably not escaped all the people who are turning to stare at her galumphing by. He pushes her ahead of him suddenly into a dark corridor, presses his back to the wall, cranes his head around the corner. 'It's clear!' he hisses. 'There's a plane waiting out behind the camel barns. We've got to move fast!' 'Wait a minute,' she pants, 'I know this guy, it's all right.' 'No, you don't! It's not who you think it is! This is his evil twin brother! Didn't you notice the telltale scar, the missing birthmark? Through forged papers he has stolen his brother's rightful inheritance! He'll stop at nothing! That's why you're involved!' 'What?' It's getting pretty complicated. 'Look, I'm not particular, they're both pretty cute.' He seizes her wrist. 'Let me show you something.'

He drags her down more corridors, more stairs, more narrow passages. 'Talk about stopping at nothing,' she grumbles. They're now deep in the labyrinth of the palace. He puts his fingers to his lips, sidles cautiously toward a locked door. 'This is the room of the favorites,' he whispers. 'First they dance for the sheik, they become his bride, and then they come here.' He picks the lock with a piece of wire concealed mysteriously on his person. Inside: a whole roomful of severed heads! She screams. It's a kind of reflex. 'I'm sorry, I don't know what came over me,' she whispers. They can hear footsteps approaching. He strokes the stone wall like a blind man trying to guess what it is. Suddenly, just as the footsteps come clattering down the stairs into the corridor, a piece of the wall slides open and they slip behind it, pressing the wall quickly together again like completing a puzzle.

The secret passage leads back to the harem pool. 'Grab your clothes and let's get out of here!' he rasps. It's hardly worth it, all that's left are her raggedy blouse and bikini pants, and it's a hot climate anyway, but she does as she's told, having always been an easygoing sort. While she's pulling them on, the other eunuchs and serving girls crowd around, trying to herd her back into the pool again, but her friend makes a slicing gesture at his throat and grabs her by the hair. They all understand this and back away. If they're so good at sign language, she wonders, why didn't they get her something to eat when she asked them? It's only slowly dawning on her just how sinister this place really is. He drags her away by the hair, which she thinks is pushing the realism a bit too far, but before she can complain, they run into some of the apes who kidnapped her in the first place.

The head-chopping act doesn't work with these guys. 'You! Dance!' once of them grunts, pushing her brusquely toward the sheik's bedroom. She trips and falls. If she can't even walk, do these mugs think she can dance? Her eunuch chum helps her to her feet, whispering furtively in her ear, 'All right, this is it, kid!' 'But I'm a rotten dancer!' she whimpers. 'All I can do is polka!' 'All you gotta do is be yourself – believe me, you can do it! Now, get in there and show 'em your stuff! I'll be waiting at the plane!'

She gets shoved into the sheik's bedroom where there's a big crowd gathered for her show, and the sheik asks her in his clumsy unpleasant accent, which she still suspects must be some kind of put-on, why she hasn't got out of her dirty old rags ('feelty olt wrecks', he calls them), and, thinking fast, she tells him that what she'd planned to do as her first number is the 'Dance of the Filthy Pig'. He looks sceptical and she tells him that it's very popular right now where she comes from and just to sit back and have a good time. She's never danced alone in public before, but once she's thought up the title, the rest comes easy. Anyone can do a dancing pig, especially if they've had a little cheerleading practice. She throws in a bit of dancing duck and dancing cow, which has the sheik boggling his eyes and twisting the ends of his moustache, and she might have gone on and done the whole barnyard (already – she can't help herself – she's thinking career) if they hadn't interrupted her with a loud gong and presented her with a covered platter: a banquet, after all! Her stomach gurgles shamelessly in anticipation.

What she finds when she lifts the lid, however, is the severed head of her eunuch friend, now wearing his old cloth driving cap, something metal between his pale blue lips. A key! She's crying on the inside, or maybe even throwing up, but on the outside she laughs crazily and snatches up the cloth cap with one hand, subtly cops the key with the other: bless his heart, his jaws are clamped around the key and she has to push on his face to get it out, sending the head rolling around on the marble floor, but this only adds authenticity to her second rendition, which she has just announced as 'Follow the Bouncing Head'. She tugs the cap down tight over her eyebrows and starts dancing wildly around the room, kicking the head ahead of her and chasing after, and, before they can recover from their amazement, boots it out the door and down the hall.

By the time she's found a way out of this pretzely loonybin, she can hear them clattering and shouting right behind her. This is going to be close! She sends her friend back down the corridor on one last mission, hoping to bowl a few of them over, and races out into the moonlight. She has no idea where the camel barns might be, but she just follows her nose and finds them soon enough. She lets the camels loose to confuse her pursuers, but the stupid things just stand there, chewing their cuds. 'Next time I'm going to do the "Dance of the Camelburgers"!' she screams furiously at them, and dashes out back where the old museum-piece of an airplane is parked. Even as she jumps up into the cockpit, she can hear the barns filling up behind her with rabid scimitar-swinging soreheads.

Her hands are trembling as she tries to figure out where to put the key in (she can just hear her girlfriend saying, 'Honey, put it anywhere it feels good!'), and she realises, as though it's just dawning on her, that she hasn't got the dimmest notion how to fly one of these clunkers. She doesn't even know how to drive a car, and on bicycles she's the town joke. Even walking is not easy for her. Still, those head-hunting goons are already clambering up on the wing with blood in their eyes, so what choice has she got? When she finally does locate the slot, everything happens violently at once: she's suddenly gunning madly down the field at full throttle, bouncing and careening, shedding startled assassins, probably there's a clutch or some-thing she should have used, but too late now, all that's ancient history, right now she's got only one problem and that's how to get this gazunkas up in the air before she hits something – like those camel barns, for example, coming straight at her. She seems to have got spun around, and all those guys in the pyjamas who were chasing her have stopped in their tracks, gaped a moment in wild-eyed shock, and are now racing each other for the barns once more.

She pulls, punches, twists, kicks, flicks, slaps, and screams at every doobob on the panel in front of her, but nothing works, so she finally just closes her eyes, hugs the steering gidget between her legs (maybe she's thinking about one of the old chewed-up dolls she still sleeps with on lonely nights, which is to say, most all the time, or else maybe that scrawny ginger cat she used to have, may he rest in peace), and shrinks back from the impending blow. Which doesn't come. She opens her eyes to find the old clattertrap miraculously rattling straight up into the moonlit sky, the palace and then the oasis itself disappearing into the darkness behind her. Startled, she pushes the control stick away and – woops! – she's diving straight back to where she came from! All right, she's not completely stupid, a little pushing and pulling on that gizmo, and pretty soon the roller-coaster flattens out to something more like a horse race with hurdles.

Not bad for a jellybean, as her friend would say; in fact she'd be pretty proud of flying this contraption, first time like this, and by the seat of her pants as it were, if, one, that seat weren't so wet (listen, it was pretty *scary* back there for a while – who knows if all those terrorised movie heroines do any better, they don't show you *every*thing), and, two, there were some way of parking it and getting out without having to go all the way back down to the ground again. She pokes around for instructions, or even a bag of peanuts to calm her nerves, and comes on a sort of clockface on the panel in front of her with the minute hand pointing to EMPTY. Oh boy, that's all she needed. Even now, the motor's making a funny choking noise like it's got something stuck in its windpipe, and what the little lights way down below seem to be telling her is 'Goodnight, Sweetheart, Goodnight'.

She fumbles in her seat, under it, behind it, finds a pack of cards, a cigar butt, a jar of hair oil, a thumbworn Western, an empty gin bottle (just not her night: even the smell is gone), a plastic ring with a secret code inside, a used bar of soap coated with dustballs, and finally what she's looking for, a parachute. The old crate is wheezing and snorting like a sick mule by now and has already started to take a noser, so she harnesses herself in the chute, flicks the cockpit open, and launches herself out into the starry night, amazed at her own aplomb at such an altitude since even sitting up in the balcony at the movies makes her dizzy.

She's not sure where she's going to land or who's going to be waiting for her or what kind of impression she's going to make, dropping in on them in a cloth cap, moist undies, and a few streamers of bleached-out blouse, but she's hoping the element of surprise will give her the lead time she needs to vanish before they figure out what they've seen. She does wish she had her lost lashes back, though, or at least a tube of lipstick and maybe some deodorant, not to mention the common comb. As though triggered by that thought, the cap flies off and she glances up through her streaming tangle of hair to watch it vanish into the night sky, thinking as she gazes up into the starry dome: wait a minute, something's wrong – *where's the parachute?!* Don't these things open by *themselves?*

Then she remembers something from all those old war movies about a ring. It's like a window shade or a wedding, you have to put your finger in a ring, then pull. She scrabbles around for it but she can't find it. She can't find *anything* with this dumb thing strapped on her back, she's getting a crick in her neck from trying, so she peels it off and searches it. Nothing. It's like a pillow. Should she just hold it under her and hope for the best? She's dropping so fast! Then she discovers a placket and buttons like a man's fly. She fumbles with the buttons, regretting tearfully, not for the first time in her life, her lack of practice. What she finds inside is a kind of nozzle with a nipple on the end. What? Is she supposed to blow this thing up? This is crazy! She jerks irritably on the nipple, there's a windy hissing sound, and – *pop!* – she finds herself suddenly afloat under a gigantic gas balloon.

Wow! Here she comes, hanging on desperately by one hand and whooshing down over lit-up Main Street, causing cars to screech and crash, dogs to yap hysterically, pedestrians to stumble all over one another in gap-mouthed amazement. She's still too shaken to revel in all this attention, her heart's hammering away in her chest like the drum of a restless native and her nose is either running or bleeding, all she really wants right now is to go sit down somewhere for a few years, even her appetite seems to have failed her. And it's not over yet! She doesn't know how long she can hang on to the nozzle, and the balloon, sweeping down the street toward the movie theater now, seems if anything to be rising again.

Just when all seems lost, her hand sweaty and slipping its grip, the balloon itself caught in a sudden updraft of hot air from the movie lobby which might take her off who knows where, she spies the awning out over the hardware store next door and lets go, dropping onto the awning as though onto a haystack and sliding down it into a pile of rubbish on the curb – not the prettiest of all landings maybe, a canvas burn or two to remember it by, but she's an all-in-one piece, as her girlfriend would say, she still has her ticket stub, and in the theater the intermission buzzer is just this moment sounding its final warning and everyone is rushing back to his seat.

Luckily the usher is looking the other way as she goes

streaking past, the doors swinging closed behind her, the auditorium already dark, some children's cartoon starting up on the
screen: loud screeching and banging noises, tinkling music, one
animal stomping another one, the usual thing, and distracting
enough, she's pretty sure, that no one notices how she's dressed,
or rather, not. Her friend has crawled into the row behind and
is curled up with the cowboy, her hand in his lap, and just as
well because she's too poohed out to put up with any wisecracks
just now about all-night suckers or pimple specials or what has
she been doing in the ladies' so long, was it fun, can we all do
it, who'll bring the buns? Her friend sometimes can be a pain,
especially when she's trying to ring some guy's bell.

She scrunches down in her seat, feeling a strange chill and
wishing she'd brought along a sweater or something, not to
mention some spare bluejeans and an extra pair of shoes. Her
teeth start to chatter and her flesh goes all shivery, but it can't
be that cold in here, probably it's just nerves (she's never sat
this *close* to one of these seats before, so to speak), so she tries to
focus on the cartoon to calm herself down. But there's something odd. One of the animals has been twisted into a kind of
coiled spring and is boing-boinging around in a way that usually
has people hooting and yipping and rolling around in the aisles
– but no one's laughing. No one's making *any* kind of sound
whatsoever. She twists around uneasily and peeks over the back
of her seat: the auditorium, lit only by the light from the
projector, is full of people, all right, but they're all sitting stiffly
in their seats with weird flattened-out faces, their dilated eyes
locked onto the screen like they're hypnotised or dead or
something. Uh oh. She reaches back and taps her friend to ask
her what she thinks is going on, and her friend, jostled, slides
lifelessly off the guy's lap onto the floor between the seats.
There's a soft bump, clearly audible under the tinny whistle and
crash up on the screen, the burlesque rattle up there as of things
tumbling down a thousand stairs. The guy's not looking too
great either, just sprawled out there with his cowboy hat down
over his nose, his slobbery mouth hanging open, his belt buckle
undone, his hand cupped rigidly around a skinny behind that
isn't there anymore. She's about to let out a yell, when she feels
this icy clawlike grip on her shoulder, and she can't even

squeak. The claw twists her around in her seat until she's facing the screen again and holds her there, peering up in the creepy silence at all that hollow tomfoolery and wondering how she's going to get out of *this* one. If how is the word. It's like some kind of spell, and there's probably a way to break it, but right now she can't think of it, she almost can't think at all: it's like that hoodoo behind her has stuck one of those bony fingers deep in her ear and pushed the 'OFF' button. So what can she do, she stares up at the screen and pretends to watch the mayhem (one of the animals, having been pressed into an ice-cube tray, is now being emptied out in cubes: there are exaggerated pops and clunks as various bodily parts tumble from the tray), wishing only that she'd at least picked up that soft drink on the way in, or better yet, a tub of popcorn and half a dozen chilidogs, it might be a long night. Like her friend would say, if she were still alive: 'Sometimes, sweetie, you just have to hunker down, spread your cheeks, and let nature take its curse.' Anyway, as far as she can tell, the claw only wants her to watch the movie, and, hey, she's been watching movies all her life, so why stop now, right? Besides, isn't there always a happy ending? Has to be. It comes with the price of the ticket . . .

KATHERINE MANSFIELD

Pictures

Eight o'clock in the morning. Miss Ada Moss lay on a black iron bedstead, staring up at the ceiling. Her room, a Bloomsbury top-floor back, smelled of soot and face powder and the paper of fried potatoes she brought in for supper the night before.

'Oh dear,' thought Miss Moss, 'I am cold. I wonder why it is that I always wake up so cold in the mornings now. My knees and feet and my back – especially my back; it's like a sheet of ice. And I always was such a one for being warm in the old days. It's not as if I was skinny – I'm just the same full figure that I used to be. No, it's because I don't have a good hot dinner in the evenings.'

A pageant of Good Hot Dinners passed across the ceiling, each of them accompanied by a bottle of Nourishing Stout . . .

'Even if I were to get up now,' she thought, 'and have a sensible substantial breakfast . . .' A pageant of Sensible Substantial Breakfasts followed the dinners across the ceiling, shepherded by an enormous, white, uncut ham. Miss Moss shuddered and disappeared under the bedclothes. Suddenly, in bounced the landlady.

'There's a letter for you, Miss Moss.'

'Oh,' said Miss Moss, far too friendly, 'thank you very much, Mrs Pine. It's very good of you, I'm sure, to take the trouble.'

'No trouble at all,' said the landlady. 'I thought perhaps it was the letter you'd been expecting.'

'Why,' said Miss Moss brightly, 'yes, perhaps it is.' She put her head on one side and smiled vaguely at the letter. 'I shouldn't be surprised.'

The landlady's eyes popped. 'Well, I should, Miss Moss,' said she, 'and that's how it is. And I'll trouble you to open it, if you please. Many is the lady in my place as would have done it for you and have been within her rights. For things can't go on like this, Miss Moss, no indeed they can't. What with week in week out and first you've got it and then you haven't, and then it's another letter lost in the post or another manager down at Brighton but will be back on Tuesday for certain – I'm fair sick and tired and I won't stand it no more. Why should I, Miss Moss, I ask you, at a time like this, with prices flying up in the air and my poor dear lad in France? My sister Eliza was only saying to me yesterday – "Minnie," she says, "you're too soft-hearted. You could have let that room time and time again," says she, "and if people won't look after themselves in times like these, nobody else will," she says. "She may have had a College eddication and sung in West End concerts," says she, "but if your Lizzie says what's true," she says, "and she's washing her own wovens and drying them on the towel rail, it's easy to see where the finger's pointing. And it's high time you had done with it," says she.'

Miss Moss gave no sign of having heard this. She sat up in bed, tore open her letter and read:

Dear Madam,
Yours to hand. Am not producing at present, but have filed photo for future ref.
                              Yours truly,
                              Backwash Film Co.

This letter seemed to afford her peculiar satisfaction; she read it through twice before replying to the landlady.

'Well, Mrs Pine, I think you'll be sorry for what you said. This is from a manager, asking me to be there with evening dress at ten o'clock next Saturday morning.'

But the landlady was too quick for her. She pounced, secured the letter.

'Oh, is it! Is it indeed!' she cried.

'Give me back that letter. Give it back to me at once, you bad, wicked woman,' cried Miss Moss, who could not get out of bed because her nightdress was slit down the back. 'Give me back my private letter.' The landlady began slowly backing out of the room, holding the letter to her buttoned bodice.

'So it's come to this, has it?' said she. 'Well, Miss Moss, if I
don't get my rent at eight o'clock tonight, we'll see who's a bad,
wicked woman – that's all.' Here she nodded mysteriously. 'And
I'll keep this letter.' Here her voice rose. 'It will be a pretty little
bit of evidence!' And here it fell, sepulchral, '*My lady.*'

The door banged and Miss Moss was alone. She flung off the
bedclothes, and sitting by the side of the bed, furious and
shivering, she stared at her fat white legs with their great knots
of greeny-blue veins.

'Cockroach! That's what she is. She's a cockroach!' said Miss
Moss. 'I could have her up for snatching my letter – I'm sure I
could.' Still keeping on her nightdress she began to drag on her
clothes.

'Oh, if I could only pay that woman, I'd give her a piece of
my mind that she wouldn't forget. I'd tell her off proper.' She
went over to the chest of drawers for a safety-pin, and seeing
herself in the glass she gave a vague smile and shook her head.
'Well, old girl,' she murmured, 'you're up against it this time,
and no mistake.' But the person in the glass made an ugly face
at her.

'You silly thing,' scolded Miss Moss. 'Now what's the good of
crying: you'll only make your nose red. No, you get dressed and
go out and try your luck – that's what you've got to do.'

She unhooked her vanity bag from the bedpost, rooted in it,
shook it, turned it inside out.

'I'll have a nice cup of tea at an ABC to settle me before I go
anywhere,' she decided. 'I've got one and thrippence – yes, just
one and three.'

Ten minutes later, a stout lady in blue serge, with a bunch of
artificial 'parmas' at her bosom, a black hat covered with purple
pansies, white gloves, boots with white uppers, and a vanity bag
containing one and three, sang in a low contralto voice:

'Sweet-heart, remember when days are forlorn,
It al-ways is dar-kest before the dawn.'

But the person in the glass made a face at her, and Miss Moss
went out. There were grey crabs all the way down the street
slopping water over grey stone steps. With his strange, hawking
cry and the jangle of the cans the milk-boy went his rounds.

Outside Brittweiler's Swiss House he made a splash, and an old brown cat without a tail appeared from nowhere, and began greedily and silently drinking up the spill. It gave Miss Moss a queer feeling to watch – a sinking, as you might say.

But when she came to the ABC she found the door propped open; a man went in and out carrying trays of rolls, and there was nobody inside except a waitress doing her hair and the cashier unlocking the cashboxes. She stood in the middle of the floor but neither of them saw her.

'My boy came home last night,' sang the waitress.

'Oh, I say – how topping for you!' gurgled the cashier.

'Yes, wasn't it,' sang the waitress. 'He brought me a sweet little brooch. Look, it's got "Dieppe" written on it.'

The cashier ran across to look and put her arm round the waitress's neck.

'Oh, I say – how topping for you.'

'Yes, isn't it,' said the waitress. 'Oh-o, he is brahn. "Hullo," I said, "hullo, old mahogany."'

'Oh, I say,' gurgled the cashier, running back into her cage and nearly bumping into Miss Moss on the way. 'You are a *treat*!' Then the man with the rolls came in again, swerving past her.

'Can I have a cup of tea, Miss?' she asked.

But the waitress went on doing her hair. 'Oh,' she sang, 'we're not *open* yet.' She turned round and waved her comb at the cashier.

'*Are* we, dear?'

'Oh no,' said the cashier. Miss Moss went out.

'I'll go to Charing Cross. Yes, that's what I'll do,' she decided. 'But I won't have a cup of tea. No, I'll have a coffee. There's more of a tonic in coffee . . . Cheeky, those girls are! Her boy came home last night; he brought her a brooch with "Dieppe" written on it.' She began to cross the road . . .

'Look out, Fattie; don't go to sleep!' yelled a taxi-driver. She pretended not to hear.

'No, I won't go to Charing Cross,' she decided. 'I'll go straight to Kig and Kadgit. They're open at nine. If I get there early Mr Kadgit may have something by the morning's post . . . "I'm very glad you turned up so early, Miss Moss. I've just heard from a manager who wants a lady to play . . . I think you'll just suit him. I'll give you a card to go and see him. It's three pounds a week and all found. If I were you I'd hop round as fast as I could. Lucky you turned up so early . . ."'

But there was nobody at Kig and Kadgit's except the char-woman wiping over the lino in the passage.

'Nobody here yet, Miss,' said the char.

'Oh, isn't Mr Kadgit here?' said Miss Moss, trying to dodge the pail and brush. 'Well, I'll just wait a moment, if I may.'

'You can't wait in the waiting-room, Miss. I 'aven't done it yet. Mr Kadgit's never 'ere before 'leven-thirty Saturdays. Sometimes 'e don't come at all.' And the char began crawling towards her.

'Dear me – how silly of me,' said Miss Moss. 'I forgot it was Saturday.'

'Mind your feet, *please*, Miss,' said the char. And Miss Moss was outside again.

That was one thing about Beith and Bithems; it was lively. You walked into the waiting-room, into a great buzz of conver-sation, and there was everybody; you knew almost everybody. The early ones sat on chairs and the later ones sat on the early ones' laps, while the gentlemen leaned negligently against the walls or preened themselves in front of the admiring ladies.

'Hello,' said Miss Moss, very gay. 'Here we are again!'

And young Mr Clayton, playing the banjo on his walking-stick, said: 'Waiting for the Robert E. Lee.'

'Mr Bithem here yet?' asked Miss Moss, taking out an old dead powder-puff and powdering her nose mauve.

'Oh yes, dear,' cried the chorus. 'He's been here for ages. We've all been waiting here for more than an hour.'

'Dear me!' said Miss Moss. 'Anything doing, do you think?'

'Oh, a few jobs going for South Africa,' said young Mr Clayton. 'Hundred and fifty a week for two years, you know.'

'Oh!' cried the chorus. 'You *are* a weird, Mr Clayton. Isn't he a *cure*? Isn't he a *scream*, dear? Oh, Mr Clayton, you do make me laugh. Isn't he a *comic*?'

A dark, mournful girl touched Miss Moss on the arm.

'I just missed a lovely job yesterday,' she said. 'Six weeks in the provinces and then the West End. The manager said I would have got it for certain if only I'd been robust enough. He said if my figure had been fuller, the part was made for me.' She stared at Miss Moss, and the dirty dark red rose under the brim of her hat looked, somehow, as though it shared the blow with her, and was crushed, too.

'Oh dear, that was hard lines,' said Miss Moss, trying to appear indifferent. 'What was it – if I may ask?'

But the dark, mournful girl saw through her and a gleam of spite came into her heavy eyes.

'Oh, no good to you, my dear,' said she. 'He wanted someone young, you know – a dark Spanish type – my style, but more figure, that was all.'

The inner door opened and Mr Bithem appeared in his shirt sleeves. He kept one hand on the door ready to whisk back again, and held up the other.

'Look here, ladies – ' and then he paused, grinned his famous grin before he said – '*and bhoys.*' The waiting-room laughed so loudly at this that he had to hold both hands up. 'It's no good waiting this morning. Come back Monday; I'm expecting several calls on Monday.'

Miss Moss made a desperate rush forward. 'Mr Bithem, I wonder if you've heard from . . .'

'Now let me see,' said Mr Bithem slowly, staring; he had only seen Miss Moss four times a week for the past – how many weeks? 'Now, who are you?'

'Miss Ada Moss.'

'Oh yes, yes; of course, my dear. Not yet, my dear. Now I had a call for twenty-eight ladies today, but they had to be young and able to hop it a bit – see? And I had another call for sixteen – but they had to know something about sand-dancing. Look here, my dear, I'm up to the eyebrows this morning. Come back on Monday week; it's no good coming before that.' He gave her a whole grin to herself and patted her fat back. 'Hearts of oak, dear lady,' said Mr Bithem, 'hearts of oak!'

At the North-East Film Company the crowd was all the way up the stairs. Miss Moss found herself next to a fair little baby thing about thirty in a white lace hat with cherries round it.

'What a crowd!' said she. 'Anything special on?'

'*Didn't* you know, dear?' said the baby, opening her immense pale eyes. 'There was a call at nine-thirty for *attractive* girls. We've all been waiting for *hours*. Have you played for this company before?' Miss Moss put her head on one side. 'No, I don't think I have.'

'They're a lovely company to play for,' said the baby. 'A friend of mine has a friend who gets thirty pounds a day . . . Have you *arcted* much for the *fil*-ums?'

'Well, I'm not an actress by profession,' confessed Miss Moss. 'I'm a contralto singer. But things have been so bad lately that I've been doing a little.'

'It's *like* that, isn't it, dear?' said the baby.

'I had a splendid education at the College of Music,' said Miss Moss, 'and I got my silver medal for singing. I've often sung at West End concerts. But I thought, for a change, I'd try my luck . . .'

'Yes, it's *like* that, isn't it, dear?' said the baby.

At that moment a beautiful typist appeared at the top of the stairs.

'Are you all waiting for the North-East call?'

'Yes!' cried the chorus.

'Well, it's off. I've just had a 'phone through.'

'But look here! What about our expenses?' shouted a voice.

The typist looked down at them, and she couldn't help laughing.

'Oh, you weren't to have been *paid*. The North-East never *pay* their crowds.'

There was only a little round window at the Bitter Orange Company. No waiting-room – nobody at all except a girl, who came to the window when Miss Moss knocked, and said: 'Well?'

'Can I see the producer, please?' said Miss Moss pleasantly. The girl leaned on the window-bar, half shut her eyes and seemed to go to sleep for a moment. Miss Moss smiled at her. The girl not only frowned; she seemed to smell something vaguely unpleasant; she sniffed. Suddenly she moved away, came back with a paper and thrust it at Miss Moss.

'Fill up the form!' said she. And banged the window down.

'Can you aviate – high-dive – drive a car – buck-jump – shoot?' read Miss Moss. She walked along the street asking herself those questions. There was a high, cold wind blowing; it tugged at her, slapped her face, jeered; it knew she could not answer them. In the Square Gardens she found a little wire basket to drop the form into. And then she sat down on one of the benches to powder her nose. But the person in the pocket mirror made a hideous face at her, and that was too much for Miss Moss; she had a good cry. It cheered her wonderfully.

'Well, that's over,' she sighed. 'It's one comfort to be off my feet. And my nose will soon get cool in the air . . . It's very nice in here. Look at the sparrows. Cheep. Cheep. How close they come. I expect somebody feeds them. No, I've nothing for you, you cheeky little things . . .' She looked away from them. What was the big building opposite – the Café de Madrid? My goodness, what a smack that little child came down! Poor little mite! Never mind – up again . . . By eight o'clock to-night . . . Café de Madrid. 'I could just go in and sit there and have a coffee, that's all,' thought Miss Moss. 'It's such a place for artists too. I might just have a stroke of luck . . . A dark handsome gentleman in a fur coat comes in with a friend, and sits at my table, perhaps. "No, old chap, I've searched London for a contralto and I can't find a soul. You see, the music is difficult; have a look at it."' And Miss Moss heard herself saying: '"Excuse me, I happen to be a contralto, and I have sung that part many times . . ." Extraordinary! "Come back to my studio and I'll try your voice now." . . . Ten pounds a week .．. Why should I feel nervous? It's not nervousness. Why shouldn't I go to the Café de Madrid? I'm a respectable woman – I'm a contralto singer. And I'm only trembling because I've had nothing to eat today . . . "A nice little piece of evidence, *my lady*." . . . Very well, Mrs Pine. Café de Madrid. They have concerts there in the evenings . . . "Why don't they begin?" The contralto has not arrived . . . "Excuse me, I happen to be a contralto; I have sung that music many times."'

It was almost dark in the café. Men, palms, red plush seats, white marble tables, waiters in aprons, Miss Moss walked through them all. Hardly had she sat down when a very stout gentleman wearing a very small hat that floated on the top of his head like a little yacht flopped into the chair opposite hers.

'Good evening!' said he.

Miss Moss said, in her cheerful way: 'Good evening!'

'Fine evening,' said the stout gentleman.

'Yes, very fine. Quite a treat, isn't it?' said she.

He crooked a sausage finger at the waiter – 'Bring me a large whisky' – and turned to Miss Moss. 'What's yours?'

'Well, I think I'll take a brandy if it's all the same.'

Five minutes later the stout gentleman leaned across the table and blew a puff of cigar smoke full in her face.

'That's a tempting bit o' ribbon!' said he.

Miss Moss blushed until a pulse at the top of her head that she had never felt before pounded away.

'I always was one for pink,' said she.

The stout gentleman considered her, drumming with her fingers on the table.

'I like 'em firm and well covered,' said he.

Miss Moss, to her surprise, gave a loud snigger.

Five minutes later the stout gentleman heaved himself up. 'Well, am I goin' your way, or are you comin' mine?' he asked.

'I'll come with you, if it's all the same,' said Miss Moss. And she sailed after the little yacht out of the café.

ROBERTSON DAVIES

extracts from
The Papers of Samuel Marchbanks

WEDNESDAY

To the movies this evening, and saw yet another of those films in which a young married couple, for no reason which would impress anyone outside Hollywood, see fit to behave as though they were an unmarried couple. By this feeble device it is possible to slip scenes past the Censors' Office – scenes in bedrooms, bathrooms and hotel rooms – which would otherwise be deemed salacious. Why the spectacle of a young unmarried woman brushing her teeth should be considered inflammatory and lewd, whereas the same scene is merely cosy and chummy when she is married, I cannot understand, but such is the power of the wedding ring to anæsthetise and insulate the passions according to the Censors . . . The mess concerned a young couple who met, married and laid the foundation for a posterity in four days, after which the husband went to war and faced the foe for a year and a half. He returned to find his wife a stranger, with a baby which looked, and talked, like Charles Laughton. This dreary incident, which was unfolded at a turtle's pace, failed to grip my attention, and my right knee got a cramp; my right knee is an infallible critic.*

---

* Marchbanks has lived to see the whole world of sexual activity revealed in the movies, the goatishness of which frequently appals him. His delicate mind shrinks from the thought of the day-long rehearsals that must lie behind these depictions of what appears to Hollywood as the Chief End of Man. He has lived to see Sex replaced by Fat as the Ultimate Sin, and at the annual shows of the Ontario Society of Watercolourists pictures of Christ Forgiving the Woman Taken in Adultery have given way to a new theme – Christ Forgiving the Woman Surprised in Laura Secord's.

FRIDAY

To the movies tonight and saw yet another picture about a girl who marries a soldier on short acquaintance. In this particular Hollywood nugacity the girl was a multimillionairess, who tested her suitor by pretending to be a secretary, to discover whether he loved her for herself alone; of course, he did so, and I think this was a fault in the plot, for money, especially in very large quantities, is so much more desirable than the average young woman that no man of real wisdom would hesitate for an instant between the two. Of course, money will not bring happiness to a man who has no capacity for happiness, but neither will the possession of a woman who has no more brains than himself. But money will greatly increase the happiness of a man who is already happy (like me). Wisdom is the greatest possession in the world; money comes next; the intimate caresses of Hollywood stars come a long way down the list . . . The hero of this movie was noticeably fat; he was greasy, too. Is the fat, greasy man to be the Adonis of the future?

TUESDAY

To the movies tonight to see a film dedicated to the exposition of one of the Thirty-Nine Articles of the Hollywood Faith, to wit, that a fellow who chews gum, wears his hat in the house, and rapes the English language every time he opens his mouth is a better matrimonial choice for a nice girl than a suave fellow who has lots of money and has been successfully exposed to education. The Apotheosis of the Yahoo is one of the primary objects of Hollywood.

MONDAY

I see that the movie magnates think of reviving *The Sign Of The Cross*, with Charles Laughton having his feet tickled, Elissa Landi being eaten by lions, and Claudette Colbert bouncing up and down prettily in a bath of asses' milk. It was one of those films in which Christianity and Romantic Love were inextricably confused; Christianity and Pure Love were equated with marrying the girl and restraining premarital caresses to an occasional light kiss on the lips; Paganism and Impure Love meant not marrying the girl, and occasionally joining her in her asses' milk bathtub. But the most fascinatingly repulsive confusion of Christianity and Hollywood Mush that I have ever seen was in *Ben Hur* in which lovers were shown in the foreground of the scene of the Crucifixion, with the caption, 'He died, but Love goes on forever'.

TUESDAY

To the movies tonight to see a film in which Ingrid Bergman and Gregory Peck played the parts of a female psychiatrist and an amnesia patient respectively. I can feast my eyes on Miss Bergman's beauty without paying too much attention to what she says or does, but Master Peck is another matter. His notion of acting is directly contrary to that of such exponents of the art as Irving, Coquelin and Stanislavsky; he does not use his head, but casts the full burden upon his face, which he works furiously, breathing meanwhile through his mouth. His resemblance to Buster Keaton is disturbing to me also; I am always expecting him to be hit with a pie, or to fall into a tub of cement.

SUNDAY

Not long ago a friend of mine opened the door of the garage at her summer cottage, and found a man inside who had hanged himself about two months before; what is more he had been cut down. She is deeply anxious to know (a) why he hanged himself; (b) if he hanged himself or was hanged; (c) who cut him down; (d) what it was about her garage that appealed to his morbid fancy. She will probably never know any of these things. It is thus that life falls short of the movies; in a film she would immediately have been accepted by the detective in the case as a full partner and would have shared his risks of life and limb until the criminal was in the hoosegow, and the full story in the newspapers. But the real-life detective never even asked her to sit all night in the haunted garage and shoot on sight anyone who came down the ladder from the loft. We deplore this lack of imagination on the part of detectives, who never seem to catch anybody, anyway.

TUESDAY

Received a letter written on Reform School stationery from a little girl who takes me to task because I spoke slightingly of Gregory Peck; she tells me that *Photoplay Magazine* esteems this Peck highly. I do not care a fig for *Photoplay Magazine*; I write for a highly exclusive public, subtle and pernickety in its tastes, and they are not to be bamboozled by any such pretentious tripe, nor by the antics of Master Peck, either. She concludes, 'you better apologise.' The day I apologise to you, you contumacious mammothrept,* there will be two moons in the sky.

WEDNESDAY

To the movies tonight to see *The Song of Bernadette*, which opened with these words: 'To those who believe, no explanation is necessary; to those who do not believe, no explanation is possible.' This seemed a very fair statement of the case, calculated to please all the Catholics, Orangemen and nullifidians present. The audience seemed to find Bernadette amusing at times. Up in the gallery something stirred; was it a bird, was it a bird? . . . I wonder what the Church of Rome thinks of Hollywood, its new ally? With so many Catholic films appearing, and a firm hold on the Hays Office, things are looking up for the

---

* *This was a favourite term of objurgation with Marchbanks and there were people who insisted that he had made it up. But no: innovative in so much, he was no neologist. The word is of Greek derivation and suggests that someone has been brought up by his or her grandmother, and is therefore a peevish, self-willed, obstinate, pasty-faced brat of hell.*

Propaganda Fide. But I warn the hierarchy that Hollywood is fickle; five years ago it was whooping it up for the Jews; any time I expect a series of films extolling the spiritual grace and mystical fervour of the Continuing Presbyterians, in which Gregory Peck, Bing Crosby, and Jennifer Jones will all be pressed into service as pawky Scots, hooting and skirling the granite pieties of the Auld Lichts.

SATURDAY

To the movies tonight, and was given a seat next to a woman who brought a baby, which was certainly not more than eight months old. It was suffering with gas on its stomach, so she had laid it upside down over her knees, and was rolling it to and fro as she watched the picture . . . So I moved to a seat next to an elderly woman who was enjoying the film in her bare feet; she had a pair of shoes, but she held them in her lap – to save them, I suppose. These incidents made me thankful for Rita Hayworth who was young, beautiful, clothed, right side up, and apparently in excellent health.

TUESDAY

I see that an English film studio is going to make a film of the life of Karl Marx. Now how will they do that, I wonder? The real life of Marx would not do for the movies: he was an incorrigible borrower, an indifferent father and lived his whole life in the extreme of bourgeois dullness. What is there here to engage the talents of a handsome star, or even Paul Muni, whose special line is playing great men?. . . But I suppose it will emerge that Karl's father was a miner, greatly oppressed, and that Karl's mother is the hired help in the mine-owner's palatial residence, and the mine-owner's son lusts after Karl's sister and wants to put her in a Boudoir, instead of qualifying as a teacher and organising the sweated teachers. In the culminating scene Karl will lead The Workers to burn down the mine-owner's mansion, as Bernard Shaw (played by Shirley Temple) stands on one side, urging caution, but wittily. In the last sequence Karl, now entirely overgrown with whiskers, will be seen in the British Museum, writing *Das Kapital*. The whole thing will be in Technicolor, inclining toward the redder shades of the spectrum. Oh, and at some point Karl must express fawning admiration for George Washington, or the film will never export.

TUESDAY

In the paper I see a picture of Shirley Temple buying her trousseau. Deary me, how time flies! Surely 'twas but yesterday that this lovable mite held all the world in chubby thrall. Even the Dionne Quintuplets, five to one, could not get the better of her in the great battle of publicity. And now she is a grown woman, trying to find a few pairs of step-ins with real elastic in the top . . . A Hollywood tycoon once explained to me that the whole of Shirley's grip on the film public began and ended with the way in which she said 'Oh my goodness!' This line appeared in all her films, and where the ordinary moppet would say 'Oh my goodness!' with perfect, if nasal, articulation, Shirley said 'Oh my gooness!' This bit of delicious juvenility reduced strong men to doting tears, and caused fond mothers to smack their children whenever the aforesaid young dared to sound the 'd' in 'goodness'. When Shirley said 'Oh my gooness!' and flashed dimples like Neon signs, she aroused the essential jellyfish in us all; we were at her mercy, even when she sang 'The Good Ship Lollipop' and clumped laboriously through a tap-dance. But Ichabod, Ichabod, the gooness is departed from Shirley.

* * *

KING OF THE BEASTS AT LUNCH

To an excellent film about Africa, with some of the best pictures of wild animals that I have ever seen. I was particularly interested in close-ups of a group of lions eating a zebra. Now I was brought up on picture books which insisted that the lion was a noble beast, that killed its prey with a single violent blow, and then stood upon the fallen carcass for a time, roaring; when it had thus worked up an appetite it tore off a leg, devoured it in lonely splendour and rushed off for further spectacular mischief. But here was a picture of five or six lions, all pushing and shoving like human beings, gobbling the guts of the zebra; there was no roaring, no defiance and no loneliness. One lion lay on its side near the feast, gorged and apparently slightly drunk. Vultures stood nearby, like waiters hoping to clear away the dirty plates. The lions ate messily, dropping bits and slobbering on their fronts. It seems that life in the jungle is rather more like life at a short-order lunch wagon than I had supposed. I do not know whether to be pleased or not.

ORGY

To a movie called *Faust and the Devil*, made in Italy, which I enjoyed greatly, and particularly an Orgy scene, where Faust made genteel and ineffective plays for several girls in filmy frocks. The Devil, meanwhile, sat at a table loaded with goodies, but ate nothing save a few grapes. Watching his weight, I suppose. Have not seen an Orgy in a movie since the days of the silent film; they often had Orgies, and they always took the form of a light meal, eaten in the company of jolly girls in peek-a-boo nighties. I have never been at an Orgy, though I suppose my garbage this morning filled the neighbourhood with dark suspicion.

PRIMEVAL FILM

To the movies, to see Charlie Chaplin and Marie Dressler in *Tilly's Punctured Romance*, which they made in 1913. In my younger days I was an ardent follower of Charlie, but as I watched this relic from the Old Red Sandstone Period of the cinematic art, I realised that time had bathed the humour of another day in a golden but untruthful light. It was the most restless film I have seen in years. Nobody stood up if he could possibly fall down. Nobody fell down without at once leaping to his feet in order to fall down again. Nobody entered a door without slapping somebody else in the face with it. Food was never eaten, it existed only to be thrown. Liquid was not taken into the mouth in order to be swallowed, but only that it might be squirted into somebody else's face. The usual method of attracting a lady's attention was to kick her; she invariably responded with a blow. The life of man in the comedies of the silent films was solitary, poor, nasty, brutish and short. And viewed from this distance it does not appear to have been especially funny, at that.

FASHION IN KISSES

To the movies, and as I sat through a double feature I was interested to observe that the audible kiss has come back into fashion. When the first talking pictures appeared, kisses were all of the silent variety; it was just then that silent plumbing made its first appearance, and there may have been some connection. But now the shadow-folk of Hollywood kiss with a noise like a cow pulling its foot out of deep mud. In my younger days there were two types of kiss: the Romantic Kiss was for private use and was as silent as the grave; the Courtesy Kiss, bestowed upon aunts, cousins and the like was noisy and wet, generally removing two square inches of mauve face powder. A visiting aunt, having been welcomed by two or three nephews, needed substantial repairs. The Romantic Kiss also involved closing the eyes, to indicate extreme depth of feeling, though it often occurred to me that if one cannot see what one is kissing, a pretty girl and a kid glove of good quality are completely indistinguishable.

MARTIN AMIS

Career Move

When Alistair finished his new screenplay, 'Offensive from Quasar 13', he submitted it to the *LM*, and waited. Over the past year, he had had more than a dozen screenplays rejected by the *Little Magazine*. On the other hand, his most recent submission, a batch of five, had been returned not with the standard rejection slip but with a handwritten note from the screenplay editor, Hugh Sixsmith. The note said:

> I was really rather taken with two or three of these, and seriously tempted by 'Hotwire', which I thought close to being fully achieved. Do please go on sending me your stuff.

Hugh Sixsmith was himself a screenplay writer of considerable, though uncertain, reputation. His note of encouragement *was* encouraging. It made Alistair brave.

Boldly he prepared 'Offensive from Quasar 13' for submission. He justified the pages of the typescript with fondly lingering fingertips. Alistair did not address the envelope to the Screenplay Editor. No. He addressed it to Mr Hugh Sixsmith. Nor, for once, did he enclose his curriculum vitae, which he now contemplated with some discomfort. It told, in a pitiless staccato, of the screenplays he had published in various laptop broadsheets and comically obscure pamphlets; it even told of screenplays published in his university magazine. The truly disgraceful bit came at the end, where it said 'Rights Offered: First British Serial *only*'.

Alistair spent a long time on the covering note to Sixsmith – almost as long as he had spent on 'Offensive from Quasar 13'. The note got shorter and shorter the more he worked on it. At last he was satisfied. There in the dawn he grasped the envelope and ran his tongue across its darkly luminous cuff.

That Friday, on his way to work, and suddenly feeling completely hopeless, Alistair surrendered his parcel to the sub post office in Calchalk Street, off the Euston Road. Deliberately – very deliberately – he had enclosed no stamped, addressed envelope. The accompanying letter, in its entirety, read as follows: 'Any use? If not – w.p.b.'

'W.p.b.' stood, of course, for 'wastepaper basket' – a receptacle that loomed forbiddingly large in the life of a practising screenplay writer. With a hand on his brow, Alistair sidled his way out of there – past the birthday cards, the tensed pensioners, the envelopes, and the balls of string.

When Luke finished the new poem – entitled, simply, 'Sonnet' – he Xeroxed the printout and faxed it to his agent. Ninety minutes later he returned from the gym downstairs and prepared his special fruit juice while the answering machine told him, among many other things, to get back to Mike. Reaching for another lime, Luke touched the preselect for Talent International.

'Ah. Luke,' said Mike. 'It's moving. We've already had a response.'

'Yeah, how come? It's four in the morning where he is.'

'No, it's eight in the evening where he is. He's in Australia. Developing a poem with Peter Barry.'

Luke didn't want to hear about Peter Barry. He bent, and tugged off his tank top. Walls and windows maintained a respectful distance – the room was a broad seam of sun haze and river light. Luke sipped his juice: its extreme astringency caused him to lift both elbows and give a single, embittered nod. He said, 'What did he think?'

'Joe? He did backflips. It's "Tell Luke I'm blown away by the new poem. I just know that 'Sonnet' is really going to happen."'

Luke took this coolly. He wasn't at all old but he had been in poetry long enough to take these things coolly. He turned. Suki, who had been shopping, was now letting herself into the apartment, not without difficulty. She was indeed cruelly encumbered. Luke said, 'You haven't talked numbers yet. I mean like a ballpark figure.'

Mike said, 'We understand each other. Joe knows about Monad's interest. And Tim at TCT.'

'Good,' said Luke. Suki was wandering slenderly towards him, shedding various purchases as she approached – creels and caskets, shining satchels.

'They'll want you to go out there at least twice,' said Mike. 'Initially to discuss . . . They can't get over it that you don't live there.'

Luke could tell that Suki had spent much more than she intended. He could tell by the quality of patience in her sigh as she began to lick the sweat from his shoulder blades. He said, 'Come on, Mike. They know I hate all that LA crap.'

On his way to work that Monday, Alistair sat slumped in his bus seat, limp with ambition and neglect. One fantasy was proving especially obdurate: as he entered his office, the telephone on his desk would actually be *bouncing* on its console – Hugh Sixsmith, from the *Little Magazine*, his voice urgent but grave, with the news that he was going to rush Alistair's screenplay into the very next issue. (To be frank, Alistair had had the same fantasy the previous Friday, at which time, presumably, 'Offensive from Quasar 13' was still being booted round the floor of the sub post office.) His girlfriend, Hazel, had come down from Leeds for the weekend. They were so small, he and Hazel, that they could share his single bed quite comfortably – could sprawl and stretch without constraint. On the Saturday evening, they attended a screenplay reading at a bookshop on Camden High Street. Alistair hoped to impress Hazel with his growing ease in this milieu (and managed to exchange wary leers with a few shambling, half-familiar figures – fellow screenplay writers, seekers, knowers). But these days Hazel seemed sufficiently impressed by him anyway, whatever he did. Alistair lay there the next morning (her turn to make tea), wondering about this business of being impressed. Hazel had impressed him mightily, seven years ago, in bed: by not getting out of it when he got into it. The office telephone rang many times that Monday, but none of the callers had anything to say about 'Offensive from Quasar 13'. Alistair sold advertising space for an agricultural newsletter, so his callers wanted to talk about creosote admixes and offal reprocessors.

He heard nothing for four months. This would normally have been a fairly good sign. It meant, or it might mean, that your screenplay was receiving serious, even agonised, consideration. It was better than having your screenplay flopping back on the mat by return post. On the other hand, Hugh Sixsmith might have reponded to the spirit and the letter of Alistair's accompanying note and dropped 'Offensive from Quasar 13' into his wastepaper basket within minutes of its arrival: four months ago. Rereading his fading carbon of the screenplay, Alistair now cursed his own (highly calibrated) insouciance. He shouldn't have said, 'Any use? If not – w.p.b.' He should have said, 'Any use? If not – s.a.e.'! Every morning he went down the three flights of stairs – the mail was there to be shuffled and dealt. And every fourth Friday, or thereabouts, he still wrenched open his *LM*, in case Sixsmith had run the screenplay without letting him know. As a surprise.

'Dear Mr Sixsmith,' thought Alistair as he rode the train to Leeds. 'I am thinking of placing the screenplay I sent you elsewhere. I trust that . . . I thought it only fair to . . .' Alistair retracted his feet to accommodate another passenger. 'My dear Mr Sixsmith: In response to an enquiry from . . . In response to a most generous enquiry, I am putting together a selection of my screenplays for . . .' Alistair tipped his head back and stared at the smeared window. 'For Mudlark Books. It seems that the Ostler Press is also interested. This involves me in some paper-work, which, however tedious . . . For the record . . . Matters would be considerably eased . . . Of course if you . . .'

Luke sat on a Bauhaus love seat in Club World at Heathrow, drinking Evian and availing himself of a complimentary fax machine – clearing up the initial paperwork on the poem with Mike.

Everyone in Club World looked hushed and grateful to be there, but not Luke, who looked exhaustively displeased. He was flying first class to LAX, where he would be met by a uniformed chauffeur who would convey him by limousine or courtesy car to the Pinnacle Trumont on the Avenue of the

Stars. First class was no big thing. In poetry, first class was something you didn't need to think about. It wasn't discussed. It was statutory.

Luke was tense: under pressure. A lot – maybe too much – was riding on 'Sonnet'. If 'Sonnet' didn't happen, he would soon be able to afford neither his apartment nor his girlfriend. He would recover from Suki before very long. But he would never recover from not being able to afford her, or his apartment. If you wanted the truth, his deal on 'Sonnet' was not that great. Luke was furious with Mike except about the new merchandising clause (potential accessories on the poem – like toys or T-shirts) and the improved cut he got on tertiaries and sequels. Then there was Joe.

Joe calls, and he's like 'We really think "Sonnet" 's going to work, Luke. Jeff thinks so, too. Jeff's just come in. Jeff? It's Luke. Do you want to say something to him? Luke. Luke, Jeff's coming over. He wants to say something about "Sonnet".'

'Luke?' said Jeff. 'Jeff. Luke? You're a very talented writer. It's great to be working on "Sonnet" with you. Here's Joe.'

'That was Jeff,' said Joe. 'He's crazy about "Sonnet".'

'So what are we going to be talking about?' said Luke. 'Roughly.'

'On "Sonnet"? Well, the only thing we have a problem on "Sonnet" with, Luke, so far as I can see, anyway, and I know Jeff agrees with me on this – right, Jeff? – and so does Jim, incidentally, Luke,' said Joe, 'is the form.'

Luke hesitated. Then he said, 'You mean the form "Sonnet" 's written in.'

'Yes, that's right, Luke. The sonnet form.'

Luke waited for the last last call and was then guided, with much unreturned civility, into the plane's nose.

'Dear Mr Sixsmith,' wrote Alistair,

Going through my files the other day, I vaguely remembered sending you a little effort called 'Offensive from Quasar 13' – just over seven months ago, it must have been. Am I right in assuming that you have no use for it? I might bother you with another one (or two!) that I have completed since then.

I hope you are well. Thank you so much for your encouragement in the past.

   Need I say how much I admire your own work? The
austerity, the depth. When, may I ask, can we expect another
'slim vol.'?

He sadly posted this letter on a wet Sunday afternoon in Leeds.
He hoped that the postmark might testify to his mobility and
grit.

   Yet, really, he felt much steadier now. There had been a
recent period of about five weeks during which, Alistair came
to realise, he had gone clinically insane. That letter to Sixsmith
was but one of the many dozens he had penned. He had also
taken to haunting the Holborn offices of the *Little Magazine*: for
hours he sat crouched in the coffee bars and sandwich nooks
opposite, with the unsettled intention of springing out at
Sixsmith – if he ever saw him, which he never did. Alistair
began to wonder whether Sixsmith actually existed. Was he,
perhaps, an actor, a ghost, a shrewd fiction? Alistair telephoned
the *LM* from selected phone booths. Various people answered,
and no one knew where anyone was, and only three or four
times was Alistair successfully connected to the apparently
permanent coughing fit that crackled away at the other end of
Sixsmith's extension. Then he hung up. He couldn't sleep, or he
thought he couldn't, for Hazel said that all night long he
whimpered and gnashed.

   Alistair waited for nearly two months. Then he sent in three
more screenplays. One was about a Machine hit man who
emerges from early retirement when his wife is slain by a serial
murderer. Another dealt with the infiltration by the three
Gorgons of an escort agency in present-day New York. The third
was a heavy-metal musical set on the Isle of Skye. He enclosed
a stamped, addressed envelope the size of a small knapsack.

   Winter was unusually mild.

'May I get you something to drink before your meal? A
cappuccino? A mineral water? A glass of sauvignon blanc?'

   'Double decaf espresso,' said Luke. 'Thanks.'

   'You're more than welcome.'

'Hey,' said Luke when everyone had ordered. 'I'm not just welcome any more. I'm more than welcome.'

The others smiled patiently. Such remarks were the downside of the classy fact that Luke, despite his appearance and his accent, was English. There they all sat on the terrace at Bubo's: Joe, Jeff, Jim.

Luke said, 'How did "Eclogue by a Five-Barred Gate" do?'

Joe said, 'Domestically?' He looked at Jim, at Jeff. 'Like — *fifteen*?'

Luke said, 'And worldwide?'

'It isn't *going* worldwide.'

'How about "Black Rook in Rainy Weather"?' asked Luke.

Joe shook his head. 'It didn't even do what "Sheep in Fog" did.'

'It's all remakes,' said Jim. 'Period shit.'

'How about "Bog Oak"?'

'"Bog Oak"? Ooh, maybe twenty-five?'

Luke said sourly, 'I hear nice things about "The Old Botanical Gardens".'

They talked about other Christmas flops and bombs, delaying for as long as they could any mention of TCT's ''Tis he whose yester-evening's high disdain', which had cost practically nothing to make and had already done a hundred and twenty million in its first three weeks.

'What happened?' Luke eventually asked. 'Jesus, what was the publicity budget?'

'On "'Tis"?' said Joe. 'Nothing. Two, three.'

They all shook their heads. Jim was philosophical. 'That's poetry,' he said.

'There aren't any other sonnets being made, are there?' said Luke.

Jeff said, 'Binary is in post-production with a sonnet. "Composed at — Castle". *More* period shit.'

Their soups and salads arrived. Luke thought that it was probably a mistake, at this stage, to go on about sonnets. After a while he said, 'How did "For Sophonisba Anguisciola" do?'

Joe said, '"For Sophonisba Anguisciola"? Don't talk to me about "For Sophonisba Anguisciola".'

*

It was late at night and Alistair was in his room working on a screenplay about a high-I.Q. homeless black man who is transformed into a white female junk-bond dealer by a South Moluccan terrorist witch doctor. Suddenly he shoved this aside with a groan, snatched up a clean sheet of paper, and wrote:

Dear Mr Sixsmith,
It is now well over a year since I sent you 'Offensive from Quasar 13'. Not content with that dereliction, you have allowed five months to pass without responding to three more recent submissions. A prompt reply I would have deemed common decency, you being a fellow-screenplay writer, though I must say I have never cared for your work, finding it, at once, both florid and superficial. (I read Matthew Sura's piece last month and I thought he got you *bang to rights*.) Please return the more recent screenplays, namely 'Decimator', 'Medusa Takes Manhattan' and 'Valley of the Stratocasters', immediately.

He signed it and sealed it. He stalked out and posted it. On his return he haughtily threw off his drenched clothes. The single bed felt enormous, like an orgiast's fourposter. He curled up tight and slept better than he had done all year.

So it was a quietly defiant Alistair who the next morning came plodding down the stairs and glanced at the splayed mail on the shelf as he headed for the door. He recognised the envelope as a lover would. He bent low as he opened it.

Do please forgive this very tardy reply. Profound apologies. But allow me to move straight on to a verdict on your work. I won't bore you with all my personal and professional distractions.

Bore me? thought Alistair, as his hand sought his heart.

I think I can at once give the assurance that your screenplays are unusually promising. No: that promise has already been honoured. They have both feeling and burnish.
I will content myself, for now, by taking 'Offensive from Quasar 13'. (Allow me to muse a little longer on 'Decimator'.)

I have one or two very minor emendations to suggest. Why not telephone me here to arrange a chat?

Thank you for your generous remarks about my own work. Increasingly I find that this kind of exchange – this candour, this reciprocity – is one of the things that keep me trundling along. Your words helped sustain my defences in the aftermath of Matthew Sura's vicious and slovenly attack, from which, I fear, I am still rather reeling. Take excellent care.

'Go with the lyric,' said Jim.

'Or how about a ballad?' said Jeff.

Jack was swayable. 'Ballads are big,' he allowed.

It seemed to Luke, towards the end of the second day, that he was winning the sonnet battle. The clue lay in the flavour of Joe's taciturnity: torpid but unmorose.

'Let's face it,' said Jeff. 'Sonnets are essentially hieratic. They're strictly period. They answer to a formalised consciousness. Today, we're talking consciousnesses that are in *search* of form.'

'Plus,' said Jack, 'the lyric has always been the natural medium for the untrammelled expression of feeling.'

'Yeah,' said Jeff. 'With the sonnet you're stuck in this thesis-antithesis-synthesis routine.'

Joan said, 'I mean what are we doing here? Reflecting the world or illuminating it?'

It was time for Joe to speak. 'Please,' he said. 'Are we forgetting that "'Tis" was a sonnet, before the rewrites? Were we on coke when we said, in the summer, that we were going to go for the *sonnet*?'

The answer to Joe's last question, incidentally, was yes; but Luke looked carefully round the room. The Chinese lunch they'd had the secretary phone out for lay on the coffee table like a child's experiments with putty and paint and designer ooze. It was four o'clock and Luke wanted to get away soon. To swim and lie in the sun. To make himself especially lean and bronzed for his meeting with the young actress Henna Mickiewicz. He faked a yawn.

'Luke's lagged,' said Joe. 'Tomorrow we'll talk some more, but I'm pretty sure I'm recommitted to the sonnet.'

*

'Sorry,' said Alistair. 'Me yet again. Sorry.'

'Oh yes,' said the woman's voice. 'He *was* here a minute ago
. . . No, he's there. He's there. Just a second.'

Alistair jerked the receiver away from his ear and stared at it.
He started listening again. It seemed as if the phone itself were
in paroxysm, all squawk and splat like a cabby's radio. Then the
fit passed, or paused, and a voice said tightly but proudly, 'Hugh
Sixsmith?'

It took Alistair a little while to explain who he was. Sixsmith
sounded surprised but, on the whole, rather intrigued to hear
from him. They moved on smoothly enough to arrange a
meeting (after work, the following Monday), before Alistair
contrived to put in: 'Mr Sixsmith, there's just one thing. This is
very embarrassing, but last night I got into a bit of a state about
not hearing from you for so long and I'm afraid I sent you a
completely mad letter which I . . .' Alistair waited. 'Oh, you
know how it is. For these screenplays, you know, you reach
into yourself, and then time goes by and . . .'

'My dear boy, don't say another word. I'll ignore it. I'll throw
it away. After a line or two I shall simply avert my unpained
eye,' said Sixsmith, and started coughing again.

Hazel did not come down to London for the weekend. Alistair
did not go up to Leeds for the weekend. He spent the time
thinking about that place in Earl's Court Square where screenplay writers read from their screenplays and drank biting
Spanish red wine and got stared at by tousled girls who wore
thick overcoats and no make-up and blinked incessantly or not
at all.

Luke parked his Chevrolet Celebrity on the fifth floor of the
studio car park and rode down in the elevator with two minor
executives in tracksuits who were discussing the latest records
broken by ''Tis he whose yester-evening's high disdain'. He put
on his dark glasses as he crossed the other car park, the one
reserved for major executives. Each bay had a name on it. It
reassured Luke to see Joe's name there, partly obscured by his
Range Rover. Poets, of course, seldom had that kind of clout. Or
any clout at all. He was glad that Henna Mickiewicz didn't seem
to realise this.

Joe's office: Jim, Jack, Joan, but no Jeff. Two new guys were there. Luke was introduced to the two new guys. Ron said he spoke for Don when he told Luke that he was a great admirer of his material. Huddled over the coffee percolator with Joe, Luke asked after Jeff, and Joe said, 'Jeff's off the poem,' and Luke just nodded.

They settled in their low armchairs.

Luke said, 'What's "A Welshman to Any Tourist" doing?'

Don said, 'It's doing good but not great.'

Ron said, 'It won't do what "The Gap in the Hedge" did.'

Jim said, 'What did "Hedge" do?'

They talked about what 'Hedge' did. Then Joe said, 'OK. We're going with the sonnet. Now. Don has a problem with the octet's first quatrain, Ron has a problem with the second quatrain, Jack and Jim have a problem with the first quatrain of the sestet, and I think we *all* have a problem with the final couplet.'

Alistair presented himself at the offices of the *LM* in an unblinking trance of punctuality. He had been in the area for hours, and had spent about fifteen quid on teas and coffees. There wasn't much welcome to overstay in the various snack parlours where he lingered (and where he moreover imagined himself unfavourably recollected from his previous *LM* vigils), holding with both hands the creaky foam container, and watching the light pour past the office windows.

As Big Ben struck two, Alistair mounted the stairs. He took a breath so deep that he almost fell over backward – and then knocked. An elderly office boy wordlessly showed him into a narrow, rubbish-heaped office that contained, with difficulty, seven people. At first Alistair took them for other screenplay writers and wedged himself behind the door, at the back of the queue. But they didn't look like screenplay writers. Not much was said over the next four hours, and the identities of Sixsmith's supplicants emerged only partially and piecemeal. One or two, like his solicitor and his second wife's psychiatrist, took their leave after no more than ninety minutes. Others, like the VAT man and the probation officer, stayed almost as long as Alistair. But by six-forty-five he was alone.

He approached the impossible haystack of Sixsmith's desk.
Very hurriedly, he started searching through the unopened
mail. It was in Alistair's mind that he might locate and intercept
his own letter. But all the envelopes, of which there were a
great many, proved to be brown, windowed, and registered.
Turning to leave, he saw a Jiffy bag of formidable bulk addressed
to himself in Sixsmith's tremulous hand. There seemed no
reason not to take it. The old office boy, Alistair soon saw, was
curled up in a sleeping bag under a worktable in the outer
room.

On the street he unseamed his package in a ferment of grey
fluff. It contained two of his screenplays, 'Valley of the Stratocasters' and, confusingly, 'Decimator'. There was also a note:

I have been called away, as they say. Personal ups and downs.
I shall ring you this week and we'll have – what? Lunch?

Enclosed, too, was Alistair's aggrieved letter – unopened. He
moved on. The traffic, human and mechanical, lurched past his
quickened face. He felt his eyes widen to an obvious and solving
truth: Hugh Sixsmith was a screenplay writer. He understood.

After an inconclusive day spent discussing the caesura of 'Sonnet''s opening line, Luke and his colleagues went for cocktails
at Strabismus. They were given the big round table near the
piano.

Jane said, 'TCT is doing a sequel to "'Tis".'

Joan said, 'Actually it's a prequel.'

'Title?' said Joe.

'Undecided. At TCT they're calling it "'Twas".'

'My son,' said Joe thoughtfully, after the waiter had delivered
their drinks, 'called me an asshole this morning. For the first
time.'

'That's incredible,' said Bo. '*My* son called me an asshole this
morning. For the first time.'

'So?' said Mo.

Joe said, 'He's six years old, for Christ's sake.'

Phil said, 'My son called me an asshole when he was five.'

'My son hasn't called me an asshole yet,' said Jim. 'And he's
nine.'

Luke sipped his Bloody Mary. Its hue and texture made him

wonder whether he could risk blowing his nose without making yet another visit to the bathroom. He hadn't called Suki for three days. Things were getting compellingly out of hand with Henna Mickiewicz. He hadn't actually promised her a part in the poem, not on paper. Henna was great, except you kept thinking she was going to suddenly sue you anyway.

Mo was saying that each child progresses at his own rate, and that later lulls regularly offset the apparent advances of the early years.

Mo said, 'My son's three. And he calls me an asshole all the time.'

Everybody looked suitably impressed.

The trees were in leaf, and the rumps of the tourist buses were thick and fat in the traffic, and all the farmers wanted fertiliser admixes rather than storehouse insulation when Sixsmith finally made his call. In the interim, Alistair had convinced himself of the following: before returning his aggrieved letter, Sixsmith had *steamed it open and then resealed it*. During this period, also, Alistair had grimly got engaged to Hazel. But the call came.

He was pretty sure he had come to the right restaurant. Except that it wasn't a restaurant, not quite. The place took no bookings, and knew of no Mr Sixsmith, and was serving many midday breakfasts to swearing persons whose eyes bulged over mugs of flesh-coloured tea. On the other hand, there was alcohol. All kinds of people were drinking it. Fine, thought Alistair. Fine. What better place, really, for a couple of screen-play writers to . . .

'Alistair?'

Confidently, Sixsmith bent his long body into the booth. As he settled, he looked well pleased with the manoeuvre. He contemplated Alistair with peculiar neutrality, but there was then something boyish, something consciously remiss, in the face he turned to the waiter. As Sixsmith ordered a gin-and-tonic, and as he amusingly expatiated on his weakness for prawn cocktails, Alistair found himself wryly but powerfully drawn to this man, to this rumpled screenplay writer with his dreamy gaze, the curious elisions of his somewhat slurred voice,

and the great dents and bone shadows of his face, all the faulty
fontanels of vocational care. He knew how old Sixsmith was.
But maybe time moved strangely for screenplay writers, whose
flames burnt so bright . . .

'And as for my fellow-artisan in the scrivener's trade, Alistair.
What will *you* have?'

At once Sixsmith showed himself to be a person of some
candour. Or it might have been that he saw in the younger
screenplay writer someone before whom all false reticence could
be cast aside. Sixsmith's estranged second wife, it emerged,
herself the daughter of two alcoholics, was an alcoholic. Her
current lover (ah, how these lovers came and went!) was an
alcoholic. To complicate matters, Sixsmith explained as he
rattled his glass at the waiter, his daughter, the product of his
first marriage, was an alcoholic. How did Sixsmith keep going?
Despite his years, he had, thank God, found love, in the arms of
a woman young enough (and, by the sound of it, alcoholic
enough) to be his daughter. Their prawn cocktails arrived,
together with a carafe of hearty red wine. Sixsmith lit a cigarette
and held up his palm towards Alistair for the duration of a
coughing fit that turned every head in the room. Then, for a
moment, understandably disoriented, he stared at Alistair as if
uncertain of his intentions, or even his identity. But their bond
quickly re-established itself. Soon they were talking away like
hardened equals – of Trumbo, of Chayevsky, of Towne, of
Eszterhas.

Around two-thirty, when, after several attempts, the waiter
succeeded in removing Sixsmith's untouched prawn cocktail,
and now prepared to serve them their braised chops with a third
carafe, the two men were arguing loudly about early Puzo.

Joe yawned and shrugged and said languidly, 'You know
something? I was never that crazy about the Petrarchan rhyme
scheme anyway.'

Jan said, '"Composed at — Castle" is ABBA ABBA.'

Jen said, 'So was "'Tis". Right up until the final polish.'

Jon said, 'Here's some news. They say "Composed at —
Castle" is in turnaround.'

'You're not serious,' said Bo. 'It's released this month. I heard they were getting great preview reaction.'

Joe looked doubtful. ' "'Tis" has made the suits kind of antsy about sonnets. They figure lightning can't strike twice.'

'ABBA ABBA,' said Bo with distate.

'Or,' said Joe. '*Or . . . or* we go unrhymed.'

'*Un*rhymed?' said Phil.

'We go blank,' said Joe.

There was a silence. Bill looked at Gil, who looked at Will.

'What do you think, Luke?' said Jim. 'You're the poet.'

Luke had never felt very protective about 'Sonnet'. Even its original version he had regarded as no more than a bargaining chip. Nowadays he rewrote 'Sonnet' every night at the Pinnacle Trumont before Henna arrived and they called room service. 'Blank,' said Luke. 'Blank. I don't know, Joe. I could go ABAB ABAB or even ABAB CDCD. Christ, I'd go AABB if I didn't think it'd tank the final couplet. But blank. I never thought I'd go *blank*.'

'Well, it needs something,' said Joe.

'Maybe it's the pentameter,' said Luke. 'Maybe it's the iamb. Hey, here's one from left field. How about syllabics?'

At five-forty-five Hugh Sixsmith ordered a gin-and-tonic and said, 'We've talked. We've broken bread. Wine. Truth. Screen-play writing. I want to talk about your work, Alistair. Yes, I do. I want to talk about "Offensive from Quasar 13".'

Alistair blushed.

'It's not often that . . . But one always knows. That sense of pregnant arrest. Of felt life in its full . . . Thank you, Alistair. Thank you. I have to say that it rather reminded me of my own early work.'

Alistair nodded.

Having talked for quite some time about his own maturation as a screenplay writer, Sixsmith said, 'Now. Just tell me to shut up any time you like. And I'm going to print it anyway. But I want to make one *tiny* suggestion about "Offensive from Quasar 13".'

Alistair waved a hand in the air.

'Now,' said Sixsmith. He broke off and ordered a prawn

cocktail. The waiter looked at him defeatedly. 'Now,' said Sixsmith. 'When Brad escapes from the Nebulan experiment lab and sets off with Cord and Tara to immobilise the directed-energy scythe on the Xerxian attack ship – where's Chelsi?'

Alistair frowned.

'Where's Chelsi? She's still in the lab with the Nebulans. On the point of being injected with a Phobian viper venom, moreover. What of the happy ending? What of Brad's heroic centrality? What of his avowed love for Chelsi? Or am I just being a bore?'

The secretary, Victoria, stuck her head into the room and said, 'He's coming down.'

Luke listened to the sound of twenty-three pairs of legs uncrossing and recrossing. Meanwhile he readied himself for a sixteen-tooth smile. He glanced at Joe, who said, 'He's fine. He's just coming down to say hi.'

And down he came: Jake Endo, exquisitely Westernised and gorgeously tricked out and perhaps thirty-five. Of the luxury items that pargetted his slender form, none was as breathtaking as his hair, with its layers of pampered light.

Jake Endo shook Luke's hand and said, 'It's a great pleasure to meet you. I haven't read the basic material on the poem, but I'm familiar with the background.'

Luke surmised that Jake Endo had had his voice fixed. He could do the bits of the words that Japanese people were supposed to find difficult.

'I understand it's a love poem,' he continued. 'Addressed to your girlfriend. Is she here with you in LA?'

'No. She's in London.' Luke found he was staring at Jake Endo's sandals, wondering how much they could possibly have cost.

A silence began its crescendo. This silence had long been intolerable when Jim broke it, saying to Jake Endo, 'Oh, how did "Lines Left Upon a Seat in a Yew-Tree, Which Stands Near the Lake of Easthwaite, on a Desolate Part of the Shore, Commanding a Beautiful Prospect" do?'

' "Lines"?' said Jake Endo. 'Rather well.'

'I was thinking about "Composed at — Castle",' said Jim weakly.

The silence began again. As it neared its climax Joe was suddenly reminded of all this energy he was supposed to have. He got to his feet saying, 'Jake? I guess we're nearing our tiredness peak. You've caught us at kind of a low point. We can't agree on the first line. First line? We can't see our way to the end of the first *foot*.'

Jake Endo was undismayed. 'There always are these low points. I'm sure you'll get there, with so much talent in the room. Upstairs we're very confident. We think it's going to be a big summer poem.'

'No, we're very confident, too,' said Joe. 'There's a lot of belief here. A lot of belief. We're behind "Sonnet" all the way.'

'Sonnet?' said Jake Endo.

'Yeah, sonnet. "Sonnet".'

'"Sonnet"?' said Jake Endo.

'It's a sonnet. It's called "Sonnet".'

In waves the West fell away from Jake Endo's face. After a few seconds he looked like a dark-age warlord in mid-campaign, taking a glazed breather before moving on to the women and the children.

'Nobody told me,' he said as he went toward the telephone, 'about any *sonnet*.'

The place was closing. Its tea trade and its after-office trade had come and gone. Outside, the streets glimmered morbidly. Members of the staff were donning macs and overcoats. An important light went out. A fridge door slammed.

'Hardly the most resounding felicity, is it?' said Sixsmith.

Absent or unavailable for over an hour, the gift of speech had been restored to Alistair – speech, that prince of all the faculties. 'Or what if . . .' he said. 'What if Chelsi just leaves the experiment lab earlier?'

'Not hugely dramatic,' said Sixsmith. He ordered a carafe of wine and enquired as to the whereabouts of his braised chop.

'Or what if she just gets wounded? During the escape. In the leg.'

'So long as one could avoid the wretched cliché: girl impeded, hero dangerously tarrying. Also, she's supernumerary to the raid on the Xerxian attack ship. We really want her out of the way for that.'

Alistair said, 'Then let's kill her.'

'Very well. Slight pall over the happy ending. No, no.'

A waiter stood over them, sadly staring at the bill in its saucer.

'All right,' said Sixsmith. 'Chelsi gets wounded. Quite badly. In the arm. *Now* what does Brad do with her?'

'Drops her off at the hospital.'

'Mm. Rather hollow modulation.'

The waiter was joined by another waiter, equally stoic; their faces were grained by evening shadow. Now Sixsmith was gently frisking himself with a deepening frown.

'What if,' said Alistair, 'what if there's somebody passing who can take her to the hospital?'

'Possibly,' said Sixsmith, who was half standing, with one hand awkwardly dipped into his inside pocket.

'Or what if,' said Alistair, 'or what if Brad just gives her *directions* to the hospital?'

Back in London the next day, Luke met with Mike to straighten this shit out. Actually it looked OK. Mike called Mal at Monad, who had a thing about Tim at TCT. As a potential finesse on Mal, Mike also called Bob at Binary with a view to repossessing the option on 'Sonnet', plus development money at rolling compound, and redeveloping it somewhere else entirely – say, at Red Giant, where Rodge was known to be very interested. 'They'll want you to go out there,' said Mike. 'To kick it around.'

'I can't believe Joe,' said Luke. 'I can't believe I knocked myself out for that flake.'

'Happens. Joe forgot about Jake Endo and sonnets. Endo's first big poem was a sonnet. Before your time. "Bright star, would I were steadfast as thou art". It opened for like one day. It practically bankrupted Japan.'

'I feel used, Mike. My sense of trust. I've got to get wised up around here.'

'A lot will depend on how "Composed at — Castle" does and what the feeling is on the "'Tis" prequel.'

'I'm going to go away with Suki for a while. Do you know

anywhere where there aren't any shops? Jesus, I need a holiday. Mike, this is all bullshit. You know what I *really* want to do, don't you?'

'Of course I do.'

Luke looked at Mike until he said, 'You want to direct.'

When Alistair had convalesced from the lunch, he revised 'Offensive from Quasar 13' in rough accordance with Sixsmith's suggestions. He solved the Chelsi problem by having her noisily eaten by a Stygian panther in the lab menagerie. The charge of gratuitousness was, in Alistair's view, safely anticipated by Brad's valediction to her remains, in which sanguinary revenge on the Nebulans was both prefigured and legitimised. He also took out the bit where Brad declared his love for Chelsi, and put in a bit where Brad declared his love for Tara.

He sent in the new pages, which three months later Sixsmith acknowledged and applauded in a hand quite incompatible with that of his earlier communications. Nor did he reimburse Alistair for the lunch. His wallet, he had explained, had been emptied that morning -- by which alcoholic, Sixsmith never established. Alistair kept the bill as a memento. This startling document showed that during the course of the meal Sixsmith had smoked, or at any rate bought, nearly a carton of cigarettes.

Three months later he was sent a proof of 'Offensive from Quasar 13'. Three months after that, the screenplay appeared in the *LM*. Three months after that, Alistair received a cheque for £12.50, which bounced.

Curiously, although the proof had incorporated Alistair's corrections, the published version reverted to the typescript, in which Brad escaped from the Nebulan lab seemingly without concern for a Chelsi last glimpsed on an operating table with a syringe full of Phobian viper venom being eased into her neck. Later that month, Alistair went along to a reading at the Screenplay Society in Earl's Court. There he got talking to a gaunt girl in an ash-stained black smock who claimed to have read his screenplay and who, over glasses of red wine and, later, in the terrible pub, told him he was a weakling and a hypocrite with no notion of the ways of men and women. Alistair had not been a published screenplay writer long enough to respond to, or even recognise, this graphic proposition (though he did keep the telephone number she threw at his feet). It is anyway doubtful whether he would have dared to take things further. He was marrying Hazel the following weekend.

In the new year he sent Sixsmith a series – one might almost say a sequence – of screenplays on group-jeopardy themes. His follow-up letter in the summer was answered by a brief note stating that Sixsmith was no longer employed by the *LM*. Alistair telephoned. He then discussed the matter with Hazel and decided to take the next day off work.

It was a September morning. The hospice in Cricklewood was of recent design and construction; from the road it resembled a clutch of igloos against the sheenless tundra of the sky. When he asked for Hugh Sixsmith at the desk, two men in suits climbed quickly from their chairs. One was a writ-server. One was a cost-adjuster. Alistair waved away their complex requests.

The warm room contained clogged, regretful murmurs, and defiance in the form of bottles and paper cups and cigarette smoke, and the many peeping eyes of female grief. A young woman faced him proudly. Alistair started explaining who he was, a young screenplay writer come to . . . On the bed in the corner the spavined figure of Sixsmith was gawkily arranged. Alistair moved toward it. At first he was sure the eyes were gone, like holes cut out of pumpkin or blood orange. But then the faint brows began to lift, and Alistair thought he saw the light of recognition.

As the tears began, he felt the shiver of approval, of consensus, on his back. He took the old screenplay writer's hand and said, 'Goodbye. And thank you. Thank you. Thank you.'

Opening in four hundred and thirty-seven theatres, the Binary sonnet 'Composed at — Castle' did seventeen million in its first weekend. At this time Luke was living in a two-bedroom apartment on Yokum Drive. Suki was with him. He hoped it wouldn't take her too long to find out about Henna Mickiewicz. When the smoke cleared he would switch to the more mature Anita, who produced.

He had taken his sonnet to Rodge at Red Giant and turned it into an ode. When that didn't work out he went to Mal at

Monad, where they'd gone for the villanelle. The villanelle had become a triolet, briefly, with Tim at TCT, before Bob at Binary had him rethink it as a rondeau. When the rondeau didn't take, Luke lyricised it and got Mike to send it to Joe. Everyone, including Jake Endo, thought that now was surely the time to turn it back into a sonnet.

Luke had dinner at Rales with Joe and Mike.

'I always thought of "Sonnet" as an art poem,' said Joe. 'But things are so hot now, I've started thinking more commercially.'

Mike said, 'TCT is doing a sequel *and* a prequel to "'Tis" and bringing them out at the same time.'

'A sequel?' said Joe.

'Yeah. They're calling it "'Twill".'

Mike was a little fucked up. So was Joe. Luke was a little fucked up, too. They'd done some lines at the office. Then drinks here at the bar. They'd meant to get a little fucked up. It was OK. It was good, once in a while, to get a little fucked up. The thing was not to get fucked up too often. The thing was not to get fucked up to excess.

'I mean it, Luke,' said Joe. He glittered potently. 'I think "Sonnet" could be as big as "—".'

'You think?' said Luke.

'I mean it. I think "Sonnet" could be another "—".'

'"—"?'

'"—".'

Luke thought for a moment, taking this in. '"—". . .' he repeated wonderingly.

ETHAN CANIN

Lies

What my father said was, 'You pays your dime, you takes your choice,' which, if you don't understand it, boils down to him saying one thing to me: Get out. He had a right to say it, though. I had it coming and he's not a man who says excuse me and pardon me. He's a man who tells the truth. Some guys my age are kids, but I'm eighteen and getting married and that's a big difference. It's a tough thing to get squeezed from your own house, but my father's done all right because he's tough. He runs a steam press in Roxbury. When the deodorant commercials come on the set he turns the TV off. That's the way he is. There's no second chance with him. Anyway, I'll do all right. Getting out of the house is what I wanted, so it's no hair off my head. You can't get everything you want. This summer two things I wanted were to get out of the house finally and to go up to Fountain Lake with Katy, and I got both. You don't have that happen to you very often, so I'm not doing so bad.

It's summer and I'm out of High. That's a relief. Some guys don't make it through, but they're the ones I was talking about – the kids. Part of the reason I made it is that my folks pushed me. Until I was too old to believe it my mother used to tell me the lie that anybody can be what you want to. 'Anybody can rise up to be President of the United States,' she used to say. Somewhere along the line you find out that's not true and that you're either fixed from the start or fixed by something you do without really thinking about it. I guess I was fixed by both. My mother, though, she doesn't give up. She got up twenty minutes early to make me provolone on rye for four years solid and cried when I was handed my diploma.

After graduation is when I got the job at Able's. Able's is the movie theater – a two-hundred-fifty-seat, one-aisle house on South Huntington. *Able's, where the service is friendly and the popcorn is fresh.* The bathrooms are cold-water-only though, and Mr Able spends Monday mornings sewing the ripped seat upholstery himself because he won't let loose a few grand to re-cover the loges, which for some reason are coming apart faster than the standard seats. I don't know why that is. I sell maybe one-third loge tickets and that clientele doesn't carry penknives to go at the fabric with. The ones who carry knives are the ones who hang out in front. They wouldn't cut anybody but they might take the sidewall off your tire. They're the ones who stopped at tenth grade, when the law says the state doesn't care any more. They hang out in front, drinking usually, only they almost never actually come in to see the movie.

I work inside, half the time selling tickets and the other half as the projectionist. It's not a bad job. I memorise most movies. But one thing about a movie theater is that it's always dark inside, even in the lobby because of the tinted glass. (You've seen that, the way the light explodes in when someone opens the exit door.) But when you work in the ticket booth you're looking outside to where it's bright daylight, and you're looking through the metal bars, and sometimes that makes you think. On a hot afternoon when I see the wives coming indoors for the matinee, I want to push their money back under the slot. I want to ask them what in the world are they doing that for, trading away the light and the space outside for a seat here.

The projectionist half of the job isn't so bad, even though most people don't even know what one is. They don't realise some clown is sitting up in the room where the projectors are and changing the reels when it's time. Actually, most of the time the guy's just smoking, which he's not supposed to do, or he has a girl in there, which is what I did sometimes with Katy. All there is to do is watch for the yellow dot that comes on in the corner of the screen when it's time to change the reel. When I see that yellow dot there's five seconds before I have to have the other projector running. It's not hard, and after you do it a while you develop a sense. You get good enough so you can walk out to the lobby, maybe have popcorn or a medium drink, then sit on the stairs for a while before you go back to the booth, perfectly timed to catch the yellow spot and get the next reel going.

Anyway, it's pretty easy. But once I was in the booth with Katy when she told me something that made me forget to change the reel. The movie stopped and the theater was dark, and then everybody starts to boo and I hear Mr Able's voice right up next to the wall. 'Get on the ball, Jack,' he says, and I have the other projector on before he even has time to open the door. If he knew Katy was in there he'd have canned me. Later he tells me it's my last warning.

What Katy told me was that she loved me. Nobody ever told me they loved me before except my mother, which is obvious, and I remember it exactly because suddenly I knew how old I was and how old I was getting. After she said that, getting older wasn't what I wanted so much. It's the way you feel after you get your first job. I remember exactly what she said. She said, 'I love you, Jack. I thought about it and I know what I mean. I'm in love with you.'

At the time the thing to do was kiss her, which I did. I wanted to tell her that I loved her too, but I couldn't say it. I don't mind lying, but not about that. Anyway, we're up there in the booth together, and it's while we have our tongues in each other's mouths that the reel runs out.

The first time I met Katy was at the theater. She's a pretty girl, all eyes, hair that's not quite blonde. It falls a certain way. It was the thing I noticed first, the way it sat there on her shoulders. But it more than just sat; it touched her shoulders like a pair of hands, went in around the collar of her shirt and touched her neck. She was three rows in front. I wasn't working at the theater yet. It was end of senior year and I was sitting in two seats and had a box of popcorn in my lap. My friend LeFranc was next to me. We both saw Katy when she came in. LeFranc lit a match. 'Put me out,' he said, 'before we all burn.' LeFranc plays trumpet. He doesn't know what to say to a girl.

During the bright parts of the movie I keep looking at her neck. She's with three other girls we don't recognise. It turns out they go to Catholic school, which is why we don't know them. Then about half-way through she gets up by herself and heads back up the aisle. LeFranc breathes out and lights another match. I smile and think about following her back to the candy counter, where I might say something, but there's always the chance that she's gone out to the ladies' room instead and then where would I be? Time is on my side, so I decide to wait. The movie is *The Right Stuff*. They're taking up the supersonic planes when this is happening. They're talking about the envelope, and I don't know what that means, and then suddenly Katy's sitting next to me. I don't know where she came from. 'Can I have some popcorn?' she says.

'You can have the whole box,' I answer. I don't know where this comes from either, but it's the perfect thing to say and I feel a little bit of my life happening. On the other side LeFranc is still as an Indian. I push the bucket toward Katy. Her hands are milk.

She takes a few pieces and holds them with her palm flat up. Already I'm thinking, That's something I would never do – the way she holds the little popped kernels like that. Then she chews them slowly, one by one, while I pretend to watch the movie. Things come into my head.

After the movie I talk to her a little and so we go on a few dates. In the meantime I get the theater job and in August she invites me to her sister's wedding. Her sister's marrying a guy twenty years older named Hank. It's at a big church in Saugus. By this time Katy and I've kissed maybe two hours total. She always bites a piece of Juicy Fruit in two when we're done and gives me half.

Anyway, at the wedding I walk in wearing a coat and tie and have to meet her parents. Her father's got something wrong with one of his eyes. I'm not sure which one's the bad one, and I'm worried he's thinking I'm shifty because I'm not sure which one to look at. We shake hands and he doesn't say anything. We put our hands down and he still doesn't say anything.

'I've been at work,' I say. It's a line I've thought about.

'I don't know what the hell you kids want,' he says then. That's exactly what he says. I look at him. I realise he's drunk or been drinking, and then in a second Katy's mother's all over him. At practically the same time she's also kissing me on the cheek and telling me I look good in my suit and pulling Katy over from where she's talking with a couple of her girlfriends.

For the ceremony we sit in the pews. I'm on the aisle, with her mother one row in front and a couple of seats over so that I can see all the pleats and hems and miniature flowers sewn into her dress. I can hear her breathing. The father, who's paid for the whole bagful, is pacing behind the nave door waiting to give away the bride. Katy's back there too, with the other maids. They're wearing these dresses that stay up without straps. The wedding starts and the maids come up the aisle finally, ahead of the bride, in those dresses that remind you all the time. Katy's at the front, and when they pass me, stepping slowly, she leans over and gives me half a piece of Juicy Fruit.

So anyway, we've already been to a wedding together and maybe thanks to that I'm not so scared of our own, which is coming up. It's going to be in November. A fall wedding. Though actually it's not going to be a wedding at all but just something done by a justice of the peace. It's better that way. I had enough the first time, seeing Katy's father pace. He had loose skin on his face and a tired look and I don't want that at our wedding.

And besides, things are changing. I'm not sure who I'd want to come to a big wedding. I'm eighteen in two months and so is Katy, and to tell the truth I'm starting to get tired of my friends. It's another phase I'm coming into, probably. My friends are Hadley and Mike and LeFranc. LeFranc is my best friend. Katy doesn't like Hadley or Mike and she thinks LeFranc is OK mostly because he was there when we met. But LeFranc plays amazing trumpet, and if there's a way for him to play at the justice-of-the-peace wedding I'm going to get him to do it. I want him to play because sometimes I think about how this bit with Katy started and how fast it's gone, and it kind of stuns me that this is what happened, that of all the ways a life can turn out this is the way mine is going to.

We didn't get up to Fountain Lake until a couple of months after her sister's wedding. It's a Sunday and I'm sitting on the red-and-black carpet of Able's lobby steps eating a medium popcorn and waiting for the reel change to come. Able himself is upstairs in the office, so I'm just sitting there, watching the sun outside through the ticket window, thinking this is the kind of day I'd rather be doing something else. The clowns out front have their shirts off. They're hanging around out there and I'm sitting in the lobby when a car honks and then honks again. I look over and I'm so surprised I think the sun's doing something to my eyes. It's Katy in a red Cadillac. It's got whitewalls and chrome and she's honking at me. I don't even know where she learned to drive. But she honks again and the guys out front start to laugh and point inside the theater. What's funny is that I know they can't see inside because of the tint, but they're pointing right at me anyway.

There's certain times in your life when you do things and then have to stick to them later, and nobody likes to do that. But this was one of them, and Katy was going to honk again if I didn't do something. My father has a saying about it being like getting caught between two rocks, but if you knew Mr Able and you knew Katy, you'd know it wasn't really like two rocks. It was more like one rock, and then Katy sitting in a Cadillac. So I get up and set the popcorn down on the snack bar, then walk over and look through the door. I stand there maybe half a minute. All the while I'm counting off the time in my head until I've got to be back in to change the reel. I think of my father. He's worked every day of his life. I think of Mr Able, sewing on the loge upholstery with fishing line. They're banking on me, and I know it, and I start to feel kind of bad, but outside there's Katy in a red Fleetwood. 'King of the Cadillac line,' I say to myself. It's a blazing afternoon, and as soon as I open the door and step outside I know I'm not coming back.

On the street the sun's thrashing around off the fenders and the white shirts, and it's like walking into a wall. But I cross the street without really knowing what I'm doing and get into the car on the driver's side. All the time I'm crossing the street I know everybody's looking, but nobody says anything. When I get into the car I slip the seat back a little.

'How'd you get this?'

'It's Hank's,' she says. 'It's new. Where should we go?'

I don't know what she's doing with Hank's car, but my foot's pushing up and down on the gas and the clowns out front are looking, so I have to do something and I say, 'The lake, let's go up to Fountain Lake.' I put it in drive and the tires squeal a second before we're gone.

The windows are up and I swear the car's so quiet I'm not sure there's an engine. I push the gas and don't hear anything but just feel the leather seats pushing up under our backs. The leather's cool and has this buttered look. The windshield is tinted at the top. After about three blocks I start thinking to myself, I'm out, and I wheel the Cadillac out Jamaicaway toward the river. I really don't know the way up to Fountain Lake. Katy doesn't either, though, so I don't ask her.

We cross over the river at BU and head up Memorial Drive, past all the college students on the lawns throwing Frisbees and plastic footballs. Over by Harvard they're pulling rowing sculls out of the water. They're all wearing their red jackets and holding big glasses of beer while they work. The grass is so green it hurts my eyes.

On the long stretch past Boylston I put down the electric window and hold my arm out so that the air picks it up like a wing when we speed up, and then, just before we get out to the highway, something clicks in my head and I know it's time to change the reel. I touch the brakes for a second. I count to five and imagine the theater going dark, then one of the wives in the audience saying something out loud, real irate. I see Mr Able opening the door to the projection booth, the expression on his face just like one my father has. It's a certain look, half like he's hit somebody and half like somebody's hit him. But then as we come out onto Route 2 and I hit the gas hard one of my father's sayings comes to me, that it's all water over the bridge, and it's like inside my head another reel suddenly runs out. Just like that, that part of my life is gone.

By the time we're out past Lincoln I'm really not thinking anything except Wow, we're out of here. The car feels good. You get a feeling sometimes right after you do something. Katy's next to me with her real tight body and the soft way girls look, and I'm no kid anymore. I think about how nice it would be to be able to take the car whenever you want and go up to the lake. I'm thinking all this and floating the car around big wide turns, and I can see the hills now way up the road in front of us. I look over at Katy, and then at the long yellow line sliding under the front of the car, and it seems to me that I'm doing something big. All the time Katy's just sitting there. Then she says, 'I can't believe it.'

She's right. I'm on the way to Fountain Lake, going fast in a car, the red arrow shivering around seventy-five in the dial, a girl next to me, pretty, smelling the nice way girls do. And I turn to her and I don't know why except you get a feeling when you finally bust out, and I say, 'I love you, Katy,' in a certain kind of voice, my foot crushing the accelerator and the car booming along the straightaways like it's some kind of rocket.

JAMES THURBER

The Man Who Hated Moonbaum

After they had passed through the high, grilled gate they walked for almost a quarter of a mile, or so it seemed to Tallman. It was very dark; the air smelled sweet; now and then leaves brushed against his cheek or forehead. The little, stout man he was following had stopped talking, but Tallman could hear him breathing. They walked on for another minute. 'How we doing?' Tallman asked, finally. 'Don't ask me questions!' snapped the other man. 'Nobody asks me questions! You'll learn.' The hell I will, thought Tallman, pushing through the darkness and the fragrance and the mysterious leaves; the hell I will, baby; this is the last time you'll ever see me. The knowledge that he was leaving Hollywood within twenty-four hours gave him a sense of comfort.

There was no longer turf or gravel under his feet; there was something that rang flatly: tile, or flagstones. The little man began to walk more slowly and Tallman almost bumped into him. 'Can't we have a light?' said Tallman. 'There you go!' shouted his guide. 'Don't get me screaming! What are you trying to do to me?' 'I'm not trying to do anything to you,' said Tallman. 'I'm trying to find out where we're going.'

The other man had come to a stop and seemed to be groping around. 'First it's wrong uniforms,' he said, 'then it's red fire – red fire in Scotland, red fire three hundred years ago! I don't know why I ain't crazy!' Tallman could make out the other man dimly, a black, gesturing blob. 'You're doing all right,' said Tallman. Why did I ever leave the Brown Derby with this guy? he asked himself. Why did I ever let him bring me to his house – if he has a house? Who the hell does he think he is?

Tallman looked at his wristwatch; the dial glowed wanly in

the immense darkness. He was a little drunk, but he could see that it was half past three in the morning. 'Not trying to do anything to me, he says!' screamed the little man. 'Wasn't his fault! It's never anybody's fault! They give me ten thousand dollars' worth of Sam Browne belts for Scotch Highlanders and it's nobody's fault!' Tallman was beginning to get his hangover headache. 'I want a light!' he said. 'I want a drink! I want to know where the hell I am!' 'That's it! Speak out!' said the other. 'Say what you think! I like a man who knows where he is. We'll get along.' 'Contact!' said Tallman. 'Camera! Lights! Get out that hundred-year-old brandy you were talking about.'

The response to this was a soft flood of rose-coloured radiance; the little man had somehow found a light switch in the dark. God knows where, thought Tallman; probably on a tree. They were in a courtyard paved with enormous flagstones which fitted together with mosaic perfection. The light revealed the dark stones of a building which looked like the Place de la Concorde side of the Crillon. 'Come on, you people!' said the little man. Tallman looked behind him, half expecting to see the shadowy forms of Scottish Highlanders, but there was nothing but the shadows of trees and of oddly shaped plants closing in on the courtyard. With a key as small as a dime, the little man opened a door that was fifteen feet high and made of wood six inches thick.

Marble stairs tumbled down like Niagara into a grand canyon of a living-room. The steps of the two men sounded sharp and clear on the stairs, died in the soft depths of an immensity of carpet in the living-room. The ceiling towered above them. There were highlights on dark wood medallions, on burnished shields, on silver curves and edges. On one wall a forty-foot tapestry hung from the ceiling to within a few feet of the floor. Tallman was looking at this when his companion grasped his arm. 'The second rose!' he said. 'The second rose from the right!' Tallman pulled away. 'One of us has got to snap out of this baby,' he said. 'How about that brandy?' 'Don't interrupt me!' shouted his host. 'That's what Whozis whispers to What's-His-Name – greatest love story in the world, if I do say so myself – king's wife mixed up in it – knights riding around with spears – Whozis writes her a message made out of twigs bent together to make words: "I love you" – sends it floating down a stream past her window – they got her locked in – goddamnedest thing in the history of pictures. Where was I? Oh – "Second rose from the right," she says. Why? Because she seen it twitch, she seen it move. What's-His-Name is bending over her, kissing her maybe. He whirls around and shoots an arrow at the rose – second from the right, way up high there – down comes the whole tapestry, weighs eleven hundred pounds, and out rolls this spy, shot through the heart. What's-His-Name sent him to watch the lovers.' The little man began to pace up and down the deep carpet. Tallman lighted a fresh cigarette from his glowing stub and sat down in an enormous chair. His host came to a stop in front of the chair and shook his finger at its occupant.

'Look,' said the little man. 'I don't know who you are and I'm telling you this. You could ruin me, but I got to tell you. I get Moonbaum here – I get Moonbaum himself here – you can ask Manny or Sol – I get the best arrow shot in the world here to fire that arrow for What's-His-Name – '

'Tristram,' said Tallman. 'Don't prompt me!' bellowed the little man. 'For Tristram. What happens? Do I know he's got arrows you shoot bears with? Do I know he ain't got caps on 'em? If I got to know that, why do I have Mitnik? Moonbaum is sitting right there – the tapestry comes down and out rolls this guy, shot through the heart – only the arrow is in his stomach. So what happens? So Moonbaum laughs! That makes Moonbaum laugh! The greatest love story in the history of pictures, and Moonbaum laughs!' The little man raced over to a large chest, opened it, took out a cigar, stuck it in his mouth, and resumed his pacing. 'How do you like it?' he shouted. 'I love it,' said Tallman. 'I love every part of it. I always have.' The little man raised his hands above his head. 'He loves it! He hears one – maybe two – scenes, and he loves every part of it! Even Moonbaum don't know how it comes out, and you love every part of it!' The little man was standing before Tallman's chair again, shaking his cigar at him. 'The story got around,' said Tallman. 'These things leak out. Maybe you talk when you're drinking. What about that brandy?'

The little man walked over and took hold of a bell rope on

the wall, next to the tapestry. 'Moonbaum laughs like he's dying,' he said. 'Moonbaum laughs like he's seen Chaplin.' He dropped the bell rope. 'I hope you really got that hundred-year-old brandy,' said Tallman. 'Don't keep telling me what you hope!' howled the little man. 'Keep listening to what I hope!' He pulled the bell rope savagely. 'Now we're getting somewhere,' said Tallman. For the first time the little man went to a chair and sat down; he chewed on his unlighted cigar. 'Do you know what Moonbaum wants her called?' he demanded, lowering his heavy lids. 'I can guess,' said Tallman. 'Isolde.' 'Birds of a feather!' shouted his host. 'Horses of the same colour! Isolde! Name of God, man, you can't call a woman Isolde! What do I want her called?' 'You have me there,' said Tallman. 'I want her called Dawn,' said the little man, getting up out of his chair. 'It's short, ain't it? It's sweet, ain't it? You can say it, can't you?' 'To get back to that brandy,' said Tallman, 'who is supposed to answer that bell?' 'Nobody is supposed to answer it,' said the little man. 'That don't ring, that's a fake bell rope; it don't ring anywhere. I got it to remind me of an idea Moonbaum ruined. Listen: Louisiana mansion – guy with seven daughters – old-Southern-colonel stuff – Lionel Barrymore could play it – we open on a room that looks like a million dollars – Barrymore crosses and pulls the bell rope. What happens?' 'Nothing,' said Tallman. 'You're crazy!' bellowed the little man. 'Part of the wall falls in! Out flies a crow – in walks a goat, maybe – the place has gone to seed, see? It's just a hulk of its former self, it's a shallows!' He turned and walked out of the room. It took him quite a while.

When he came back he was carrying a bottle of brandy and two huge brandy glasses. He poured a great deal of brandy into each glass and handed one to Tallman. 'You and Mitnik!' he said, scornfully. 'Pulling walls out of Southern mansions. Crows you give me, goats you give me! What the hell kind of effect is that?' 'I could have a bad idea,' said Tallman, raising his glass. 'Here's to Moonbaum. May he maul things over in his mind all night and never get any spontaneity into 'em.' 'I drink nothing to Moonbaum,' said the little man. 'I hate Moonbaum. You know where they catch that crook – that guy has a little finger off one hand and wears a glove to cover it up? What does Moonbaum want? Moonbaum wants the little finger to *flap*! What do I want? I want it stuffed. What do I want it stuffed with? Sand. Why?' 'I know,' said Tallman. 'So that when he closes his hand over the head of his cane, the little finger sticks out stiffly, giving him away.' The little man seemed to leap into the air; his brandy splashed out of his glass. 'Suitcase!' he screamed. 'Not cane! Suitcase! He grabs hold of a suitcase!' Tallman didn't say anything; he closed his eyes and sipped his brandy; it was wonderful brandy. He looked up presently to find his host staring at him with a resigned expression in his eyes. 'All right, then, suitcase,' the little man said. 'Have it suitcase. We won't fight about details, I'm trying to tell you my story. I don't tell my stories to everybody.' 'Richard Harding Davis stole that finger gag – used it in *Gallegher*,' said Tallman. 'You could sue him.' The little man walked over to his chair and flopped into it. 'He's beneath me,' he said. 'He's beneath me like the dirt. I ignore him.'

Tallman finished his brandy slowly. His host's chin sank upon his chest; his heavy eyelids began to close. Tallman waited several minutes and then tiptoed over to the marble stairs. He took off his shoes and walked up the stairs, carefully. He had the heavy door open when the little man shouted at him. 'Birds of a feather, all of you!' he shouted. 'You can tell Moonbaum I said so! Shooting guys out of tapestries!' 'I'll tell him,' said Tallman. 'Good night. The brandy was wonderful.' The little man was not listening. He was pacing the floor again, gesturing with an empty brandy glass in one hand and the unlighted cigar in the other. Tallman stepped out into the cool air of the courtyard and put on one shoe and laced it. The heavy door swung shut behind him with a terrific crash. He picked up the other shoe and ran wildly towards the trees and the oddly shaped plants. It was daylight now. He could see where he was going.

Acknowledgements

Thanks are due to the copyright holders of the following stories for permission to reprint them in this volume:

Martin Amis: 'Career Move', first published in the *New Yorker*, 29 June 1992. Copyright © 1992 by Martin Amis. Reprinted by permission of the Peters, Fraser and Dunlop Group Ltd.

J. G. Ballard: 'The Screen Game' from the collection *Vermilion Sands* (Orion Publishers, London). Copyright © 1971 by J. G. Ballard. Reprinted by permission of Margaret Hanbury Literary Agents.

Ethan Canin: 'Lies' from *Emperor of the Air* (Picador, 1988). Copyright © 1988 by Ethan Canin. Reprinted by permission of Picador and Houghton Mifflin Co. All rights reserved.

Robert Coover: 'Intermission' from *A Night at the Movies* (William Heinemann Ltd, 1987). Copyright © 1987 by Robert Coover. Reprinted by permission of Georges Borchardt Inc. for the author, and Reed International Books.

Robertson Davies: extracts from *The Papers of Samuel Marchbanks* (Viking, 1987). Copyright © 1986 by Robertson Davies. Reprinted by permission of Penguin Books Ltd and Stoddart Publishing Co. Ltd.

Graham Greene: 'The Blue Film' from *Twenty-One Stories* (William Heinemann Ltd, 1954). Copyright © 1954 Verdant S.A. Reprinted by permission of the author's estate and David Higham Associates.

Alison Lurie: extract from *The Nowhere City* (William Heinemann Ltd). Copyright © 1965 by Alison Bishop. Reprinted by permission of Reed International Books and Aitken, Stone & Wylie Ltd.

Jay McInerney: 'The Business' published in *Granta 24*, Summer 1988. Copyright © 1988 by Jay McInerney. Reprinted by permission of International Creative Management Inc.

Alberto Moravia: 'The Film Test' from *Roman Tales* (Martin Secker & Warburg, 1956). Copyright © 1954 Valentino Bompiani & Co. Reprinted by permission of Reed International Books.

R. K. Narayan: 'The Antidote' from *Under the Banyan Tree* (William Heinemann Ltd, 1985, and Viking USA). Copyright © 1956, 1985 by R. K. Narayan. Reprinted by permission of Sheil Land Associates Ltd and Reed International Books.

John O'Hara: 'Malibu from the Sky' from *Good Samaritan* (Hodder and Stoughton, 1976). Copyright © 1968 and 1974 by United States Trust Company New York, as executor of and trustee under the will of John O'Hara. Reprinted by permission of Curtis Brown Group Ltd on behalf of the Estate of John O'Hara.

William Saroyan: 'OK, Baby, This is the World' from *The Trouble With Tigers* (Faber and Faber Ltd, 1939). Reprinted by permission of the William Saroyan Foundation, San Francisco, California, USA, and Laurence Pollinger Ltd.

James Thurber: 'The Man Who Hated Moonbaum' from *My World – And Welcome To It* (Hamish Hamilton, 1952 and Harcourt Brace and Co.). Copyright © 1942 by James Thurber. Copyright © 1970 Helen Thurber and Rosemary A. Thurber. Reprinted by permission of Helen and Rosemary Thurber and Hamish Hamilton Ltd.

P. G. Wodehouse: 'The Rise of Minna Nordstrom' from *Blandings Castle and Elsewhere*, first published by Herbert Jenkins Ltd, 1935. Copyright © the Estate of P. G. Wodehouse. Reprinted by permission of the Estate of P. G. Wodehouse and Hutchinson as publisher.